"I never told you how much I appreciated all your help back in high school. I never said thank you."

Chris placed his big, strong hands on her shoulders and squeezed. "I'm sorry. This is fifteen years too late. Thank you, Tiffany, for everything you did for me."

Her heart sped up, her pulse tripping through her veins. It had never occurred to her that she'd needed to hear a thank-you from him. He'd paid her, after all. But his appreciation was worth ten times what she'd earned.

He was gazing at her as though she might try to deny his words. He searched her face with a probing look, eyes falling to her lips.

Whatever had gripped him for that heady, fervent moment dissipated. His hands fell away, leaving her wishing could step closer and wrap his arms around her.

Dear Reader,

It has long been my dream to write a book featuring a contemporary Chinese-American heroine. Tiffany and I share the same cultural background, raised as first-generation North-American-born Chinese, except I was raised in multicultural metropolitan Toronto, while she grew up in the fictional town of Everville, New York. While many rural and suburban communities are becoming increasingly diverse, I wanted to explore how being isolated and torn between cultures affected the way my characters grew up.

All her life, Tiffany has felt like she doesn't belong anywhere. Her parents criticized her constantly and her schoolmates teased her because she was different. She retreated into herself as a result, becoming a shy, standoffish girl whose driving ambition was to leave Everville. It's only when she opens herself up that she begins to find her place. Wouldn't it be nice if it were with her old high school crush, Chris Jamieson?

I hope you enjoy this story of reconnection. May you find good fortune and happiness wherever you look for it!

Vicki Essex

PS—I like to hear from readers! Please contact me at vicki@vickiessex.com.

Back to the Good Fortune Diner

VICKI ESSEX

HARLEQUIN®
entertain, enrich, inspire™

Recycling programs
for this product may
not exist in your area.

ISBN-13: 978-0-373-71828-3

BACK TO THE GOOD FORTUNE DINER

Copyright © 2013 by Vicki So

ABOUT THE AUTHOR

Vicki Essex was born and bred in Toronto, Canada, and has lived most of her life within spitting distance of downtown Chinatown. She still doesn't get the appeal of chicken balls, but she loves sweet and sour sauce, especially on deep-fried pork intestines. Her left-handed husband has better chopstick form than she does. She loves dim sum, her mom's soups and roast beef dinners with Yorkshire pudding. Her Cantonese is atrocious—she considers herself *jook-sing*. Visit her at www.vickiessex.com, on Facebook at www.facebook.com/vickiessexauthor or follow her on Twitter @VickiEssex.

Books by Vicki Essex

HARLEQUIN SUPERROMANCE

1718—HER SON'S HERO

This book is dedicated with love to
my mom and dad.

Thank you for everything in my life that is good and true.

To my sister Jenny,
who I don't appreciate enough—I'm proud of you.

Thanks for taking care of Smartikus and for surprising
me regularly with your awesomeness.

Thanks to Stephanie Doig for all her insights into
small-town life and for all the hours of brainstorming,
critiquing and delicious food.

Thanks to my editor, Megan Long,
who believed in me and cheered me on.

A Kermit arm-flail to everyone at Harlequin Enterprises
who has supported me in this second venture.
(Yaaay! *flail*)

And as always, to John. Luboo!

CHAPTER ONE

TIFFANY KNEW THE EXACT MOMENT when her family arrived in the E.R.

"Say joh may-ah?" *Poh-poh*'s voice creaked.

"No, Grandma, she's not dead." She heard Daniel reassure in that too-smooth voice of his. Tiffany grabbed the edges of the pillow and stuffed them against her ears. With her family hovering on the other side of the curtain, the pleasant buzz of the painkillers evaporated, and her stomach churned.

Shadows streaked into her cubicle from beneath the partition. "Tiffany?"

For a moment, she considered pretending to be comatose, or ducking away and hiding somewhere until they left. But there was no avoiding the inevitable. Sighing, she propped herself up in the hospital bed, smoothing the blanket over her knees. "I'm here," she called in a rusty voice.

The rings on the curtain railing clattered as the partition was yanked aside. Mom, Dad, Daniel and *Poh-poh* took her in with dark, wide eyes.

"Ai-ya!" Her grandmother began speaking rapidly in Cantonese, waving her hands.

"Bah, she's fine. I told you she was fine," her father said impatiently, giving her a cursory once-over. His stained white kitchen apron still clung to his narrow hips, the front dangling to his knees, and he smelled strongly of fryer oil. "You're fine, right?" he asked.

She didn't reply, knowing any answer apart from "yes" would cause only more trouble.

"What were you doing driving so fast in the rain?" Her mother placed her dry, papery palm against Tiffany's forehead as if she had a fever. Her fingers brushed the bruises along her cheek and jaw and Tiffany flinched. "It's that car, I bet. I told you not to buy used."

"There's nothing wrong with used cars," her dad said. "She's just a bad driver. She should have learned from me instead of paying for those classes. 'Defensive driving'—bah." He snorted in disgust. "Daniel learned from me, and now he *teaches* driving."

Poh-poh cycled through relief, exasperation and hysterics as she berated her only granddaughter in her native tongue. She was reckless; drivers today were careless; the weather had cursed her; her face was all bruised and now she wouldn't be able to find a husband and why hadn't she stayed in Everville with the family instead of moving to New York City?

"I'm sorry, *Poh-poh*." She felt bad for making her grandmother worry.

"Sit down, Grandma. Don't work yourself up." Daniel pulled the cubicle's lone chair next to the bed, but their grandmother argued that her dad should sit after his long day in the kitchen. Tony insisted his wife sit. Rose insisted Daniel sit. Tiffany closed her eyes as they argued, voices rising until a nurse asked them to quiet down. Grudgingly, *Poh-poh* sat.

The E.R.'s attending physician interrupted to talk to the family about Tiffany's condition. Dr. Frewer was a nice-looking middle-aged man with salt in his dark hair and a fat gold wedding ring on his finger. Tiffany bet he was wondering the same thing she did whenever her family got together: How did four people manage to make such a racket? He greeted each family member and ran through the list of Tiffany's injuries: a few bruises, a sprained wrist, but nothing serious.

"Sounds like nothing she can't sleep off," her dad said once the doctor finished speaking. "You don't need to stay here, right?"

"For God's sake, she was in an accident," her mom said in exasperation, adding in Cantonese, "Have some compassion. The doctor will think you're cruel."

"No point coddling her if she's fine." Tony folded his arms across his chest. "They didn't have to drag us all out here for a few bruises."

"Let's listen to what the doctor says," her brother interrupted. That was Daniel. Always coming to the rescue.

"Of course, of course." Tony switched back to English and said to the doctor, "My kids are strong. They heal fast. Tiffany doesn't heal as fast as her brother, though." He turned to Daniel. "Remember that time she broke her arm? She had that cast on for six weeks. You only had it on for five."

Daniel rolled his eyes. "You guys stay here with Tiff. I'm going to talk to the officer out front and see about Tiff's car."

Rose looked at her. "Why didn't you tell us you were driving up?" she asked.

"It was a last-minute decision."

Concern became suspicion, and small lines appeared around her mother's dark eyes. "Last minute? With no phone call? What happened?"

Tiffany didn't want to get into it while she was wearing nothing but a hospital gown. She sat up and forced a smile. "Can I be discharged?" she asked the doctor to stave off her mother's interrogation.

"There's nothing to keep you here," Dr. Frewer said, shrugging, "though I would recommend you see your family doctor if anything gets worse. He or she can prescribe you physical therapy, in case you have any difficulties with your wrist. In the meantime, I'll write a prescription for some painkillers."

"We have Tylenol at home," Tony said. "She doesn't need a prescription."

"Of course we'll take the prescription," Rose insisted, shooting a look at her husband.

Tony growled in Cantonese, "It's a waste of money."

"No one asked *you* to pay for anything."

Their glares locked over her bed. Tiffany closed her eyes and sank into her pillow. *Please, not here, not now, and not over me.*

"I'll make soup." *Poh-poh*'s declaration broke the stalemate, and Tiffany's parents withdrew to their respective corners. No one would argue with the respected elder. After all, her grandma's soups could cure anything.

An hour later, they were all packed into her dad's old minivan. Tiffany sat alone in the middle row of seats while her mother and grandmother breathed down her neck and her father glanced at her over his shoulder from the front passenger seat. Daniel's gaze met hers in the rearview mirror, and the interrogation resumed as the van got up to speed.

"What happened out there?" her mother demanded. "How did your car end up in the ditch? Why were you driving out of the city on a Monday night?"

"Maybe we should wait till we get home to discuss things," Daniel said as he methodically checked all his mirrors. Tiff knew he hated it when his passengers distracted him.

"She could have been killed," her mom exclaimed. "I want to know why she put herself in such danger."

"It was an accident, Mom. I'm fine." Tiffany couldn't suppress her irritation. Her body ached, her arm was in a sling and she'd just had the worst day of her life, so she figured she had a right to be cranky.

"The cops said something about your rearview mirror being blocked by garbage bags in the backseat." Daniel picked his words carefully.

Dammit. Why'd he have to bring that up? "That had nothing to do with it. The road was slippery, and I lost control."

"You haven't come to visit since Christmas," Mom said. "Why drive up now?"

Tiffany wished she could have pleaded exhaustion, waited until morning to tell them the awful truth. But the last of her strength left her and she gave in. "I…I lost my apartment."

Stunned silence crowded into the vehicle, but only for a second. "Why did you lose your apartment?" her father asked slowly.

"I…didn't pay my landlady in time."

Tony's jaw clenched so hard she could hear his teeth grinding. His fingers curled around the armrest.

"So, you got evicted?" Daniel's tone wavered. He knew she was standing on thin ice with their parents. "Why didn't you stay at a friend's place?"

"You could have stayed with Jennifer," *Poh-poh* added helpfully.

Tiffany's eyes burned. Reality had slammed home today. She didn't want to humiliate herself further by describing all the doors that had been shut in her face, how her cousin Jennifer must have moved without telling her. But then, they'd never kept in touch. "I didn't want to impose on anyone."

"Well, how are you supposed to get to work?" Mom asked. "Are you going to drive three hours every day to get to the city? I hope your insurance will cover a rental."

"That's not going to be a problem—" she took a deep breath and took the final plunge "—because I was laid off."

"You were fired?" her parents cried simultaneously.

"Laid off," she emphasized. "The company was restructuring, and there isn't that much room to cut out fat. I was a junior assistant to the publisher, so—"

"If you were worth keeping, they wouldn't have laid you off." Her father's proclamation was as final as the fall of an ax. She'd done the unforgivable and come home in disgrace, homeless and unemployed. He snorted and grumbled, *"Moh gwai young."*

Useless.

She straightened her shoulders, despite the ache that shot through her bones. "I did my job well. Really well," she said, echoing her employer's words from the exit interview. "It was a budgeting decision. It wasn't personal."

That, at least, had been what her boss had told her. But since none of her colleagues would let her crash at their place, she wondered if he was just trying to be kind.

"Well, what's done is done." Her mother said it with a touch of asperity. "Your room's still empty. We'll change the bed-sheets and move the sewing machine...."

Tiffany tuned out as her mother listed what needed to be done to accommodate her daughter's return to the house-hold. She stared at the black road ahead, watching the night rush toward her.

She was going home to Everville, the last place she wanted to be.

"THAT'S ONE HELL OF A WRECK."

Chris Jamieson inspected the crumpled hatchback sitting in Frank Konietzko's auto body shop. He'd stopped in to pick up some parts for the tractor when he spotted the mangled ve-hicle in the garage. It looked like a giant had clapped the car between its hands. The side-view mirrors dangled off both sides like sad bunny ears. Both front air bags had deployed and all the windows had shattered. He hoped the driver was okay.

The dark-haired mechanic stood staring at the little black car. "It looks worse than it is. The engine is fine, but consid-ering the cost for repair, it's probably better off sold for parts. I told Daniel I'd have a look at it, though."

"Daniel Cheung?" The man had taught half of the people in town how to drive. Chris couldn't believe he'd been in this wreck.

"My ears are burning. You guys talking about me?" Daniel strode in, grinning broadly. He didn't look like he'd been in an accident. "Been a while, Chris. How're you doing?"

"All right. We were just talking about—" He nodded toward the car.

"Man. It looks a lot worse in daylight." He rubbed his jaw as he studied the wreck. At Chris's quizzical look, he explained, "Tiffany was driving up when she spun out on the 87 and rolled into a ditch."

Tiffany Cheung. Now, there was a blast from the past. He pictured the girl with the straight, long hair, the big wire-rimmed glasses and the frown that rivaled the sour-faced librarian's at their old high school. "Is she okay?"

"A little banged up, but she's fine otherwise. Got lucky, I guess."

"You don't sound entirely convinced of that."

Daniel blew out a breath. "Well...you know my parents. They've always been kind of hard on her."

"They blame her for the accident?"

"No. She got laid off. That's why she was driving up..." He clamped his lips together. Chris got the sense Daniel had said more than he meant to and didn't prod further.

Frank gave Daniel the rundown of repairs on the hatchback, and Chris winced when he overheard the estimated total to fix the car. Daniel called his sister on his cell phone. Chris pictured her stony face as her brother relayed Frank's assessment. Getting a smile out of Tiffany had been a real challenge back in high school—he could only imagine how she'd receive this grim news.

"Are you sure?" Daniel asked incredulously. A pause, and he wiped a hand down his face. "Well...okay. If you say so."

He hung up and turned to Frank. "Tiff wants you to fix it however you can."

The mechanic shoved his hands into his pockets. "All right. But it's going to take some time. I'll get you a preinvoice. Show that to her, and we can work out a payment schedule."

"Why don't you help Chris out first?" Daniel offered. "I know he's got work to do, and this'll take some time. Wouldn't want your dad to get mad." He gave Chris a sympathetic look.

"Right. I appreciate that."

Once Chris had loaded up his truck with the tractor parts, he headed home. He tried to enjoy the gorgeous June weather and the long, lush country road stretching before him, but as he sped by a monolithic wind turbine, the slowly spinning blades reminded him of the long list of chores ahead. It seemed something was always breaking down, falling apart or being torn to shreds by the local wildlife. And those repairs were on top of all the usual farm duties. Sometimes he felt like that turbine blade, being pushed by the winds, spinning in place, never actually getting anywhere.

He pulled onto the long gravel driveway in front of the main house, which his grandfather had built. Chris's father had added cedar shingles and siding to the two-story brick home, but the place was sorely in need of some TLC. A decorative shutter hung at a precarious angle from a second-story window, and one of the eaves troughs had come loose, swinging off the corner of the house. The roof would need to be replaced soon, too, and the house could use a coat of fresh paint. Unfortunately, fixing up the homestead was low on the priority list.

The storm door banged open. "Where have you been?" William Jamieson demanded, crutches thumping across the veranda.

"I was at Frank's getting parts." Chris didn't look at him as he unloaded the white 4x4's bed.

"For two hours? I could have been there and back in one. Just because the days are getting longer, doesn't mean you can waste time lollygagging around town."

Chris groaned inwardly. Preempting another diatribe, he asked, "Where's Simon?"

"Barn. I assume *he's* doing his chores."

He ignored the dig. "Did you work those numbers out for me?"

"You mean the ones that say we're going to have to sell our kidneys to make it through the winter?"

Chris closed his eyes briefly. "I mean the numbers for delivering to Greenboro Market."

"I already told you, selling to them's a waste of time and resources. They're too far out. They won't order enough to make the trip there and back worthwhile."

"Do you have the numbers to support that?"

"I don't need numbers to tell you it's not going to work. Greenboro's full of regular working folk who want good, cheap food, not these fancy organic vegetables you want to sell them. You have a hard enough time in the market competing against imports."

Chris tugged off his work gloves and slapped them down on the truck bed. He did not want to drag himself into another argument about market competition. "Look, Dad, I asked you to do this one thing for me. I appreciate your advice—" *yeah, right* "—but I'm the one in charge."

"You think because you run the day-to-day, you own this place? Back in my day and my father's day, we knew who our customers were and we gave them what they wanted. We didn't try to sell them chichi designer vegetables for rich snobs."

A headache pressed at Chris's temples, and he pinched the flesh between his eyes. "Organic farming isn't chichi, Dad. It's practical business sense."

"It's environmental bullshit, is what it is. It's a way for the government to pull subsidies away from honest farmers. You don't know anything about the farm life, boy. It isn't about numbers and marketing, it's about heart and sweat and hard work, and I haven't seen you give an ounce of that...."

Chris started to walk away.

"Where do you think you're going? Don't you turn your back on me. Just because I'm missing a leg doesn't mean I can't kick your ass, you disrespectful—"

"I'm leaving before I hear something *you'll* regret. Now, get me those numbers. I want them by the end of the day." He stalked off before his dad could get the last word in.

CHAPTER TWO

CHRIS HEADED TO THE BARN, a stiff, dust-laden breeze stinging his cheeks instead of cooling him off. His dad really knew how to push his buttons. If he didn't know any better, he'd say his father enjoyed riling him up, probably because it gave him something to do.

He rounded the paddock where the horses stood soaking up the sun. One of Simon's jobs was to clean out the stalls, but when Chris walked into the barn, he could see it hadn't been done yet.

"Simon?" His voice echoed through the stuffy enclosure. Electronic *bleeps* and *bloops* from above caught his attention. He climbed the ladder into the loft and found his son slouched in the straw, his earbuds blaring some raspy, bass-heavy music while he played on his handheld video game.

Chris thumped the floorboard, and Simon jumped. He glared through his dark, shaggy bangs as he removed his earbuds.

"What are you doing? The stalls haven't been cleaned out yet."

"I'll do it in a minute. I just got back from school. I need a break."

"You shouldn't have your music turned up so loud," Chris told him. "You never know who might be calling for you, or if there's danger."

Simon's lip curled as he returned to his game. "Whatever."

A low moaning meow emanated from the corner of the

loft, drawing their attention. Chris went to investigate. In the far corner, the straw had been loosened and dug into a nest. Chris crouched down and found the big black barn cat Simon had named Shadow lying in the straw, panting hard. "Simon, come here."

"What?" He scrambled from his seat and peered over his dad's shoulder.

"If you hadn't had that music so loud, you would have heard her. Look, Shadow's having kittens."

And right then, a slimy ball of fur slid out of the cat and landed in the soft straw.

"Whoa." Simon backed off. "Should we call a vet or something?"

"She'll be fine. This is perfectly natural. She's probably getting ready to give birth to a few more." As the cat licked the newborn clean, Chris peeked up at his son's slightly green face. Simon had never been much for watching the miracles of life, even though he'd grown up on the farm. "Why don't you get a few towels and see if we can't make Shadow more comfortable?" Though Chris had other things on his plate, Shadow was Simon's cat, and his son looked slightly panicked. He couldn't abandon either of them now.

They fashioned a bed in the straw for the cat. Within the hour, Shadow gave birth to five kittens, a mixture of tabbies and solid black with white markings. Simon wasn't given to oohing and aahing, but once the grosser parts of birth were over, his eyes shone.

"Can we keep them?"

Chris grimaced. "We can't afford to have them all spayed and neutered—" he was already regretting not getting Shadow fixed "—and I don't want them running amok. We'll probably have to give them away."

Simon's shoulders slumped, and Chris felt a twinge of guilt. He might as well have told him he'd canceled Christmas. His son didn't understand that animals were a huge responsibility. Despite working with chickens, pigs and horses, he had very little interest in their lives and well-being. His 4-H project hadn't been anything special, either—in fact, Chris was almost certain the whole thing had been pulled off the internet.

Maybe looking after the kittens would be a good lesson for him.

"Tell you what. If you want, you keep an eye on them. Visit them regularly, feed them, clean up their messes, make sure they're safe. It'll be a few weeks before they're ready to go to new homes, anyhow, and if things go all right, you can keep one of them."

"Deal." Simon plunged into the straw to caress Shadow's head. The cat meowed plaintively as she gathered her babies closer. A smile softened his son's face, and Chris was reminded of the baby Simon had been, the sensitive child he'd raised. Lately, Simon had morphed into a surly, defiant teen. He had no idea where he'd sprung from.

"By the way," Chris ventured, knowing his next question would shatter their tentative truce, "did you get your report card yet?"

Simon's smile vanished. He shoved away from the kittens and started pitching straw down from the loft without meeting his father's eye.

So much for bonding time. Chris hated it when he ignored him like that. "I asked you a question, Simon."

"Yeah, I got it," he answered gruffly.

"I'd like to see it."

"Why?"

"Because I want to know how you did."

"What does it matter? It's not as if I need good marks to run this place." He tossed down a heavy bale then flung the pitchfork into it before Chris could stop him.

"Jesus, don't go throwing tools around like that. What if someone had walked in? You could have hurt them."

His son glanced down belatedly. "No one's there."

"Simon." He glared hard. "Don't throw tools. I mean it."

His son shrugged as he started down the ladder.

"And of course you need good marks," Chris continued, following him. "And who says you have to run this place?" But of course, he knew the answer to that. He stared icily through the open barn doors toward the house.

"It's not like I have a choice," Simon said. "If all I'm going to do is shovel shit and dig around in the dirt for the rest of my life, what the hell would I need Shakespeare for?" He rolled the wheelbarrow around to the first stall.

"Shakespeare?" Chris flinched. "You failed English?"

"It was a stupid class. Why would anyone need to learn that stuff? No one talks like that anymore."

"You failed English?" Chris asked again incredulously. They were more alike than he thought.

Simon stabbed the pitchfork into the dirty straw. "Yeah, I failed English. I'm a dummy. You happy?"

"Of course I'm not happy. And I didn't mean it to come out like that." Chris raked his fingers through his hair. "I didn't realize you were having trouble. Why didn't you say something?"

He snorted. "Like you would've been able to help."

"Maybe I could've." Although that was unlikely. Shakespeare had been his Achilles' heel, too. But that wasn't the point. "All you had to do was ask."

"Well, it's too late now."

The hopelessness in his son's voice made Chris ache. He didn't want to give his Gandhi-inspired take-charge-of-your-future lecture again. It obviously wasn't working. And yelling at him wasn't going to do him any good. He hooked his thumbs in his belt loops and tried to act casual. "So, do you have to retake the course?"

"Why should I? I'm turning sixteen in January. I can quit school and work here like you want me to."

"What I want is for you to be happy. If you want to stay and work on the farm, that's fine, but I still expect you to finish high school. And I'm not making you choose a future you don't want."

"Coulda fooled me." Simon attacked the mounded horse droppings as though he were digging a trench in enemy territory.

Chris was steadily losing patience. "Listen, this is part of your chore list. You chose it, remember? I need you to help out where you can. With Grandpa's leg—"

"Yeah, okay, I know, whatever." Simon flung a pitchfork full of manure into the wheelbarrow, scattering dung all over the ground. Chris compressed his lips.

"You're making more work for yourself by doing that."

Simon skewered him with a look as sharp as the pitchfork. He put his earbuds back in and continued shoveling, letting crap fly.

TIFFANY STARED AT THE BOWL of soup *Poh-poh* set in front of her. A chicken foot waved to her from the thin, murky concoction of ginseng and herbs. "Good for you," Sunny urged in broken English. "For your bruises. Make your skin nice, *la*."

Tiff sighed inwardly, but obediently sipped the broth, avoiding the pale, clawless fingers poking up at her. What she wouldn't give for a bagel and lox and a plate of latkes from the deli near her old apartment. Sunny only ever cooked traditional Chinese food for the family, and Tiffany was starting to get tired of white rice every night. This evening, her grandmother had made braised soy sauce chicken, steamed grouper with ginger and scallions and a stir-fried vegetable medley including snow peas, carrots, celery, onions, water chestnuts and cashews. Tiffany ate without complaint—her grandmother's cooking was good, after all—but she longed for something that hadn't been made in a wok.

When she was ten, Tiff had complained how their family never ate pizza and chicken fingers and fries like the other kids in school did. Most of the lunches her grandmother had packed had consisted of leftovers, with their colorful pieces of meat and vegetables on rice. To her classmates, most of whom had bland-looking sandwiches, her lunches had been strange and exotic, garnering a lot of the wrong kind of attention. They'd started asking if she ate dog meat, or if their family caught stray cats and turned them into chop suey.

"Just ignore those kids," her mother had told her. "Our food is part of our culture. This is part of who we are."

"But I don't want to be who we are," Tiffany had cried in frustration. "I want to be normal."

Silence had fallen at the table, and she'd been buried beneath her parents' flinty glares. It had been years before she'd understood what she'd really meant.

"You eat what we eat," was all her father had said.

Her mother joined them at the table. Dad and Daniel were working the dinner shift. Mom worked the lunchtime rush and stayed later if needed. On weekends, the whole family worked together. That schedule hadn't changed in the twenty-five years the Good Fortune had been under their management. It meant they rarely ate together, but *Poh-poh* still cooked as if they did.

"Are you still using a fork?" her mother asked, exasperated.

Tiffany shrugged. She'd always preferred a fork over chopsticks, even as a child. She gave her mother a look that dared her to comment further, but she didn't.

"So, what did you do today?" Rose asked, slurping her soup down and deftly attacking her chicken foot.

Tiffany spooned her own chicken foot into her mom's bowl. "I'm still going through my stuff." Daniel had retrieved the bags from her car earlier. She'd left a lot behind, yet still had a ton of stuff to go through, most of it clothing. She hadn't gotten very far in the culling process.

"How's your wrist?"

She held it out, turned it gingerly. "Not bad. It still hurts to lift anything heavy."

"Your face looks better," her mom remarked as she inspected Tiffany carefully. "The bruises are pretty light. A little makeup and you won't see them at all."

Dread filled her. Rose wouldn't be asking after her well-being unless she had something on her mind.

"What are you doing tomorrow?"

"Oh, you know. Sitting around the house and eating bon-bons. Watching bad TV until my eyeballs fall out."

Her mother cut her a disapproving look.

"I'm kidding. I've been looking for a job. Updating my résumé, that kind of thing."

"And then?"

"And then I'll be busy interviewing for a job. Probably driving back to the city for those interviews, in fact."

"Well, no one's going to be so impressed by your résumé that they'll call you in for an interview tomorrow." Good old Mom. A realist to the bitter end. "You should come and work at the diner."

"I can't come in," Tiff argued, panic setting in. "I'm going to be busy. Finding a job is a full-time job." At her mother's stiff silence, she blurted, "I'll find a job in town."

"Doing what? Bagging groceries? Waiting tables? You can do that with us."

Tiffany sucked in a breath, forcing patience into her tone.

"Look, Mom. I appreciate that you want to help me. I know I'm costing you and Dad groceries and stuff. As soon as I get some cash, I'll write you a check to cover my expenses."

"It's not about money or rent or groceries." She sighed disparagingly. "I don't see why you're so against working for us. We could use the extra help. And we're only trying to help you."

Tiffany knew that, and guilt made her resolve waver. But there was more than one reason she wanted to avoid the family restaurant. "I need to do this my way."

"Humph. You do everything your way, Tiffany, just like when you went off to college." She spooned a piece of fish into her bowl, talking without meeting her eye. "You wasted your intelligence on an English degree. What has it gotten you except a bunch of low-level jobs?"

"I haven't found a good fit yet, that's all." She hated how defensive she sounded. Since finishing college, Tiff had held three jobs, all as assistants. She'd been at her most recent junior assistant's position for the past two years. The problem was that upward mobility in the industry was limited, and senior positions rarely opened up. "But I was living in Manhattan and making okay money. I loved my work. I loved my life."

"You were probably living in a shoe box full of cockroaches, and 'okay money' to you means mac and cheese for breakfast, lunch and dinner."

"I like mac and cheese," Tiff said defiantly, though she had to admit that was only because instant ramen noodles had been getting tiresome.

"You should have gone into medicine," Mom said. "You never see any doctors getting laid off."

"Well, I didn't," she snapped. *So, live with it.* Tiffany gripped her fork hard. "I don't want to argue about this over dinner."

Her mother gave her a long, inscrutable look, then stopped talking altogether as she ate. Tiffany's appetite waned.

"Only one bowl of rice?" her grandmother asked, alarmed when Tiff pushed up from the table. She hadn't said a single word during the exchange between her and her mother, though usually *Poh-poh* broke up any arguments and made everyone save it until after meals.

"I'm full. Thanks. I need to work on my résumé now."

"*Ai-ya*. Always working." Sunny cast her own daughter a disapproving look. "Just like your mother."

Rose shoveled rice into her mouth as if she were trying to dig a hole through her bowl.

Tiffany quickly washed her dishes and left the kitchen. *It's like I'm a teen all over again. Only back then I used homework to escape the dinner table.*

She hurried through the house. Nothing about it had changed since she'd left. The decor was trapped in an awkward era between the seventies and eighties with faux wood cabinets, faded gray carpets and textured wallpaper that was stained in places. The only thing fresh and new about the place was the vase of red and yellow carnations on the mantel by the picture of *Kung-kung,* her grandfather, who'd died before the whole Cheung family left New York.

Once in her room, Tiffany shut her door and leaned her forehead against the cool wood. Like everything else in the house, her room had remained untouched. Glossy animal posters were still tacked up on the walls. Mementos of her childhood still sat on the shelves, including the many plastic trophies and medals for spelling bees and mathletics, and her one big trophy for highest academic achievement in high school. Her high school diploma sat in the center of her achievements, its gold, foil-embossed letters declaring highest honors. And tucked in one corner was the blue ribbon she'd won at the county fair for one of her watercolors.

All those achievements mocked her now. What good had any of those bits of plastic done her? Dejectedly, she waded through the garbage bags full of clothing and sat on her old sticker-covered twin bed. She shouldn't be here. She'd had a plan, goals, and considering how hard she'd worked, she refused to believe she was back to square one.

She took out a sheet of paper. Making lists always helped smooth things out in her mind, and she desperately needed the mental balm.

1. Pay off car repairs.

The old hatchback meant escape and freedom, and she'd need her car if she was going to get to job interviews. It would also be a roof over her head if things got desperate.

2. Get a job.

Naturally. Though how she'd get it was another question.

Steps three through five listed the bills she needed to pay off in order of highest interest. Of course, she didn't have anything to pay them with.

Looking at the piles of clothing-filled garbage bags, it wasn't hard to figure out where most of her paycheck had gone. But almost all her clothes had been on sale, and she'd had to stay fashionable and look the part of a professional if she was going to work in New York. That, at least, had been her justification when she'd seen her latest credit card bill.

A whole lot of good her fashion sense did her now. She remembered there was a consignment store on the far end of Main Street. Perhaps she could sell her clothes there. Most of her wardrobe was in good condition—plenty of items hadn't even been worn yet. But even if they sold, it wouldn't be enough to pay all her bills. And if her credit score sucked, she wouldn't be able to rent an apartment in the city.

She crumpled up the sheet and rewrote her list. Her number one priority now had to be making money. She needed to work off that debt. Nothing else could happen until she paid her bills.

Determined, she went online to search the town's classified ads.

CHAPTER THREE

"THINK YOU'VE MIXED that soil enough?"

Chris looked up at the sound of Jane Orbach's voice echoing through the greenhouse where the seedlings and more delicate crops were raised. The farm overseer nodded at the pile of black earth before him. "Trying to bury your troubles, or is there a body we haven't accounted for?"

"Maybe I'm digging for answers." He stuck the spade into the ground and wiped his brow. Jane had two grown children and was divorced. She'd always been a willing sounding board, and today, Chris really needed her guidance.

"William or Simon?" Count on Jane to know the source of his problems.

"Both. We had a big fight last night. Simon failed English, and he didn't do so well in his other classes, either." The scene from the barn had been replayed at the dinner table, except that his father hadn't taken issue with Simon's poor grades. In fact, he'd seemed delighted. "Dad encouraged him to quit school and work on the farm, and told him we couldn't afford to send him to college, which is a lie." It infuriated him that William would try to manipulate Simon like that.

"Sending your kids to college ain't cheap," Jane agreed solemnly. "But if it were going to be a cakewalk, I assume you wouldn't look like you were facing the executioner on your birthday."

"There are…issues." Chris sat heavily on a stool. "I thought I'd have a better handle on the finances by now. But I had to dip into his college fund to pay a few bills." He pinched the furrows between his eyebrows.

"That's the farming business for you. You can't blame yourself." She gave him a reassuring smile. "Things'll get better, you'll see. Have you tried talking to Daphne about helping out?"

His lips thinned with distaste. "I'm not getting my hopes up there. Frankly, I'm not sure she could rouse herself to make a trip to the bank."

Jane pulled up her cap and wiped the back of her arm across her brow. "You've gotta give the woman a chance to say no. That way, she can't blame you later for not asking her to contribute."

She was right about that. He couldn't cut Daphne out of his son's life, even if she'd effectively done it herself.

"But I think we're getting ahead of ourselves." Jane propped a hip on the table. "Your problem is that you're always trying to see the forest instead of the trees. Fact of the matter is, if Simon wants to go to college, he'll need to bring his GPA up. And to do that, he's going to have to retake that English course and ace it. Pretty damn clear course of action, if you ask me."

It was clear to Chris, at least. But as he went about his day, he couldn't stop worrying about how he would pay for college. Simon wasn't likely to get a scholarship; he had to admit that to himself. His son lacked the motivation and drive. Chris had done his best to provide and save money, but it wasn't going to be enough.

Fists clenched, he strode into the house. He couldn't let a little thing like money stand between Simon and his future.

He picked up the phone and stabbed the number buttons.

"Daphne. It's Chris," he said tersely when she answered the phone.

"I'm waiting for a call from my decorator. What do you want?"

How about a few minutes out of your day to discuss our son? He willed the tension to drain from his voice, pushing down the resentment that surfaced whenever he talked to his ex-wife. After all, he was calling her, hat in hand. He led into the matter slowly. "I thought you might want to hear about Simon's report card. I'm not sure he'd tell you about it himself." He gave her a brief rundown of his marks.

"What do you expect me to do?" Daphne asked impatiently when he was done. "It's not as if I can fly over there to do his homework for him."

"So nice to hear you care."

"Don't get sarcastic with me," she snapped. "Of course I care. He's my son, too."

"You're right, that was uncalled for. I apologize." He blew out a breath. "Look, I've been thinking a lot about the next couple of years. Simon's going to head off for college soon and...well, he's going to need help with tuition."

The silence from the other end of the line pressed down on him. "I thought you said you'd take care of all that."

"Things on the farm haven't been easy."

"Things on the farm have *never* been easy. What is it this time? Barn fire? Swine flu? Plague of locusts?"

"It's not about the farm—"

"It's always about the farm, Chris. You never cared about anything else."

"How can you say that? I left school for you."

"You could have gotten a job in town."

"Doing what? I didn't have a degree or diploma. We needed money right away, so I had to work on the farm to provide for you and Simon and—" He cut himself off ruthlessly, willing his pulse to stop throbbing inside his skull. He would not rehash this old argument with her. "Please, Daph. Will you help with Simon's college fund?"

"You think he's going to go anywhere with those marks?"

The wryness in her voice was tinged with just a hint of bitterness. She'd never done well in school, either. "Besides, I thought you and your father would be happy. You always need help mucking out the stables, right?"

"Is that what you want for him?"

"Of course not." She sighed. "You think your father will even accept money from me?"

"Forget what my dad thinks. He doesn't matter."

"That's not what you've said in the past."

"Daphne. Please," he implored, barely clinging to the last of his patience, "will you help?"

Finally, after a lengthy pause, she replied, "I'll have to talk to Bryan. I'm sure he'll say yes, but he'll want to see some college acceptance letters first."

The muscles in his shoulders relaxed marginally. "I understand. And I appreciate it. Thank you."

"You know I care for him, right?" Daphne asked in earnest. "Simon means a lot to me. I know it doesn't seem that way but…I care, Chris. I really do."

Chris chewed the inside of his cheek. He'd told himself she'd done the best she could. And they really had been in love once. She'd cared for him and Simon. But not enough to stay. Not enough to try to work things out, to get help, not even for herself. Instead, she'd run into the arms of a man who'd taken her away from her problems, gotten her the counseling she'd needed and given her all the things she'd ever wanted. Things Chris would never have been able to provide. He'd been enough back in high school, but now… "Yeah, I know you care," he said, tired to the bone. "Do you want to talk to Simon? He's up in his room."

"Better not," she said after a brief hesitation. "I feel a headache coming on. Just tell him hi for me." She hung up without saying goodbye.

He put down the receiver and rubbed at the ache in his

chest. It wasn't for love lost—not exactly, but he did have regrets. He wondered whether getting a shift job at a factory and moving into a dingy little apartment might have kept their family together. But he knew they wouldn't have been happy. Daphne was never happy.

Though maybe Simon would have fared better in a bigger town. He'd never said it outright, but Chris was sure his son resented the hell out of being stuck on the Jamieson farm. Chris remembered being fifteen: too young to drive, too isolated to have friends with cars to pick him up to go to town. Things had changed after Chris had joined the football team and gotten his driver's license, but Simon wasn't as athletically inclined or motivated. Things might change in another year when Simon could get his learner's permit, he told himself hopefully. But he could easily picture his son taking the car for a ride and never coming back. He would drive aimlessly, in any direction that was away from the farm, until the car broke down, or he ran out of gas money....

Gripped by a sudden fervor, Chris booted up his computer. He wouldn't let Simon's future slip out of his hands. He was his father, dammit, and he would make sure Simon went to college.

Unfortunately for Simon, the only way he was going to get there was by first passing that English course.

"SUMMER SCHOOL?" Simon stared at the enrollment form Chris had printed out. "You want me to go to *summer school?*"

"It's better than doing the extra course load in the fall. Besides, you're still in school mode. Better to stay in and get it over with."

"But...what about the farm? And the kittens? I was supposed to help out around here."

"You'll still have to do your regular chores, including keeping an eye on the kittens. But I'll figure something out with

Jane for the rest. I'd rather you focus on your grades. And I want to find you a tutor," he added. "It's easier to have someone guide you through Shakespeare rather than figuring it out on your own. And a tutor could help you brush up on a few other subjects, too."

"I don't think so."

"Why not?"

"Dad, I'm sick of school," Simon whined. "I'm not smart, and I can't do all this work. Why can't you accept that?"

A hard, hot lump lodged in his throat. He couldn't believe his son was giving up so easily. "You *are* smart. Did someone tell you otherwise?"

Simon looked away without answering.

Gentling his voice, Chris said, "You can do this, Simon. If you work hard, you'll bring your GPA up. You need it if you want to go to college."

"I don't want to. I'm lazy, okay? School's stupid. None of that stuff matters. I don't want to go to summer school. I don't want a tutor."

"So, to spite yourself and prove how lazy you are, you'd rather work on a farm for the rest of your life?" Chris laughed humorlessly. "Listen, Simon, farming is not work for a dummy. Farming is not work for someone who wants to cut corners and nap in the barn. You want to work on the farm? I'll show you what a real day's work is, mark my words." Good Lord, he was starting to sound like his dad. But he had to be firm and make Simon see how important his education was.

Simon jammed his hands into the pockets of his hoodie, belligerence in every line of his body. "Never mind. Forget I said it."

Chris pressed his advantage, hating that he always had to be the bad guy. "Summer school and the tutor, or you're up at 4:00 a.m. every day doing farmwork till it's dark."

His son shot him a hateful glare. For a heart-stopping second, Chris thought he'd have to condemn his son to hard labor. He'd called his bluff before. But then Simon threw his hands in the air. "Fine. I'll do summer school."

"And the tutor."

"Yeah, yeah. Whatever."

His insides unclenched. He hated how he had to threaten his son into wanting something better. But the battle was won. Simon would get help. He would raise his marks. And he would go to college if Chris had to sell half the farm.

Tiffany scanned the piles of clothing, lips pursed. The Sell pile wasn't nearly as big as it should be, the Keep pile was too big, and the Maybe pile was inching ever closer to the Keep pile.

She stuffed the Sell pile into a backpack and hefted it downstairs with her good arm. It would make a good test, she told herself. She could bring in more if this cream of the crop sold.

She peeked around the edge of the stairwell. She couldn't let anyone in her family see what she was doing. Her mother had never approved of using the consignment shop. She thought it made the family look cheap. And besides, Tiffany didn't want anyone knowing how much debt she was in. If her parents found out, they would insist on paying her bills, and she would never live it down. No, she had to do this on her own.

She placed the bag by the door and went to say hello to her grandmother.

"*Poh-poh,*" Tiffany greeted as she entered the kitchen. Sunny sat at the table, meticulously peeling cloves of garlic. She acknowledged her with a grunt. She'd slowed down considerably in her old age, so she didn't work in the diner much anymore. Instead, she cleaned and cooked the family meals and did prep work for the diner at home. "I'm heading out. Do you need help with anything before I go?"

Her grandmother regarded her with a small frown. "Why are you okay working here, but not at the diner?"

"I want to spend more time with you, that's all." She couldn't quite mask her false intentions, though, because Sunny simply shook her head.

"Your parents work very hard, you know. You should help them."

Tiffany didn't respond. Her grandmother didn't usually harangue her about her duty to her parents. In fact, back in high school, Sunny had often told her daughter and son-in-law that they all worked too hard and wore their children down to the bone.

"*Ai-ya,* I forgot we're out of creamed corn." She pushed up slowly. "I'll go to the grocery store."

"I can pick it up for you," Tiff volunteered.

She waved her off. "*Mm-sai, la.* I was going to get a few things anyhow."

Tiff hesitated. She wouldn't be able to drop into the consignment store if *Poh-poh* was with her. She'd have to leave that task for another day.

The grocery store was a healthy twenty-minute walk away, but at seventy-five, Sunny wasn't as fast as she used to be, so it took significantly longer. Still, she insisted on walking everywhere. The sun was bright and hot, and a stiff breeze blew dust into their faces. Tiff worried her grandmother was a little overdressed in her dark blue jogging suit, but Sunny didn't complain. She didn't even break a sweat.

Much of this part of Everville looked the same, with lines of Colonial-style houses broken up by postwar detached homes on big grass parcels, many of them remodeled and added on to over the years. A weed-choked lot, which had once housed a line of older homes leveled by fire, had been cleared, and a new development was being built. Several yellow backhoes and dump trucks were parked around piles of gravel and big lengths of pipes.

Someone needs to put a Starbucks here, Tiffany thought wistfully. She missed her daily soy latte.

"So, do you have a boyfriend yet?" her grandmother asked, managing to sound only mildly interested.

Tiffany smirked. "I've been too busy to date."

"That's no good. You're getting older, *Ah-Teen*." It had been a long time since Tiffany had heard her shortened Chinese name, *Cheung Sai Teen*. "You can't wait much longer. *Ah-Day* has a girlfriend, you know."

She startled. "Daniel's dating someone? Who?"

"She's a doctor in New York. Her name is…ah…Seelee-na?" She shook her head. "Strange name."

Her brother was dating a doctor, and no one had shoved her nose in it yet? "Do Mom and Dad know about her?"

"They know he's seeing someone. But none of us have met her yet."

She filed that bit of information away for later as they approached Main Street. It was busy for a Tuesday afternoon, or as busy as small-town thoroughfares could get. Part of that was due to the construction a couple of blocks away, where they were replacing the water mains. Annoying as the roadwork was, drivers who would otherwise be passing through stopped for gas and coffee and peeked into the shops. Tiffany was surprised to see a few of the older businesses had closed down and been replaced by new ones including a modern furniture store, a trendy café and an eco-friendly Laundromat. Fortunately, the consignment shop at the far end of the street was still open, a rack of colorful clothes displayed outside.

Everville Grocer hadn't changed. The green-and-white facade had been repainted recently. The store still advertised all their specials on hand-painted signs taped to the window glass. Inside, yellowy fluorescent lights illuminated the dingy gray linoleum.

While *Poh-poh* pushed the cart up and down the aisles, Tiffany checked the bulletin board for part-time work. Her online search had yielded nothing. Sadly, the bulletin board sported many of the same ads for local businesses and services, with the addition of a flyer for piano lessons and a sign for a lost dog.

"Ah-Teen!" Her grandmother's shout blared across the store as loudly as if she were on the PA system. *"Fai-dee lay-ah."*

Tiffany's cheeks heated as a few customers watched her hurry to the produce section. "You don't need to shout. I was coming right back."

"I can't see the price on this." Her grandmother held up a bunch of Shanghai bok choy, squinting. Tiff was surprised the Asian vegetable could even be found in Everville, though she had noticed it on plenty of non-Asian menus in New York. She glanced up at the signage and blinked at the big marquee.

C. Jamieson's Organic Produce, Everville, N.Y., U.S.A.
100-Mile Approved.

As in Chris Jamieson? Her insides fluttered as she remembered the high school quarterback with the floppy mop of gold-blond hair, sky-blue eyes and brilliant smile. What on earth was he doing back on the farm? Last she'd heard, he'd gone to Berkeley.

Tiffany told her grandmother the price of the bok choy and they continued shopping. After they paid and headed outside, *Poh-poh* paused on the sidewalk. "I need to talk to your mother at the diner."

Tiff suppressed a groan. She knew it would be childish to

drag her feet, but she dreaded stepping foot in the Good Fortune and seeing her parents.

The ugly wind chimes by the door jangled discordantly as she preceded her grandmother into the Good Fortune. The place had been an old diner before her parents had converted it into a North-American style Chinese eatery. The Formica tables and cracked red vinyl seats had been preserved, but the walls were covered in mirrors to make the space look bigger. Rose sat at the table closest to the counter rolling plastic take-out utensils in paper napkins. She glanced up. "We just got a shipment of supplies that need unloading. Go help your father and Daniel."

"Mom." Tiffany pointed at the sling.

"So, don't use your bad arm. Carry the lighter things and the bags. It's not like you broke your leg."

Tiffany set her teeth. Fine. The sooner she was done, the sooner she could leave. She dropped her purse behind the counter while *Poh-poh* eased herself into a chair across from her mother and started speaking in rapid-fire Cantonese.

Passing through the swinging door into the kitchen, she nearly walked into Daniel, who carried two large boxes of vegetables. "Finally decided to show up?" He cocked a smile.

"I only popped in because I was helping *Poh-poh* with groceries. Mom conscripted me into helping unload."

"If you do a good job, I'll fry up your favorites," he teased.

She shuddered. "Ugh. Chicken balls." When she was young, her parents had literally paid her in chicken balls to work at the diner after school and on weekends—one per hour. She'd loved the fried doughy balls smothered in bright orange sweet-and-sour sauce and had hoarded them greedily. But her palate was much more sophisticated these days, and besides, she had a figure to watch.

She followed Daniel through the kitchen and out the back door to where the delivery truck sat in the alley. Her father conversed with the driver, acknowledging her with a short wave.

"So, I was at the grocery store with *Poh-poh*," Tiffany began as she grabbed a big bag of onions with her uninjured right hand, "and I saw a display of organic produce from the Jamiesons' farm. Is that Chris Jamieson? The one from high school?"

"Yeah, he's running the family business now."

"What about his father?"

Daniel grimaced. "I guess you didn't hear about the accident. The tractor overturned while William was out in the field and it crushed his left leg. They had to amputate."

She gasped and dropped the bag of onions. "Oh, my God."

"He's all right. I mean, minus a leg. He doesn't come in much anymore, though." Daniel didn't sound too broken up about that, Tiff noted. He continued, "Actually, I saw Chris last week when I was at Frank's checking on your car. He was surprised to hear you were in town."

"He was?" A stupid little thrill shimmied down to the base of her spine. She straightened in an attempt to suppress the sensation. "I'm surprised he remembered me at all."

Daniel gave her a smarmy grin. "You still have a crush on him, don't you?"

"Don't be ridiculous. That was high school." She busied herself unpacking a box of vegetables to hide the color flaming across her cheeks. "I'm totally over him."

"That's too bad because he's available again."

Her hands stilled as the words ricocheted through her brain. "Again?"

"He and his wife divorced...wow, must be nine years ago now."

"I didn't even know he'd been married," she said slowly, her mind buzzing. She was unsure how she was supposed to feel about this news. Divorce was one of those sticky events where you didn't know whether to console or congratulate a person.

"See, this is what happens when you don't call," Daniel said. "Important gossip goes right past your radar." He sliced a hand over his head. "Anyhow, Daphne—Chris's high school girlfriend, I don't know if you remember her—left him for this real-estate developer when their son was about six. Didn't fight for custody or alimony or anything. Her new husband's loaded, apparently."

"Chris has a son?"

"Yeah, Daphne got pregnant before he left for college. Chris had to drop out before he barely finished his first year. Moved home and married her, been there ever since."

Tiffany sucked in her lip. She'd assumed Chris had come back after his father's accident, but learning he hadn't even completed his first year at Berkeley made her insides turn over. She couldn't fault him for his decision, of course. He'd done the right thing. But she'd spent hours tutoring Chris to improve his GPA. When he'd gotten that scholarship, she'd never been prouder.

And what did he do? Knock up Daphne Blaine.

She huffed as she hastily unpacked a box.

Daniel's cell phone rang and he answered. "Oh, hey, speak of the devil. How are you, Chris?" He grinned at Tiffany as he listened. "Actually, she's right here. You want to talk to her? Hang on." He held out his cell. Tiffany looked at it as though it were a bomb. Her heart rate sped up. "It's Chris Jamieson. He wants to ask you something."

She accepted the phone with cold fingers and cleared her throat. Every nerve in her body was so tight she vibrated. She listened for a moment to the background noise. Machinery echoed in the distance. A breeze distorted the birdsong for a beat. She could almost feel Chris breathing into her ear, and she imagined his breath fanning over her, trailing goose bumps down her neck. Daniel watched her, urging her to speak.

"Tiffany Cheung," she greeted crisply. Jeez, could she have sounded any more unenthusiastic?

"Hey, Tiffany, it's Chris. From high school. Remember me?"

She remembered that his favorite foods had been chocolate milk and fries. She remembered the way he'd smelled when he'd meet her at the library after football practice on Thursdays—like grass and musky boy sweat. She remembered how much he'd loved his motorbike, how he'd offered to give her a ride home after every session. She'd never accepted; she hadn't wanted her parents or anyone else to see her and make assumptions. "Yes."

"I heard you were in a car accident. How're you doing?"

"I'm fine."

Daniel's eyebrows knit at her indifferent, deadpan tone. This had always been the way she'd talked to Chris back in high school. She couldn't help it. She'd been terrified of blurting out something foolish, so she'd kept her interactions to a minimum. She tried to lighten her voice and explained, "Just a few bruises, sprained wrist."

"Sorry to hear that, but it sounds like you got lucky. I saw the wreck at Frank's."

"Daniel mentioned."

"So, how have you been otherwise?"

Terrible. I'm unemployed, I have no car and no money and I'm living with my parents. Hearing your voice has been the best thing to happen to me since I left New York.

"Fine." If she started talking now, she was afraid she wouldn't stop until she'd told him in excruciating detail all about the past fifteen years. "What do you want?"

And now she sounded like a bitch. She corrected herself brusquely, "Daniel said you had something to ask me."

"I was wondering…how long are you going to be in town?"

She paused, not sure what he wanted to hear. "I'm looking for a job right now. It might be a few weeks. But I'm not staying."

"Your brother mentioned you got laid off. Sorry to hear that. The economy's been hard on everyone."

Blood rushed into her face and she glared at her brother. What right did he have to go shouting her business all over town? He didn't see her death stare, though, since his back was to her as he shelved produce in the big stainless-steel fridge.

"Listen, I know this is kind of out of the blue…do you want to meet up for a coffee?"

Wait, did she miss something? "Coffee?"

"At the Grindery. It's where the old feed store used to be on Main. They've got great coffee."

She remembered passing the little café on the way to the diner. "When?"

"How about in an hour? I've got to pick up something down at the hardware store anyhow."

She couldn't detect any ulterior motive, couldn't sense a trap, but she was too discombobulated to examine his intentions. She answered, "Okay. Sure. An hour. The Grindery," and before she realized what she was doing, she hit End, before Chris could respond.

She gaped at the phone in her hand, appalled she'd hung up on him. Maybe she should call him back and tell him she'd been cut off. What if he'd said something more, something important, like, "Just kidding, I'd never ask you out for coffee"?

Stop that. Chris had never been that cruel, and this wasn't high school.

"Hot date?" Daniel smirked.

She threw him a contemptuous look, her fury resurfacing. "What did you tell him about me?"

"Tell him? Nothing."

"He knew I'd been laid off. You told him that?"

Daniel blinked slowly. "Oh. Yeah. I did. Sorry."

"I don't need you blabbing my business to everyone, okay?"

Her brother stepped back, hands raised. "I said I'm sorry. Jeez, what's the big deal?"

"What do you mean 'what's the big deal'? I was fired. You think I want the whole town to know it?"

"You were laid off, not fired," he said quietly.

"I know that. But I'd rather not have the whole freaking town think I was a massive failure. You know that's what Mom and Dad are going to tell everyone." She hated it when her family talked about her to other people. They'd done it her whole life, making her a living example of good Chinese upbringing, tearing her down when she didn't meet their standards, and always, always comparing her to Daniel.

She slapped his phone onto the tabletop and pushed through the swinging door. The stink of fryer oil clung to her skin.

Her mother looked up as Tiffany snatched her purse from under the counter. "The menus could use wiping down—"

"I've got to go. I'm meeting someone." Her biting tone startled her mother.

"Who?" Rose asked, surprised.

"A friend. From high school."

Her mother's eyebrows knitted together skeptically.

"I'll walk *Poh-poh* home first," Tiff said, preempting her mother's query. Hearing her name, Sunny got to her feet and said a cursory goodbye. Her grandmother was perfectly capable of walking home alone, of course, but that wasn't the point.

As they plodded home, Tiff decided she'd shower and change before she met up with Chris. Hopefully, by that point, she'd have calmed down and regained her temper and self-confidence, and put awkward Tiffany Cheung back into the darkest recesses of her mental closet.

CHAPTER FOUR

CHRIS DWARFED THE CAFÉ TABLE in the Grindery, the extralarge coffee he'd ordered cupped between his hands. His gaze jumped toward the door every time someone came in or a flash of movement caught his eye. He was inexplicably nervous about meeting Tiffany Cheung again.

Part of it was that she'd always kind of intimidated him, which was stupid since she was barely five-two and 120 pounds soaking wet. She'd always been ultraserious, goal-oriented, her mind always on schoolwork and getting top marks. Nothing distracted her. Not even him.

He remembered when he'd first approached her, asking for help with his English paper, and she'd refused, saying she didn't have time to tutor him. He'd followed her through hallways between periods and practically begged until she'd reluctantly given in.

She'd been mercilessly focused in her tutelage. She wouldn't allow him to waste a minute of their time together: she had other things she could be doing, and he was only paying her five bucks an hour. It was the best money he'd ever spent. Thanks to Tiffany, he'd earned his scholarship to Berkeley.

Maybe that was why he felt like a boy waiting to get a scolding from the principal. He was ashamed that he was begging for her assistance again. He should have been paying more attention to Simon's education.

Part of the problem was he barely got to see his son. They

spent less than an hour a day at the dinner table, where volatile tempers regularly clashed over William's greasy, salty meals. The moment he finished eating, Simon would storm up to his bedroom and slam the door. His hostility should have warned Chris something was wrong. Instead, he'd dismissed it as teenage angst.

But he hadn't noticed because instead of spending time with Simon, Chris would double-check the paperwork his father had done that day. Early on, when Chris had first taken over the farm, he'd caught his father playing with the numbers to make it look like they were in big trouble. William had claimed it was an honest mistake, but Chris wasn't about to let it happen again.

He checked his watch. He'd come ten minutes early, and now the caffeine was kicking in. His knee bounced restlessly. Damn. What did he have to be so nervous about? It wasn't as if Tiffany was going to spank him for Simon's poor grades.

The door swung open. A slender woman in slim-fitting jeans, a frilly pink short-sleeved blouse and three-inch heels strode in, her dangly silver earrings catching the light. A small designer purse hung off her elbow. Her long, waterfall-straight ebony hair, which cascaded past her shoulders, swayed as she walked to the counter. A pair of huge dark sunglasses made her delicate face look even smaller. Chris watched her place her order, admiring her figure. Definitely not a local. If he had time to flirt, he might ask her out for dinner, but he had other things to worry about.

When she picked up her drink, she gazed around the café. She looked in his direction and raised one hand in a wave.

He waved back automatically, but then his brain seized. That wasn't… It couldn't be…?

She started toward him, drink in hand. "Sorry I'm late. Didn't mean to keep you waiting." She set her coffee on the table, revealing the sling around her left arm that he hadn't noticed before. She lifted her sunglasses to rest on top of her head.

Chris faltered. "T-Tiffany?"

She quirked an eyebrow at him. "Chriiiis?" She drew out his name, uncertain.

Dear Lord. This was not the girl he remembered from high school. Where were the owlish glasses? Where was the headband and ponytail she usually wore? Mentally, he super-imposed the image of the Tiffany Cheung he knew. As she continued to scrutinize him, her mouth tightening into a steep frown, he realized this was, indeed, his old tutor.

He cleared the frog from his throat. "You look, um… different."

Her well-plucked eyebrows lowered. Ah, *there* she was. She still had those parallel lines between her eyes. "How are you?" he asked, trying to recover himself.

"Fine." She set her purse on the adjacent chair and sat pertly on the edge of her seat, arms folded over the tabletop, exactly the same way she used to when they met for tutoring. "You?"

"Good. Well, a little stressed, I suppose. One of the pigs just gave birth so there's a new litter to care for. We have new kittens, too. And coyotes have been stalking the area.…" He was blabbering. He took a gulp of his beverage and shuffled his feet beneath the table. "I don't know if you heard…I had to leave school to take over the farm after my dad's accident. He lost a leg." He cringed inwardly. That was only half-true, since he'd come home long before that. And he hadn't meant to go for the pity ploy talking about his dad's leg. He wanted to explain why he was here.

She nodded. "I heard. I'm very sorry."

Because his father's leg had been amputated or because she was disappointed in him? He rubbed his damp palms over his thighs. "He's all right. And being on the farm… It's a living, you know? I'm pretty happy. On the farm, I mean. Even with my dad…"

Verbal diarrhea. That's what this was. He snapped his jaw shut and forced himself to stop talking. She would not be interested in the goings-on at the farm.

Tiffany didn't say anything for a moment as she stirred her drink, eyes cast down. Her lashes fanned across her cheeks. "I heard you got married and had a baby."

The coffee tasted bitter suddenly. He reached for a packet of sugar. "Married, and divorced. My son, Simon, is fifteen now." He paused as regret pricked him. "Daphne's in L.A. with her new husband."

He wasn't sure that was censure in her dark eyes when she looked up, but there was definitely something. Hurt? Resentment?

"Congratulations," she said, and he quirked his eyebrow.

"On the divorce?"

"On the birth of your son. I guess it's kind of late to say it, though."

"Better late than never, right?" He chuckled weakly. Her lips lifted a fraction and she sipped her beverage.

Up close with the afternoon light bathing the café, he noticed the slight swelling in her jaw, the faint bruises beneath a light covering of powder. He'd never thought of her as someone who would wear makeup, but she certainly did now. Her lashes were sooty with mascara, her eye shadow and eyeliner glimmering with a hint of sparkle. Lip gloss made her rosebud mouth appear jeweled. Tiffany resembled a silver-screen starlet. It was all aesthetically pleasing in that glossy magazine way, but he found himself thinking about the girl beneath.

"So, you have any other kids?" she asked, interrupting his frank appraisal.

"No, just Simon…actually, he's the reason I wanted to see

you. He failed English this year. Shakespeare caused him trouble, apparently."

She gave a ghost of a smile. "Like father like son."

"I haven't been around much to help him, so it's partly my fault." He glanced into his cup. "He's going to retake the class over the summer, but I want him to have help, not only in English, but in whatever else he might want to work on. Would you be willing to tutor him?"

She lifted her eyes as if she were studying a menu above his head. "It's been a while since I've brushed up on my Shakespeare."

"What he really needs is guidance, someone to stick by him and make sure he's trying. He's not stupid—I know he's not, even if he tries to pass himself off as being below average."

"Something else the two of you share in common," she said wryly.

"Hey, I genuinely needed the help," he protested.

"You needed a babysitter."

He laughed and shook his head. "You're selling yourself short."

"I try to be humble." Her gaze remained fixed on his.

It was an apt word for her, he thought. On graduation day, when her name was called, she'd glided serenely up to accept her scholarship to NYU, her award for academic excellence and her high school diploma. Barely anyone clapped. Despite all her achievements, she'd simply accepted her prize with a smile, then descended.

That had been the last time he'd seen her. He couldn't find her after the ceremony. She hadn't shown up at any of the grad parties, either, but that was hardly a surprise. A week later, he found out she'd left for New York.

Tiffany sat back, her all-business mask dropping smoothly over her face. "I don't know how long I'll be in Everville.

I've been applying for jobs back in New York and could get called at any time."

"I appreciate that, of course. But Simon needs someone, and I'd like that someone to be you. I'd pay you, of course. I can't afford much, though." He named a reasonable hourly rate, much better than the paltry sum he'd given her back in the day, but she deserved more. "You'd come at least three times a week for two hours a session, minimum. You could probably work that around a second part-time job if you had to."

Those two lines re-formed between her eyes. "You understand if I get a job on Friday, I'm leaving, right?"

"What's the hurry?" he asked on a half laugh, but she didn't return his humor.

"I have a life to get back to. My plans have been…interrupted. I need to start working again as soon as possible." She made it sound as if she were racing against the clock.

Same old Tiffany. She knew what she wanted, knew how to get it. She was an intelligent, ambitious woman with laser-like focus and a mission. He couldn't blame her for not staying in Everville when she could have the world.

It shouldn't have bothered him as much as it did.

Tiffany needed to leave before she embarrassed herself.

Chris Jamieson was *hot*. Scalding *H-O-T*. The golden boy was now a golden man, and staring at him was like staring at the sun. She was going to go blind or melt in her seat if she stayed any longer.

Her crush hadn't abated. Not one bit. And now, as a woman who'd literally had sex a blue moon ago, she was pretty sure her panties were on fire.

Chris had always been tall, but now he was also big. Broad, with muscles that bulged beneath his fitted T-shirt. His bare forearms sported a fine thatching of dark gold hair, and his hands, with their long, strong fingers used to curving around a football, now delicately curled around his mug. He'd grown into his features, too, his chin and jaw more square and pronounced, the cleft peeking out behind the three-day growth of dark gold stubble. A dimple flashed with every easy smile. Crow's feet added a touch of worldliness to his avenging angel look. Actually, he looked more like a Norse god, minus the helmet.

He was saying something about his son, but she couldn't hear him above the silent scream ringing in her ears. His pretty, sculpted lips were moving, but she couldn't register the sound because, wow, those lips. She bet those bristles tickled.

Staring into his sky-blue eyes was her final mistake. She didn't know what drowning in another person's eyes meant until she accidentally sucked her latte down the wrong pipe.

"Are you okay?" he asked as she spluttered and coughed.

"Hot…" she rasped, praying there wasn't coffee snot hanging from her running nose. He handed her some napkins and worked on the spill around her cup, his hand brushing lightly against her elbow. She yanked it away as though scalded and nearly knocked the rest of her drink over.

"I'm fine," she snapped. Her cheeks were burning, and tears clumped in her mascara. Dammit, she knew she'd put on too much. She recomposed herself and sat up straighter. "Thank you."

He grinned. "Can't have you dying on me yet. Simon still needs help."

Oh, how she wished he wouldn't smile and push his hand through his hair like that. It made his T-shirt pull against his chest, made her think of all the wicked things she would like to do to that chest.

She wiped a palm over her mouth as if she could pocket the encroaching smile. "Tell me about Simon. What's he like?"

"Simon? Well…I guess he's a typical fifteen-year-old. He used to play baseball, but I don't think that's what he's into anymore. He's more of a video-games kind of kid. Computers and Facebook and stuff. He definitely didn't get that from me." He toyed with his nearly empty cup. "He's very intelligent when he applies himself. Once, when he was eleven, he fixed the lawn mower all by himself...."

Chris's words blurred together as he waxed on about his brilliant son. Every word out of his mouth reinforced how much he'd grown, becoming a proud father with a house and a farm. A man with responsibilities, property, a family, a life.

Inexplicably, she was a little disappointed. Where had the rebellious, intellectual, motorcycle-riding teen she'd known gone to? He used to rant about issues like how crass consumerism was destroying the environment, or how the North American obesity epidemic was a crime when children were starving in other parts of the world. He'd been one of the most intelligent and radical kids around, though he'd hidden it beneath his QB persona.

"So, do you think you can help?" he asked when he'd finished extolling his son's virtues.

She tilted her chin, considering the money. It was more than she'd make mowing lawns, certainly. And it should keep her out of the diner. "All right, I'll do it."

He slumped in his chair in relief. They discussed when she could meet Simon and when the best times to tutor would be. Chris handed her a business card, and she wrote her number down for him.

His smile was wide as he took the card from her and clasped her hand. Warmth snaked up her arm and she stuffed down a dreamy sigh. "Thank you so much for agreeing to this. I'll see you soon."

Oh, she definitely wouldn't mind seeing more of him.

DANIEL LOGGED ON to his instant messenger, cracked his knuckles and waited. He double-checked to make sure the door was closed—he hated being interrupted during his personal time, and he'd been very clear to his family that after hours, when he was in his room, he was not to be disturbed.

Not that they ever listened to him.

It was hard enough to have a long-distance relationship; having one with a general practitioner who was always on call with her patients was like trying to chase the sun as it set over the horizon. Added to the fact that his parents were on him every minute of the day, it was no wonder he hadn't told them about Selena until nearly a year after meeting her.

The window blinked as Selena88 popped up with her greeting. Hey, honey bear, how was your day?

Long, as usual, he replied. And longer than usual since Tiffany had come home, he admitted to himself. Lots of kids are signing up for summer driving lessons, but Dad wants me to spend more time at the diner. I don't know what he expects. I already work there thirty-five hours a week.

How's your sister? Maybe she can fill in for you.

Physically, she's doing better, but she won't go near the diner if she doesn't have to. She hates it there. Besides which, he couldn't imagine her doing him any favors. They'd never really gotten along, mainly because their parents had always encouraged sibling rivalry between them. He understood that his parents believed "friendly competition" would bring out the best in their children, but the constant comparisons had left a huge chip on Tiff's shoulder. He knew being home was bringing old resentments back to the surface.

You could hire someone. You should talk to your father about it. You work too hard.

We're not really a talking family. It was hard to explain his family dynamic to anyone on the outside. The Cheungs did not discuss feelings or personal problems; likewise, he did not question his father on matters about the diner. He did the books, sure, but his dad was the one who had final say in any expenditure. It drove him crazy that he wouldn't spend money on anything, not even if it meant more business. But that was Tony. Tightfisted and immovable.

Well, that's a shame, Selena wrote. You're too loyal.

He wasn't sure if she meant it as a compliment or a criticism. He decided to take it for the former. That's me. Dutiful firstborn son. He added a smiley face.

He switched topics. So, can you make it up for your vacation?

Yes! I've got the time booked off and I'm arranging to have my partners take on any emergency calls. I'll be all yours for two whole weeks. Yay!

Daniel wanted to dance around the room, but settled with sending a string of emoticons. Huzzah!

I miss you so much. I've been thinking about you a lot.

Me, too.

I think a lot about that one wild night when you came down at Christmas. Especially when I'm in the shower.

He grinned. Since the first time they'd met face-to-face, they couldn't keep their hands off each other. I can't wait for a repeat.

Though, if she was coming up to visit him in Everville, they were going to have to find a hotel in the next township. *Poh-poh* was around the house all the time, and while his parents would insist Selena stay with them to be good hosts, they'd probably give her Tiffany's room, or make her share. He didn't want to think about how Tiff would react to that.

The next words that popped up on screen made all thoughts of his family fly away. I wish you were touching me right now.

Daniel flushed hot even as his hands turned cold. He glanced at his door once more to make sure it was closed.

Is your webcam working yet?

He hesitated. She'd asked him this before, but he felt too exposed, knowing things would heat up fast if they got to see each other, play striptease, show each other what they were doing, what they wanted the other to do. As tech savvy as he was, he wasn't entirely convinced those images couldn't be intercepted or recorded and spread over the internet.

Sorry, no, he wrote back. But I'm still thinking of you.

Too bad. I bought the prettiest new bra today. It's black satin with lace and a cute little pink bow. And it pushes my tits up really high.

His cell phone buzzed. Selena had sent him a photo. With slightly shaky hands, he opened the file to see said new bra doing what bras did best.

A loud knock shattered the lusty haze. "*Ah-Day,* you want some *tong sui?*" *Poh-poh* yelled through the door.

"No, thank you," he groaned, trying hard to keep the frustration out of his tone.

"I'll leave some for you on the table."

"I don't need dessert," he yelled, mood thoroughly killed.

"What are you doing in there? Talking to your girlfriend?"

He stared up at the ceiling, praying for patience. "I'm on the computer. I'll come out later, thank you."

I've got more to show you as soon as your webcam is working, he read. I've been taking pole-dancing classes.

I'll get it working, he promised, mouth dry.

Another loud knock on his door had him shooting out of his chair. Furious, he yanked the door open to find Tiffany, knuckles poised to knock again. "What do you want?"

"I need to pick up a couple of books I saw on your shelf." She pushed past him. Little sisters apparently did not grow out of invading personal space.

He was about to toss her out, but then she stopped in front of his computer, the IM window still open on his screen and clearly readable. "Omigod, you *do* have a girlfriend," she hooted. "Are you guys having cybersex?"

Heat exploded on his face. "Get out."

"I hope you're using virus protection. Though you should wait until you're cybermarried before you jump into things," she snickered. "Seriously, she's for real?"

"Yes, she's real, her name is Selena and I'm trying to spend some quality time with her. Now, will you please respect my privacy?"

"You're expecting privacy in this house?" Tiff laughed, and dodged the bunched-up socks he whipped at her. "All right, all right, I'll come back later."

He really needed to put a lock on his door. Unfortunately, it was an older door and the old lockless hardware had become one with the wood beneath the hardened layers of paint, so it'd be a huge job to replace the doorknob. His father didn't like him putting holes in the wall or on the doors, either, so he couldn't install a latch or dead bolt. On top of that, his grandmother would get suspicious of what he was up to behind locked doors and would end up pestering him twice as often.

He really needed to move out.

Hello? You there, honey bear? he read when he returned to his computer.

Sorry. Stupid interruptions. Stupid little sister... : (

Did you talk to her?

She came in to get something.

You should talk to her. She needs her big brother.

Daniel sighed. He thought he was being a big brother by leaving his sister alone. She'd never reached out to him before.

Damn, I'm getting paged. Sorry. We'll continue this tomorrow night. If you're good, I'll show you the panties that match. ;)

Daniel swore a blue streak and wrote back. Okay. Sorry for the interruptions.

It's all right. I know how much your family means to you.

He wanted to deny it, but instead typed, Good night. xoxo
Tiffany was standing outside his door when he opened it, and he glowered down at her. "Do you still have that copy of Shakespeare's complete works?" she asked without pre-amble. "And any of the SparkNotes that go with the plays?"

He stood firmly in his doorway. "Listen. When I'm in my room and the door is closed, it's private time, okay?" He locked eyes with her. "I've made this clear to Mom and Dad and *Poh-poh*. I work with them all day, so I need this space for myself."

Her lips pursed and she nodded. "You're right. Sorry I barged in like that. Old habits."

Daniel gestured for her to come in. "What do you need these for?" he asked as he pulled the books off his shelf.

"Chris wants me to tutor his son in English."

"Ah." He'd wondered why Chris wanted to talk to his sister. He'd never asked about her before. Tiffany was trying to sound blasé, but he knew she'd been crushing on Chris since her freshman year in high school. "Sorry again that I told him about your layoff," he said.

"I overreacted. I should be the one saying sorry." She sat on the edge of his bed. Her fingers clutched the bedspread convulsively. "I hate that after all the work I put in, this is where I'm at. I was supposed to be an editor at a publishing house by now. But here I am, thirty-two and back living with my parents."

"Hey—" he jabbed his thumbs into his chest "—thirty-four, and it's like I never left."

Her mouth tugged up at the corners. "Yeah, what's with that? Can't you afford to move out?"

"Where would I go? To an apartment fifteen minutes away?" His defensiveness surprised him; others had asked this question, but coming from his sister, it sounded like an accusation. "If I live here, I can save for a down payment on a place of my own and never have to deal with rentals."

"And exactly when do you think you'll save enough?" Tiff asked cynically. "Five, ten years from now? Do you think your girlfriend's okay with that?"

"You don't know her." Anger flashed through him. "What gives you any right to judge?"

"Hey, I'm just trying to show you how she might see things. You're thirty-four and still working at our parents' restaurant. I mean, why'd you bother with an MBA if all you were going to do was wait tables and make chow mein?"

"I *like* being here. Mom and Dad needed me, so I stayed," he snapped. "I didn't run away and turn my back on the family."

Tiffany's eyes narrowed and he immediately regretted his hasty words. "I shouldn't have said that. I'm sorry."

Too late. He'd put their parents between them, made it Tiffany versus the family. Her face settled into that impassive mask she wore whenever she was mad. "You never cut the apron strings," she bit out. "Sooner or later, Selena's going to realize it, too." When Tiffany's claws emerged, they were like razors, so sharp and precise you didn't know you'd been cut until you saw the blood.

"Selena doesn't care about that," he retorted hotly. "She thinks it's good I'm so close to Mom and Dad."

"Really? That's what she said?"

Not in those exact words. But she'd never complained about his dedication to them. She had family she cherished. She would understand his situation. He sidestepped Tiff's question by saying, "She's coming in July to meet everyone." He raised his chin defiantly. "If all goes well, I've got my eye on an engagement ring."

Tiffany's lips compressed and her eyebrows rose a fraction. "So, how did you meet this paragon of virtue?" she asked lightly.

"Online. On a dating website."

"What did you put in your preferences? 'Must be a doctor or lawyer, must like Chinese food, must have wide birthing hips to produce sons'?"

"You've watched *Mulan* too many times." But he had to admit Selena's self-professed love for kung-fu movies and the profile photo of her standing on the Great Wall of China had caught his eye...as had her straight talk about wanting children.

"How many times have you two met in person?"

"Six." He left out the fact that it had been only six times in one year. "She's busy building her practice, so it's hard to make time. She's amazing and beautiful and I know Mom and Dad will approve."

"Is she Chinese?"

The blunt question pulled him up short. "Why would that matter?"

"Remember when I was dating Jordan? Mom and Dad flipped when they found out he was white."

"They flipped because he had tattoos on his neck and those disgusting hole things in his ears. *And* they found out about him on Facebook instead of from you." Of course, Daniel had been the one to show them the photo and her relationship status. But he'd only done so because the guy was clearly unsuitable for his sister. "Besides, why do you care? You broke up with him two weeks later."

"He owned his own auto body business and made three times as much as I did. But instead of taking that into consideration, Mom and Dad took one look at him and made a snap judgment. Did you know Mom actually called me and told me not to date *gwai-los* anymore?"

"That's not going to happen with Selena," he said fiercely. Daniel refused to believe his parents were that racist. "So what if she's not Chinese? She's everything they could ever want."

"Are you even listening to yourself?" Tiffany laughed nervously. "She's everything *you* could ever want, you mean. I sure hope that's what you mean."

"Of course it is," he growled, his cheeks prickling with heat. "Not that any of this is your business. Selena and I are both ready for the next step in our lives. She wants kids, and so do I."

"*You* want kids, or Mom and Dad want grandkids?"

He'd had enough. "If you're going to sit there and question my feelings all night, you can get out right now."

Tiffany crossed her feet at the ankles and her arms over her chest. "I'm just being realistic. If you're both ready for the next step, that's great. I'm happy for you." She had that infuriating matter-of-fact tone their mother sometimes used to convince someone to do something they didn't want to. "But I hope you've thought about the future. For instance, is she going to live here, share a room with *Poh-poh?*"

"Don't be ridiculous. We'll get a place of our own."

"Uh-huh. So, are you planning to leave the restaurant business?"

"Of course…" He trailed off. He was going to say, "Of course not," because what else was he going to do? He loved the diner, and his parents needed him. And one day, the Good Fortune would be his. Once Mom and Dad retired, he would renovate the dining room, redecorate, get new menus printed—he had grand plans for the place.

But what would Selena do? Work alongside him, waiting tables and taking orders over the phone? Pop out a few babies and raise them at home?

A slow, cold dread crept down his spine and puddled in his shoes. His sister went on ruthlessly. "Last I checked, the job market wasn't so good. You might have a hard time getting an entry-level position at your age." Tiffany pushed off the bed. As she headed out with her books, she said over her shoulder, "But I'm sure if you're both ready for the next step, you'll work it out, right?"

CHAPTER FIVE

TIFFANY WASN'T SURE the consignment shop would be open on a Sunday, but it had been the first opportunity she'd had to get away from her family without rousing suspicions. She'd told *Poh-poh* she was on her way to the Jamieson farm—which wasn't a complete lie, since she was heading there straight after—then slipped out with her loaded backpack.

The Good Fortune was a few doors down the street and she didn't want her family seeing her. She parked Daniel's car in the tiny lot next to the shop, out of sight of the main thoroughfare. He'd lent it to her grudgingly, and only after *Poh-poh* had badgered him to be a good big brother and help his little sister out. It was good of him, considering how harsh she'd been last night. She shouldn't have goaded him about his girlfriend or their future together. She should have been supportive and told him she was happy for him, but the misanthrope in her had insisted on pointing out the flaws in his plan. She supposed that was what came out of years of never being praised by her family. Not that it was an excuse.

The bell above the door jangled as she entered the shop. It was quiet before noon—a lot of folks were still in church. Big band jazz crooned from an old-fashioned radio in one corner. The place smelled faintly of patchouli and mothballs. Jam-packed racks of clothing barely left enough room for people to squeeze through. An adjoining room held household goods and small appliances lined up on metal shelves.

At the back of the store from behind a curtained doorway, a woman came out. For a moment, Tiff thought she'd
walked into a fifties TV show, but the woman's hair was all
wrong for the era. She wore a bright blue tea-length house-
dress and a white apron adorned with big ruffles. A pair of
cat-eye glasses hung off a beaded chain around her neck and
her pumps clicked smartly across the parquet floor. Her face
brightened, her pink lips parting in a huge smile.

"Tiffany? Tiffany Cheung?"

She had no idea who this woman was. She nodded with a
helpless, questioning smile in answer.

"Maya Hanes, from high school."

"Maya…" It was hazy at first, but then she remembered.
Maya had been in a few of her classes. Back then, she'd kept
her straight, sun-kissed brown hair in a slick ponytail. She'd
run with the sporty crowd. She was still fit-looking, but her
hair had been cut super short and was gelled into spikes. "Yes.
Of course. Hello."

"I'd heard you'd come home. Are you doing all right?
Someone told me you were hit by a car." She looked her
over, beaming. "You look fantastic."

"Um. Thanks. I wasn't hit. It was a car accident. I'm fine."

"I'm so glad you're okay."

Tiffany's awkwardness increased when Maya hugged her.
She held herself stiffly in the woman's light grip.

"You own this shop now?" she felt compelled to ask as
Maya let go.

"I bought the business and the building off the previous
owners about a year ago. I actually specialize in vintage
stuff now, but it's always been a handy place for the locals to
freshen up their wardrobes. How've you been? What are you
up to these days? Are you moved back here permanently?"

"Only temporarily," she said. Small talk was not Tiffany's
forte. She didn't think Maya truly cared about what was hap-

pening in her life. They hadn't been friends. They'd worked together on a group project in science once, but that was it.

"So, you're on vacation?"

"I'm between jobs."

"I see." She nodded sagely, waiting for more details.

Tiff wished she could just get her business over with and move on. She was starting to think her mom was right—if she sold her clothes here, Maya would know right away she needed money. Considering small-town gossip, everyone else would know it, too, and then what would her parents say?

She was about to make her excuses and walk out when Maya nodded at her overstuffed backpack. "Hey, if you have clothes to sell, I could always use more stock." She extended her hand for the bag.

Tiffany hesitated.

"Don't worry. I know what you're feeling. I assure you, I use absolute discretion when it comes to my customers. I don't tell anyone where the clothes came from, and you won't find out who bought them."

Tiffany handed Maya the backpack. Her need to pay the bills was greater than her pride or her worries. In the next moment, Maya spread her clothes across the worktable in the back for inspection.

"It's all in great condition. Nice, quality stuff. I'm not sure it'll sell too quickly, though." She pointed at the size six label on a silk blouse. "Most of my customers are above size ten. That's not to say I don't want it," she added quickly. "You never know who's going to come in here, after all, and variety is where it's at in a shop like this."

She explained the process, then wrote up all the tags and paperwork, and had Tiffany sign her designer labels away. Maya waived the seller's fee for old times' sake. It wasn't a lot, but Tiffany didn't have the luxury of wasting even a few dollars these days.

"I appreciate this," Tiffany said, putting the paperwork into her backpack.

"Hey, I've been where you are. And we're old friends. Doesn't hurt that you have such good taste."

Words stuck in her throat. Maya couldn't possibly have known about her mountain of debt, though she supposed she could have guessed. She wondered how many others had come in to trade their party dresses and hand blenders in the hopes of raising a little extra cash. "Thanks," she managed to say.

"You've got that look," Maya said, tilting her chin.

"Look?"

"Regret. Shame. Like you're giving up your babies to the orphanage." She ran her fingertips over the clothing. "I promise you, they always go to good homes. There's no shame in making sure someone else looks fabulous at a good price." Her beatific grin actually made Tiffany feel better.

"Thanks for the reassurance." She turned to go.

"Hey, when you've got time, give me a call and we'll go out for coffee." She handed her a business card. "Or pop by. It gets kinda lonely here."

She looked at the business card, then at Maya. "Okay."

"Promise?"

Tiff pursed her lips. "You need a promise from me?"

"I never knew you to break one. But then, I don't really know you. I hope we can change that."

Tiffany hesitated. She'd probably be away from Everville before she had to make good on her promise, but then again, a promise like this couldn't hurt her. It wasn't binding. "All right. I promise."

Maya grinned. If for nothing else, she'd call to see whether her clothes had sold.

On her way to the Jamieson farm, Tiff kept one eye on the map and the other on the two-lane road. The GPS on her smartphone didn't work very well, and she didn't trust it— it would probably lead her into the middle of a wheat field.

The farm was about thirty minutes south of town, and she hated long drives. It left her with too much time to think. In New York, she walked or took transit everywhere, and was constantly distracted. But on these long, deserted stretches, not even blasting the radio could keep her from navel-gazing.

Her mind went to Maya. She and her clique had been in all the clubs and teams. They'd been an active, popular bunch, and had little to nothing to do with Tiffany. She was confused as to why Maya would reach out to her all these years later. Then again, some people liked to talk and were always looking for an ear to listen. There wasn't much else Tiff could honestly offer her.

Ahead, a brightly painted sign that read Jamiesons' Organic Farm loomed. She turned onto the driveway. From the road, she could see a two-story farmhouse with a wide veranda and wood siding with flaking paint in dull shades of gray. Next to the house were the remains of something that might have been a fruit stand, though it was mostly filled with firewood and scraps now. The gravel driveway forked around a large maple tree and led to a red barn. Three horses of varying colors stood flicking their tails in the adjacent paddock, greeting her with low whinnies. On the other side, beyond a fenced-in area, sat four long, squat greenhouses.

Tiffany wasn't sure how big the farm was, exactly—it sloped up and over a hill, covered in large swathes of green and dotted with the occasional worker or animal. It was probably safe to say the Jamiesons owned all the land as far as the eye could see. From what she knew, it was one of the biggest plots in the county.

Her tires crunched along the gravel as she parked beside

a white pickup truck. The scent of hay, earth and animal poo hit her as she got out of the car, and she wrinkled her nose. The wind blew dust against her bare calves and sandal-shod feet, which slipped and caught tiny, painful rocks between her soles. It had been a while since she'd been anywhere without paved sidewalks.

A loud clatter drew her attention as a tall, middle-aged woman in a trucker cap, red T-shirt and blue jeans strode toward her through a side gate. "Would you be Tiffany Cheung?" she asked in a rough voice.

She put on what she hoped was a smile. "That's me."

"Chris sent me to bring you into the house and introduce you to his son. He says he's sorry he can't be here himself. He's fixing a fence on the other end of the property and can't get back in time. I'm Jane Orbach, the farm manager here."

They shook hands. Tiffany had to admit she was a little disappointed she wouldn't get to see Chris. Actually, she was downright crushed. Who else had she dabbed on her Obsession perfume for? "Nice to meet you." She forced herself to smile.

"He told me you used to tutor him back in high school." Jane regarded her curiously. "You don't look all that old."

"I was in the same year as Chris." She didn't mention that she'd skipped a grade. That fact had never earned her any allies.

They started toward the homestead. "I'm glad Chris is doing something about his son. It's not easy being a single parent. It's been especially difficult for them, what with Simon's mother leaving and then William losing his leg." She glanced at Tiffany to make sure she knew. Tiff nodded. "If I was more inclined, I'd probably be seeing to them myself. But frankly, I have better things to do than to play referee. Word of advice—keep out of their fights and you'll do all right."

Tiffany hummed in agreement. She'd dealt with being stuck in the middle of arguments before.

"A couple of other things. Will's on crutches. Unless he

asks, never, ever, *ever* offer to help him with anything. He's so full of pride, I swear he'll pop at the seams. Simon can be a little shit, too, sometimes, pardon my French, but don't let him boss you around. And Chris…" She glanced back over her shoulder toward the fields. Tiffany followed her gaze, saw a faraway speck of color striding across the brown dirt. Even at that distance, she could recognize his broad shoulders and sure gait. "Well, he's in and out all the time, and his head's in the clouds a lot. So, if there's something important you need to tell him, it's best to write him a note. Maybe pin it to his shirt or something."

Tiffany nodded, though she was getting more and more nervous. "Anything else?"

Jane grinned. "I like mocha lattes from the Grindery. So, if you happen to be passing by on the way over, a large with double espresso and extra foam will sweeten my mood and motivate me to swing by the house to save you if any of these fellas go for your throat."

Tiffany gave a weak laugh. What was she getting herself into? "I'll do my best."

They walked into the house through the front door. The foyer led into a large open-concept space that served as living room and dining room. Warm, earthy, masculine colors dominated, mostly tans, grays and hunter-green, and the furniture was bulky, comfortable-looking and thoroughly worn.

The tiled area in front of the door was cluttered with dirt-crusted boots and running shoes. Outerwear from all four seasons was strewn across the lower banister post and railing that led upstairs. Clumps of animal fur and dust formed large cloudy entities trapped within spiderwebs in dark corners. The place smelled like bacon grease, stale beer and old cheese. Tiffany pinched her lips tight. Ugh, men were so disgusting. No way was she taking her shoes off in here. The Jamiesons could really use a housekeeper.

"Simon, your tutor's here," Jane yelled. She nearly tripped over a pair of boots, cursing. Her sardonic look mirrored Tiffany's thoughts precisely: not our mess to clean.

"What's all this yelling about?" William Jamieson came stumping in from the kitchen. Tiffany shifted her purse from one side to the other and tried not to stare. The elder Mr. Jamieson had gained quite a bit of weight since she'd last seen him. She would have thought he'd get leaner with the exertion of having to use crutches, but apparently that wasn't the case. His hair was more white than gray now, still military-short. The lines in his leathery face and especially around his frowning mouth and eyes had deepened. She couldn't help but glance down at his leg, cut off above the knee, his cuff folded up and neatly pinned. Despite the loss, he still managed to cut an imposing figure. He gave her a critical once-over. "We're not hiring anymore seasonal laborers right now," he said.

Tiffany ground her jaw, but kept her smile stiff as she stuck out her hand. "I'm Tiffany Cheung. I guess you don't remember me, Mr. Jamieson. I'm here to tutor your grandson in English."

"*You're* going to teach my grandson *English?*"

"Bill." Jane's reprimand had him whipping his head around to give her an innocent expression.

Tiffany didn't need Jane to defend her against the likes of Will Jamieson. "In fact, I have a bachelor's in English with honors from NYU. I also used to tutor Chris in high school."

"Of course you did," he said with a careless wave, both acknowledging and dismissing the fact all at once. "You might as well head back to wherever you came from. Simon doesn't need a tutor. He should be spending the summer helping out around the farm where he's needed."

"Chris was the one who hired her, Bill," Jane interrupted, and Tiffany didn't miss her warning tone. She glanced at her watch. "Where is that boy?" She walked halfway up the stairs, shouting Simon's name.

"This is a waste of time and money," he muttered. "There're no guarantees he'll pass, anyhow."

"I'll do my best to ensure he does." Tiffany had never liked William Jamieson much, but he was Chris's father, and it wasn't in her to hate an old man who was missing a leg. Her parents had often told her that no matter what he said or did, she should respect her elders and take the high road, smile and nod politely. Now seemed like a good time to put those lessons to use. "It was nice to see you again, Mr. Jamieson."

She kept her mask on until he grumbled something and hobbled back into the kitchen.

Jane walked down the stairs still talking to Simon. "You need to get your hearing tested. I've been shouting for the past five minutes."

"I was napping." The kid's voice was husky and low, his words dragging as much as his steps.

"With your iPod thingy blasting in your ears?" Jane rolled her eyes toward Tiffany. *Teenagers.*

Simon was a pale kid with a dark mop of hair and an over-developed Adam's apple. Dark bags hung beneath his eyes, and his lips stuck out in a belligerent pout. He'd probably be taller than her if he didn't slouch like an italicized question mark. He wore a faded black hoodie sweatshirt and wide-legged blue jeans at least two sizes too big. His clothes appeared to be in the process of swallowing him whole.

"Simon, this is your tutor, Miss Cheung," Jane introduced.

Simon reluctantly stuck out a limp, clammy hand, which she shook. There was a little something about his face that reminded her of Chris, but Simon's cheeks still sported a touch of baby fat, which probably hid his father's cheekbones. His coloring was definitely Daphne's.

"I'll leave you to it," Jane said to her. "Simon, your father will be around later."

"Whatever."

The farm manager gave him an arch look. The teen shuffled his feet, stuck his hands into his pockets and murmured, "I mean, yes, ma'am. Sorry."

"Good luck, Tiffany." Jane's wave was more like a salute.

"So," Tiff began, feeling the jitters crawl around her belly, "we're not going to do any work today. I just came to get to know you and figure out how we're going to do things. Where do you prefer to study?"

"In bed." Now that Jane had left, he was glaring at her with open hostility. She sucked in her lower lip. Chris hadn't said his son would be resistant to tutoring.

She straightened to her full height, wishing she'd worn heels. "Since that's not going to work with two of us, would it be all right if we worked at the dining table?"

He lifted a shoulder. "I guess."

"Would you prefer the couch?"

"Whatever. I don't care."

"Let's work at the table, then." She was trying to offer him choices, but if he wasn't going to give his opinion, then she'd make the decisions for him. "Do you have your syllabus yet?"

He brought it down and she took note of all the books they'd be studying. Over six weeks, the class would be doing *The Tempest,* as well as *Animal Farm* and *Catcher in the Rye,* along with a handful of essays.

"These are all great books," she said pleasantly. "It's going to be fun reading them with you."

"I can't read all this in six weeks," he complained.

"Trust me, they're all really short. And *The Tempest* is easy in comparison to most of Shakespeare's other plays. What did you study this past year?"

"Hamlet."

"Another fun one, though not as fun as *Romeo and Juliet* or *Macbeth* in my opinion."

Simon stared at her as though she'd told him she ate nails for breakfast. "You're serious. You *like* this stuff?"

"Of course I do. Shakespeare's fun, once you get the hang of it. Don't tell me you're one of those guys who doesn't like reading?"

"I can read," he said, lip curling. "But I don't see why we should study Shakespeare. It's stupid and boring."

"*Boring?* You found *Hamlet* boring? Did you even read it?" Okay, maybe she was laying it on a little thick—*Hamlet* was somewhat long-winded and she thought the prince of Denmark was a crybaby. But she still loved the Bard.

Simon scowled through his curtain of bangs. "I barely understood it. All I know is that he was whining about his stepdad and wanted to have sex with his mom or something."

The English major in her died a little. But she had to admit it was more than some people got. "Was it the language that gave you trouble?"

It took him a while before he finally admitted, "I guess."

"Did your copies have the plain English translations?"

His reply came in the form of a glare. She had the feeling she'd be getting a lot of those. It confirmed her suspicions, though: Shakespeare's language had been so overwhelming, he'd probably given up reading it after a few pages. Chris had done the exact same thing.

"Shakespeare takes a lot of getting used to," she told Simon, "and if you have no idea what the basic plot or themes are, it's kind of hard to figure out when you read it cold. In fact, it's easier to have the play performed." She made a mental note to show him a DVD performance or two. "Do you know anything about *The Tempest?*"

"No."

"It's about a powerful wizard who lives alone on an island

with his daughter, but then he causes this shipwreck to land a prince on the island—"

Simon yawned so widely she could see the bright orange remains of some Cheetos lodged in his molars. "I'm sorry, am I boring you already?" she asked irately.

"Actually, yeah, you are."

She flinched. She'd heard rude in her life, but she hadn't expected attitude from Chris's son.

"Class doesn't start till next Monday," Simon said. "I don't know why we have to do anything right now." He tossed his bangs. "Look, I know Dad's paying you to teach me for two hours, but can we pretend we worked? You can take the rest of the day off and still get paid. I won't tell anyone."

Tiffany scowled at his attempt at manipulation. She couldn't believe he was already bargaining with her, and using his father's money, too. "I'm not charging for this time. I drove out here because I wanted to get to know you."

His darting look said, *Are you serious?* "I'm *exhausted,*" he groused. "This year was hard enough, and now I have to take an extra six weeks." He rubbed his temples. "My dad's the one making me do this. I don't know why. It's not like it's going to help."

"All right." She picked up her purse. "If you don't want to do this, fine. I'll let your father know you don't need me." She started toward the door. "I didn't think you'd give up before we'd even started, though."

"I'm not giving up," he shot back, voice rising in panic. She stopped in her tracks. He added hastily, "I just don't want to do this *right now.*"

Those were the words she wanted to hear. Anything that told her he wanted *something,* that he was not simply playing the victim. If there was one thing she hated, it was people who blamed everyone and everything but themselves for their problems and refused to do anything about them.

"It's your call," she said, folding her arms. "You set the schedule. I'm here for you."

Simon stuffed his fists into his hoodie pockets, shuffling in place. "I start class next Monday. I'm done at three-thirty."

"I'll see you here at four, then."

The front door crashed open. Chris's broad, tall frame filled the doorway, eyes landing squarely on her. Mud caked his jeans, and the strong musk of male sweat filled the room. "I was hoping I'd catch you in time." He beamed. "Had to rush back here to see you."

Her insides flipped and she struggled to keep from breaking into a goofy grin. "Was there something you needed?" she asked to stop herself from making ridiculous assumptions.

"Thought we might talk about how I'm going to pay you. Business stuff." He yanked off his wide-brimmed cowboy hat, running a muscled forearm across his brow. His arm halted in midswipe and he made a face. "Sorry, I'm not smelling too fresh." He gestured vaguely out the door. "How about we stand on the porch? I promise I'll stay downwind."

She didn't care how he smelled. She was still trying to get over how good he looked covered in sweat and mud, his golden skin below the T-shirt sleeves lobster-red. "You should be wearing more sunscreen," she remarked when they were outside.

He glanced at his arms and smirked. "This'll go away. I usually work with long sleeves, but it's been so hot lately, I can't stand it. Most of the time, I have to go shirtless. Not to be vain, but I hate farmers' tans."

Tiffany's brain went into meltdown. She looked away forcefully, afraid she'd end up burning a hole into his chest with her staring. She watched the horses in the field, letting herself cool off at the sight of those graceful, powerful beasts.

"Those yours?" she asked.

"The horses? No, we board them for their owners. The

extra income is handy, and the manure we get makes quality composted fertilizer." He gave her a sidelong glance. "You used to like horses a lot. I remember you had drawings of them all over your notebooks."

Her cheeks flushed anew. He'd remembered that? "I think they're beautiful animals."

"Do you ride?"

"Never tried."

"You lived in Everville and never went horseback riding?" he asked incredulously.

"Never had time." Or permission. Or money. Or the guts. They were creatures best enjoyed from afar. "You wanted to talk about payment?"

It didn't take long to work out her pay schedule. They could have had this conversation over the phone or via email, but she wasn't complaining.

"So, what do you think?" he ventured.

"About Simon?" Was he expecting her to tell him it was going to be a piece of cake? That his son was the genius he said he was? "He's got issues to work out. I won't know until we jump into it."

"I have faith in you," he said stoutly and grinned. "I know he's in good hands. I was."

She did smile and blush at that.

UNFORTUNATELY FOR TIFFANY, she couldn't go idle for a whole week while living under her parents' roof, no matter how many excuses she came up with. Once her mother promised to pay her, however, she gave in and agreed to work at the diner. She couldn't turn down the money. Besides, she was getting the feeling she was in her grandmother's way. She didn't know the reason for the tension between her and Sunny, but *Poh-poh*'s rueful gaze was like a sack of sharp, pointy rocks on her back. Perhaps her grandmother resented her intruding on her private time at home.

It was 9:00 a.m. and the kitchen was prepping for the lunch-hour rush. The sous-chef, Manny, had been doing the prep work for their family for more than seventeen years. Tiffany hollered a greeting, and he grinned toothily. *"Joh-san, mui mui."* *Good morning, little sister.*

"¿Hola, Manny, qué pasa?" She greeted him the same way she had as a teen. He'd patiently allowed her to practice her Spanish on him in exchange for a few phrases in Cantonese. There was a bit of salt to his thick, black hair, and a few more lines in his face, but his smile and his eyes were as bright as ever.

"Your parents told me you were home," he said. "All this time and you didn't come to see your *sook-sook?*" He gave her a hurt look.

"I've been busy looking for work, *tío.*"

"Why? You could work here." Her disdain must have shown because then he cackled. "C'mon, help me out here. Can you start the deep fryer going and throw in the egg rolls?"

She donned an apron and hairnet, turned on the fryer and got the egg rolls out of the freezer. *Poh-poh* used to make them from scratch, but the demand was too high to keep up with and they didn't have the manpower to produce them fresh anymore.

When the lunch rush came, Daniel took over in the kitchen, and Manny went to his afternoon job at a nearby farm. Her mother made her work at the steam table, scooping sticky food into foam take-out boxes.

A few regulars recognized Tiffany and proceeded to interrogate her about her return to Everville. The ones who didn't know her asked if she was new to town.

"That's my daughter," her mom would say proudly. And

then they'd commiserate over how young Rose looked, how she and Tiffany could be sisters, and how nice it was that her grown daughter was working for the family business. Tiff might as well have not been there—even as an adult, people treated her like some artifact on display in a gallery. She would have preferred to stay in the back where no one could gawk at her.

Tony arrived at the tail end of the lunch rush, frowning at her as he approached. "You serve people with that face?"

"Gee, thanks, Dad."

"Smile. Show everyone how pretty you are. People buy more when you treat them kindly, you know."

That was her dad. Always thinking about the bottom line. "Aren't you here a little early?" she asked.

"I'm preparing food for a catering event. When it slows down, come to the back and help me."

"I need her up front," Rose insisted. "It's still busy."

"I said *after* it slows down," he shot back. "Why don't you ever listen?"

She glowered back at him, and for a heart-stopping second, it looked like they'd go for each other's throats. Tiffany's stomach torqued.

Two heavy heartbeats later, Tony spun and pushed through the kitchen doors, uttering something in disgust. Tiffany exhaled, tension draining from her bones. Her mother continued wiping the counter. The customers in the diner didn't notice the exchange.

"Got any chicken balls left?"

She jumped at the sight of Chris standing in front of her, grinning wide.

TIFFANY'S CHEEKS CHANGED from pale to flaming red. Chris wasn't sure what had put that worried expression on her face, but he was glad to be the one to wipe it off. The lights from the steam counter bathed her in a golden light. Despite the hairnet, apron and sheen of sweat, she really was an attractive woman.

She regained herself quickly as her dark eyes dropped to his chest. "Nice T-shirt," she said wryly.

He looked down. His T-shirt had come from a poultry farm in the next county, and featured a cartoon chicken serving up eggs in a pan, the words *It's Clucking Good* hovering over its head. "Thanks. It's all the rage in Paris." He struck a pose and gave a duck-lipped moue.

She smirked. That seemed to be the closest he'd ever gotten to making her laugh. She pointed toward the golden deep-fried spheres. "I didn't realize you were a chicken-ball fan."

"I thought I'd get some for Simon. They're his favorite." He didn't want to admit he'd only stopped in to see if she was there and to say hello, even though he had a million things to do.

She filled a take-out box, studiously avoiding eye contact. Her reserved manner reminded him of the way she'd treated him in high school, and it made him smile.

"You must be hot," he drawled.

Her hand jerked, and two of the balls jumped out of the container. "Excuse me?"

"Back there. From the steam." He grinned.

She blinked slowly as her expression closed once more. "It's good for the skin." She continued filling the box with laserlike focus. He chuckled to himself. Getting any kind of reaction out of her was a private win. There'd been times as a teen when he'd wondered if she was immune to his charm, or simply hadn't been interested in the opposite sex. And though he hadn't admitted it to himself then, it had needled him that she'd been so unaffected.

He leaned up against the counter. "So, I was thinking, if

you have time this week, I wouldn't mind if you swung by and got a jump on things with Simon."

She didn't look up as she answered. "Simon doesn't start class till Monday. I'll work with him then."

"Oh." His disappointment surprised him. "I thought you might want to help him out in some of his other subjects."

"He said he wanted a break before summer school starts. I don't blame him. He looks like he could use a two-month nap."

He laughed. "I was tired all the time in high school. That didn't stop you from giving *me* a hard time."

"He needs a break," she said, mouth turning down steeply. "It'll be hard enough making him sit through an extra two hours of tutoring regularly. If I don't give him some space, he'll shut me out completely. When he and I sit down, I'll put him to the task. But I'm not going to drive him into the ground before we've even started."

Chris was stunned she'd reacted so vehemently. "I thought you'd—"

She plopped the box of chicken balls and the tub of glowing orange sweet-and-sour sauce on the counter by the register. "My mom will ring you up." She went back to the far end of the steam counter to serve the next customer.

Rose Cheung grinned brightly at him as he paid. She asked him some questions about his family, but his eyes kept going back to Tiffany, who wore an easy, bright smile as she filled a take-out container for the old man. Why he should be jealous that she smiled so easily for a stranger and not for him was something he didn't want to examine too closely.

"YOU WANT TO TELL ME what that was about?" Daniel asked over Tiffany's shoulder after Chris had left. Without his sister saying goodbye, he'd noted.

She lifted an eyebrow sardonically. "What what was about?"

"Why do you keep giving Chris the brush-off?" He'd watched the whole interaction unfold through the pass-through window. And while he knew he had no business questioning what Chris did with whom, he did feel obligated to look out for his little sister. It was plain to Daniel his friend had been flirting with her.

"He wanted me to start putting his son's nose to the grindstone. The kid's had a full year of high school. He's getting over failing a class. He deserves a break."

"You sure it's just that?" When she didn't answer, he nudged her aside while he picked up a mostly empty tray of sweet-and-sour pork from the steam table. Steam blasted him in the face and he wiped the sweat from his brow. "If you're interested in him, you should try to be more friendly instead of pushing him away."

"I *was* being friendly. And I'm not interested."

He chuckled. The roses blooming on her cheeks had come from more than just the heat. "Admit it. You're still crushing on him, but you're not going to do anything about it because you're afraid he'll laugh at you or hurt you."

"I do not— Don't go psych-101ing me," she sputtered.

"I'm only trying to be helpful. You're both grown-ups now. I'm just saying, if you decide to make a move… Well, you're a big girl."

She shot daggers at him. "You're one to give relationship advice. Have you told Mom and Dad about Selena yet?"

He glared, ice forming in his veins. Rose hadn't turned around, so he guessed she hadn't heard Tiff.

He walked back into the kitchen and dumped the hot steam tray into the sink. It felt as if a hundred pins were stabbing into his neck. A little teasing and his sister had slashed out with her razor-sharp talons.

What was Tiffany expecting him to do? Go up to their

parents and announce that, oh, by the way, that sweet doctor from Queens is a *gwai-mui?*

Okay, so maybe it was as simple as that. But Tiffany didn't have to keep provoking him about it.

His thoughts were disrupted as his father suddenly cursed and stalked out of the kitchen. Daniel watched through the narrow window as he headed straight for Rose. "You ordered the wrong brand of rice."

Trepidation ratcheted tightly in his gut as his mom rang in a customer and said blithely over her shoulder, "I didn't. This one is a better quality."

"And it's more expensive. Why did you order this one? I told you not to."

"It's more fragrant," Rose responded primly. "I'm tired of the old rice. It's too flaky and loose. Nothing like what we have at home."

Daniel glanced over at the sack sitting on the table. That brand cost about three dollars more. Were they seriously fighting over three dollars?

"It's a waste of money." Tony's voice rose. "I don't want to make fried rice for a hundred people with good rice."

"They won't know the difference."

"If they won't know the difference, then why did you buy the more expensive rice?" The pitch and volume of his father's voice made the pans in the kitchen vibrate. Daniel shot out of the kitchen door like a bullet.

"Hey!" he shouted. *"Mo gum dai seng-ah."*

Don't make so much noise. Or more accurately, *You're going to drive the customers away with your yelling.*

Tony gave his wife one final glower and stomped back into the kitchen. "Your mother is going to send us to the poorhouse."

"Calm down, Dad."

"She doesn't understand. This is a business, not a charity. She gives one special price here, one extra helping there, it all adds up. She doesn't care." He flung a ladle across the counter and it clattered noisily to the ground.

Daniel struggled not to get into it with him. "Dad, we're fine."

"I haven't been in business this long because I gave everyone special treatment," he said pointedly. "I'm not running a soup kitchen."

He groaned. "I get that you're mad. But Mom handles the front of the diner, you take care of the food and I take care of the books. That's our arrangement." And the only way to keep the peace around the diner.

His dad pointed at him accusingly with a spatula. "You need to keep a closer eye on her when she makes the orders." Tony resumed work on the fried rice, grumbling.

Daniel left his father to stew and stepped out to the front to replace a steam tray of black-bean eggplant. His mother was chatting up a customer with a winning smile. He frequently wondered whether the locals picked up on his parents' arguments by their angry tones, even if they didn't understand the words.

Tiffany's hands were shaking as she wiped the counter, and he had a flash of empathy. She'd always hated their parents' fights. It'd taken him years to toughen up, placing himself in the middle of their arguments. Some days, though, the tension pressed against him like a knife's edge.

"Hey." Daniel squeezed her shoulder. "You okay?"

She shook him off. "Fine."

"It's like this all the time, but this is nowhere near as bad as it can get." She whipped her head around to look at him, appalled. "It's got nothing to do with you."

"Why would *I* be to blame?" Her eyes narrowed.

"I was only trying— Oh, forget it." He escaped back to the kitchen, annoyed with her, with his parents and with himself.

No matter what he tried to do, however good his intentions, people always knocked him back down.

REGRET PRICKED TIFFANY as Daniel left in a huff. She really had to tone down her bitch factor. Years of being stuck behind a hot steam counter with her bickering parents should have tempered her, but Tony and Rose's row had left her feeling as queasy and scared as she'd been as a child. That sense of helplessness made her get defensive, like a porcupine with its quilt of needles.

She stared after her brother, thinking she should go apologize, but then Rose snapped at her, "Why are you standing there doing nothing?"

Tiff looked around. All the customers had gone. "Have you forgotten how to work?" her mother asked irritably.

Tiffany sucked her cheeks in. She reminded herself that she was living with her parents rent-free, that she owed them her love and respect. But it could be really trying, especially when she was being snapped at. She was tired of having everyone in her family telling her what to do instead of asking her with a please and thank-you. But as her mother turned away, she caught her swiping a palm across her cheek. She stood unmoving for a few seconds, facing the empty diner, back to the kitchen. Her shoulders pulled into a straight line and she picked up a broom and started sweeping.

Tiffany quietly went to clear the tables.

CHAPTER SIX

BY THREE-FIFTEEN THE FOLLOWING MONDAY, Tiffany was *so* done with the diner. She didn't think she'd ever wash the smell of fryer oil and onions out of her hair. Not even the thick overcast sky and stifling humidity could dampen her spirit as she sailed along the highway, far, far away from the Good Fortune.

She pulled up in front of the Jamieson house, grabbed her book bag and purse, headed up the veranda and knocked. She rocked on her heels, eager and a little nervous. Chris had come by twice more that week to say hello and to buy a box of chicken balls for his son. She'd done her best to be more pleasant. He'd said he was looking forward to seeing her at the farm, and even though there was no affection behind his words, she couldn't help the feeling of anticipation sizzling through her.

She was a little surprised when William Jamieson, dressed in jeans and a blue shirt, opened the door. She glanced behind him, then around the farm, expecting to see Chris or even Jane running toward her.

"You expecting a gong to announce you or something?" William narrowed his eyes at her as he shuffled his crutches.

She smiled with clenched teeth to hide the tic beneath her eye. "Hello, Mr. Jamieson. I'm here to tutor Simon."

"He's not home from school yet. And he has to do his chores when he gets back." He stayed firmly rooted in the doorway. Three long seconds passed before she realized he was not going to invite her in.

"May I wait inside?" She wouldn't allow this old man to intimidate her the way he used to.

William studied her, his jaw set. "You're not charging my son from the minute you step in here, are you?"

"Of course not."

He hobbled inside. She followed. "Do you want something to drink? I'm about to put some coffee on."

His offer of hospitality surprised her. "I'm fine for now, thank you. Would it be all right if I set up my things on the dining table?"

"Sure you wouldn't rather sit on the floor? Isn't that what you people do?"

She dug her fingernails into her palms. "Only after our kung-fu lessons," she deadpanned.

He didn't react. "I don't know if my son has said anything to you," William began, "but you should know I don't approve of all this tutoring business."

"You don't think Simon's education is important?" Or was he objecting to *her* teaching him?

"School curriculums are too focused on useless academic courses. They should be teaching important things like computers and accounting, and bring back home economics and shop. Those are useful classes. Everyone cries about how the arts get cut all the time, but when it comes to school budgets, the first thing that's cut is life skills and gym." His gaze lifted to her face. "English isn't a second language to Simon. He can speak and read it fine, unlike some people. He doesn't need to study Shakespeare to know how to fix a tractor engine."

She partly agreed with his view on education. But her dislike of the man and his implication that English wasn't her first language put her on a wary defensive. She drew herself up. "I respect your position, but the reality is that the state has basic requirements in order for your grandson to earn his GED. He'll need to excel in this course in order to raise his GPA and score well on his SATs if he wants to go to college."

"He doesn't need to go to college," he declared. "A diploma or degree's just a fancy, expensive piece of paper that people use to lord over others, pretend they're smarter than everyone else. It don't make a difference in the real world. Work is work, and there's plenty of it here. Simon'll learn everything he needs from me."

Remembering Jane's advice, she decided not to continue the argument. William was obviously set in his beliefs, and this was something he would have to discuss with Chris. "My only objective is to tutor Simon and get him through this summer class. How he conducts himself after that is up to him."

William didn't respond. Actually, he didn't say anything as he made his way to the kitchen where he studiously read the paper and ignored her. So much for hospitality.

It was another twenty minutes before Simon finally came stumbling into the house. He looked worn out as he dropped his bag by the door. William came out of the kitchen frowning. "You're late. Miss Chang's meter's been running."

"It's *Cheung*," she corrected, though she didn't bother to correct his lie. Considering what she was going through with him, she ought to be paid for the extra time.

"I couldn't help it. The bus made a long detour to drop three other guys off."

"You still have chores to do," William reminded him. "Don't leave 'em till it's too dark."

Simon slumped. "I have to go clean the stalls and stuff," he explained to Tiffany in a low voice. She noticed he didn't argue or sigh in disparagement around his grandfather.

"I'll go with you," she said, getting up. "You can tell me about your class today."

The rich smells of farm life assaulted her as she followed

Simon across the dirt and gravel in her ballet flats. Rocks bit through the flimsy soles of her shoes as she skirted what she was sure wasn't just dirt. They passed a large fenced-in area that housed a coop. Brown-and-white chickens roamed freely within, pecking at the spare grass. Simon hastily grabbed a scoop, opened a big plastic bucket and dug in, scattering a measure of chicken feed across the ground, which the hens hurried to gobble up.

"Are they for the eggs or for meat?" Tiffany asked.

"Eggs, mostly. Dad does sell a few for meat sometimes, though."

"Do you have to wake up at the crack of dawn to collect the eggs?"

He grimaced, eyeing the birds warily. "One of the hands usually comes by every day. Dad only makes me feed them." She heard him mutter "Thank God" under his breath and suppressed a smile as he headed for the barn. She wasn't sure she'd want to have to fight off a bunch of chickens for their eggs, either. The only place she wanted to see a chicken up close was in a grease-stained bucket.

"So, tell me about your first day."

He lifted a shoulder. "My teacher's a serious hard-ass. He jumped straight into *The Tempest*. We read the first scene in class and started the second. We have to finish scene two by tomorrow."

"Did you have any problems understanding the text?"

Simon didn't answer. His mouth firmed, and his eyes grew flinty, though they wouldn't meet hers. Wordlessly, he grabbed a pitchfork and gloves and rolled the wheelbarrow out of the corner. "Simon?" He started shoveling, and Tiffany had to move out of his way. "If you didn't understand something, you have to tell me."

Still no response. Maybe he hadn't heard her over the sound of the rustling straw. "Hello?"

"I heard you. I'm stupid, not deaf."

Tiffany reeled back. "Whoa, okay, I didn't say anything about you being stupid."

"But that's why you're here, isn't it? Because I'm too stupid to pass English." He stabbed the fork into the dirty straw. "English!"

Okay. So, he'd had a long, hard day, and now he was here, scooping poop. She'd be kind of cranky, too. His grandfather hadn't even allowed him to take a breather, get a snack. The kid was probably suffering from low blood sugar or something. Gently, she said, "Look, Shakespeare is hard for everyone at first. People are still digging up new meanings to the text."

He snorted. "I should have known you wouldn't get it." He turned his back on her.

He meant get how difficult high school was, she thought. Oh, if only he knew. She rested her fists against her hips. "Let's start with what you do know. What can you tell me about the scene you read today?"

Simon went on shoveling, and Tiffany jumped back as droppings scattered from the fork at her feet.

She scowled. "Simon, I'm here to help you. Why are you acting like this?"

"If you don't want to be here, get lost."

"Is that any way to talk to a lady?" Chris's deep voice boomed through the barn, startling them both. He crossed his forearms over his chest, leaning up against the door to the tack room. He must have been in there all this time. He caught and held his son's belligerent look. "How was school?" An edge of warning vibrated beneath his question. He didn't scold, didn't make his son apologize for his behavior right off. Tiff watched in fascination as father and son did their dance of discipline.

Simon shrugged. Chris stared him down until his son replied, "Fine, *sir*."

Chris nodded. "I thought I'd come by and say hi," he said to Tiffany. He hitched a shoulder toward his son. "Is he giving you attitude?"

It was on the tip of her tongue to say yes, but instead she smiled. "Not at all. I was just about to offer to help out." She met Simon's bang-veiled glower, flashing her teeth at him.

Chris put his hands out in refusal. "Oh, no. I'm not paying you to clean horse stalls. This is Simon's job. Besides, I wouldn't want you to dirty your nice clothes."

His approving gaze was like the lightest caress, and she became hot all over. "What, these? They're my schlupping clothes." She cringed—she sounded too much like a princess with her fancy outfit. Chris raised one eyebrow. "I can pitch in. It'll make the work go faster."

"No." He crossed over to his son and held out a hand for the pitchfork. "I'll take over just this once, Simon. You go in, clean up and work with Tiffany."

"But—"

"Just this once." Chris took the pitchfork from him. "She's here for you. You need to take advantage of her while she's around to help."

"I don't need help," Simon blurted. "I need everyone to leave me alone!" He kicked up a cloud of straw and dust as he stormed from the barn.

"Simon—" Chris stopped at the barn door. He set the pitchfork aside and rubbed his jaw. "Sorry about that, Tiffany. I don't know why he's been acting like this."

She knew why. And in some ways, she understood Simon's frustration and anger. "He's a teenager. It kind of comes with the territory."

"His behavior is unacceptable," Chris said. "If he knew what you did for me—" A forlorn look darkened his expression and he became still. With an intensity that practically vibrated off him, he stepped closer to her. "I never told you how much I appreciated all your help back in high school. I never said thank you." He placed his big, strong hands on her shoulders and squeezed. "I'm sorry. This is fifteen years too late. Thank you, Tiffany, for everything you did for me."

Her heart sped up, her pulse tripping through her veins. It had never occurred to her that she'd needed to hear a thank-you from him. He'd paid her, after all. But his appreciation was worth ten times what she'd earned.

He gazed at her as though she might try to deny his words. He searched her face with a probing look, and his eyes fell to her lips. Trembling, Tiffany held her breath wondering what he would do next, but whatever had gripped him for that heady, fervent moment dissipated. His hands fell away, leaving her wishing she could step closer and wrap her arms around him.

He turned toward the barn door where his son had escaped, steel in his eyes and voice. "Simon needs to show you more respect."

"Respect's something I'm going to have to earn myself," she told him. This was more than simply teenage rebellion, and if she was going to have a shot at getting Simon to work with her, she had to break through to him on her own. Chris wrinkled his brow skeptically. "Seriously, if you want me to work with him, let me do this my way."

He searched her face, his growing confusion clouding those gorgeous blue eyes. Then he nodded. "All right. But if he gives you any trouble…"

"He won't."

She left Chris in the barn, but couldn't help but peek over her shoulder to watch as he hoisted a bale of straw above his head, muscles rippling across his back and shoulders. Something in her chest fluttered. She really had to stop ogling him like this. He was going to catch her at it one day and—

He looked up, grinned, then went back to work.

She hurried away, body tingling everywhere. Why was she still so afraid of her attraction to him? She wouldn't be in Everville long. There wouldn't be any consequences to indulging in a little man-ogling. She glanced over her shoulder again. Chris was using the front of his T-shirt to wipe his brow, exposing the delicious expanse of his washboard abs. Yowza.

Back in the dining room, Tiffany swept aside all unsettling thoughts about Chris and sat at the table. Simon came downstairs a few minutes later, hesitating on the staircase when he saw her.

"*The Tempest* starts with a storm," she declared. "That's what a tempest is. A big storm."

He rolled his eyes as he descended that last few steps. "I *know* that."

"I thought you said you were stupid," she said, tilting her chin to one side coquettishly.

"The teacher told us about the play," he griped, flinging himself into a chair across the table.

"Okay. So, what else did your teacher say?"

She waited while he glowered at a spot on the table, eyebrows knitted. He seemed to be debating what to tell her. "Hey, if you can't remember, I'll be happy to tell you about it all over again. That way you can repeat a day's worth of lessons in two hours. Bet you'd love that. Or, if you prefer, we can sit here and stare until you want to chime in. I'm still getting paid either way."

"That's all that matters to you, isn't it?"

"Maybe. Or maybe I actually care enough to make you try your hardest so you don't end up mad at everyone for something only you can fix." She opened the book and started reading out loud. "'If by your art, my dearest father, you have put the wild waters in this roar, allay them—'"

"I know how to read," Simon said irritably.

She propped up her chin with one hand. "You probably do. But I'm going to do a translation, line by line. It goes like this—'Yo, Daddy-O, stop with the magic storm, man. I saw a ship go down, and I felt bad for the dudes on board.'"

His color went from pale to purple, the look on his face something between horror and rage—as if he'd stepped on a piece of Lego but couldn't scream. "I'm not an idiot," he choked out.

"I don't think you are, either. In fact, I'm pretty sure you're smarter than you let on. But you've been trying your hardest to prove otherwise. So, unless you start showing me what you know, I'm going to make baby talk at you and waste our time and your dad's money. Now, are we going to work together on this or not?"

He gave her a defiant snort, crossed his arms over his chest and sneered. "Fine. I'm stupid. So, go ahead. Talk to me like I'm a baby."

She leaned forward and lifted her lips in a predatory smile. "All right, then. Guess we're going to have to work together every. Single. Day."

CHAPTER SEVEN

TIFFANY WASN'T KIDDING when she promised to make Simon work. Every day after school, she'd follow him to the barn where she'd read through *The Tempest* using her terrible translations while he cleaned the stables. She wasn't sure he was learning anything, though—he never had an answer for her when she asked leading questions. Then again, cleaning the stalls was such smelly work, she wouldn't want to open her mouth while shoveling, either.

She found he was more responsive once he was back in the house at the table with a glass of chocolate milk and a couple of peanut butter sandwiches. But whenever they settled down to work, William would inevitably appear and listen in, making her self-conscious. From what she'd observed, he didn't leave the house much, thumping his way between the kitchen for a cup of coffee to the office off the living room, but rarely venturing outside. He was pretty loud about it, too—she was certain he didn't normally bang his dishes or cupboards.

"This play is idiotic," William said at one point, overhearing one of her more awful translations. He clapped a hand against Simon's thin shoulder. "Tell me the truth, Simon. Do you think you're ever going to need to know this stuff in real life? Wouldn't you rather be learning how to drive the tractor?"

Simon's impassive answer was coupled with a pointed glance at his grandfather's stump. "Dad says he won't let me until I'm sixteen."

William noticed the direction of his look and scoffed. "This was a stupid accident. I wasn't paying attention. I know you wouldn't make the same mistake."

Tiffany cleared her throat. "Mr. Jamieson, if you don't mind, I'm on a tight schedule with Simon."

His eyes locked with hers, and he gave her a brittle smile. "I'm only trying to have a heart-to-heart conversation with my grandson, Miss Chang."

"Cheung."

He ignored her. "Simon, when you want to do some real man's work, you come and find me. All this tutoring nonsense is costing your father a lot, you know. I personally think that's money better spent on a car when you get your license, eh?" He went back into the office, leaving the door wide open and turning up the volume on the radio so it blared country music into the dining room.

Tiffany seethed quietly. Undermining her like that wasn't the only thing he did to interfere with their sessions. He interrupted frequently by getting Simon to fetch things for him, made casual observations about nothing in particular. He'd sit in front of the TV and turn the volume way up, and when she asked him to turn it down, he'd tell them he was going deaf. Simon never defied the old man. He simply gave her a meek look and murmured an apology.

She couldn't work under these conditions. She was sure that was the point. She didn't want to get Chris involved, though—he had enough on his plate without her stirring up trouble between father and son. But she wouldn't allow the likes of William Jamieson to drive her out. By Wednesday, she decided she and Simon had to move.

She met him directly off the school bus and told him to get into her car. He perked up and asked, "Where are we going?"

"I cleared this with your father. I'm going to tutor you somewhere else for a while." She'd told Chris it was because

Simon would have better focus in a more formal setting. "We'll head downtown and I'll drop you back home afterward." It would be hell on gas, but she didn't have much choice. At least Simon seemed excited about it.

At first, she took him to the library, but the elderly patrons kept glaring and shushing her. Her low voice was apparently ruining their afternoon nap time. They went to the Grindery, but the jazz music was too loud and most of the tables were occupied. Besides, if they didn't buy something, the barista would probably give them the evil eye. She considered taking Simon to the house, but she knew *Poh-poh* would be as distracting as William was.

It left only one place they could go.

They walked into the Good Fortune Diner the following day. At four-thirty, the place was dead. Sitting behind the counter, her mother's eyes shifted from her daughter to the slouching boy at her side.

"Hi, Mom. This is Simon Jamieson, my student."

Rose smiled brightly. "Hello. Nice to meet you."

"Hi." He shook her outstretched hand.

"Mom, is it okay if we work here? We need to find a place where it's quiet, and there's too much going on at Simon's house and at the library for us to concentrate."

"Of course, of course." She pointed at the corner booth. "You want something to eat?" she asked Simon.

"I probably shouldn't. Grandpa will be making dinner."

"I'll get you a little something. You need food for your brain, eh?" She popped up and shouted into the kitchen.

"She seems nice," Simon said as Rose disappeared. Tiffany was surprised to hear anything like a compliment from him.

They sat and she paused to assess Simon's mood. He looked around distractedly, inspecting the vinyl seats and the scarred old table.

"My brother and I used to do our homework here after

school," she explained. "We'd work until about six and then we'd help out at the diner, taking orders and stuff."

"Cool."

Cool? Maybe she hadn't been clear. "It was hard work, doing school and working all the time."

"Tell me about it. At least you got to work after school, instead of in the morning. Sometimes I have to wake up at dawn to get things done so I can finish my homework at night. I barely have time now, working with you."

Was that supposed to be a guilt trip? He obviously hadn't ridden the Cheung family express, which made regular stops at Shameville, Honor Town and Duty City. "That's very responsible of you."

"It sucks balls," he muttered. "I'm so sick of all this. I hate the farm."

"You do?"

He shrugged again, his face pinched as guilt flashed across his features. She understood his feelings exactly. She wondered if William knew about his grandson's opinion on the matter, or whether the elder Jamieson cared. He was awfully stubborn.

"Here we go." Rose set down a plate of deep-fried chicken balls and a big bowl of sweet-and-sour sauce. "I know these are your favorite. You eat up and take home anything you can't finish, okay?"

Simon's eyes went huge. "Wow. Thanks, Mrs. Cheung."

"You're a good boy, working so hard to get your marks up. Not everyone would spend their summer vacation doing that. Although Tiffany and Daniel both went to summer school every year."

"You failed that many classes?" Simon asked incredulously.

"I took them to broaden my education," she proclaimed,

not adding that it kept her out of working at the diner for most of the summer. Simon's jaw slackened.

"Work hard," Rose said as she pattered away, adding, "Such a good boy."

Tiffany rubbed at her brow, exasperated. Rose had never coddled and praised either of her children for their dedication to their studies. Even Daniel, who'd earned his MBA with a 3.96 average, hadn't gotten much more than "good boy."

"Awesome." Simon greedily stuffed a saucy ball into his maw and chewed. "These are so good. Want one?"

"No, thanks." It would just stick in her throat anyhow.

He shrugged. "More for me."

She wanted to snatch the plate away until he had accomplished something. He needed an incentive to work. She'd have to put a Do Not Feed the Teen sign up when they came next. "I think we should do some review for your quiz tomorrow."

Sighing, Simon slowly put the chicken ball he'd picked up back onto the plate and sank deeper into the bench.

The next fifteen minutes were excruciating as she tried to draw answers out of him and got nothing but blank stares, shrugs and "I dunno." She threw her book on the table. "Are you doing this on purpose? You knew the answers two days ago. Why are you pretending like you don't know this stuff?"

"I just don't."

"I don't believe that." She leaned forward, gripping the table. "Are you only going to summer school so you won't have to work on the farm?"

"I don't see why you care," he said, looking away.

Tiffany watched him thoughtfully. Was it possible Simon had a learning disability? If that was the case, she wasn't qualified to deal with it. But everything inside her screamed that wasn't the problem. He was being deliberately unhelpful. He shut down at the first sign of pressure and seemed to have a few issues with authority. Maybe he got nervous when he was put on the spot. There were plenty of kids who weren't good at taking tests, or who got quiet when called upon by a teacher.

And then there were kids like her who didn't know how to relate to other people, who were more comfortable being alone than in a group. It was way easier to shut down and run away than it was to confront your problems and deal with life.

"I care because I've been where you are." She glanced over her shoulder and lowered her voice. "All I ever wanted was to get out of this town and move to the city. I knew the only way to do that was to go to college, so I studied my ass off and got into the program of my choice. Look, Simon—" she squeezed his shoulder "—if you really want to get away from the farm and leave Everville, college is the way to do it. Even if you don't want to go to college, you'll still need to get your high school diploma. It's a minimum requirement in practically every job."

"That's stupid," he said with a snort.

"Well, that's life."

"Lots of people get jobs without diplomas. I don't need this. I'm too smart for school."

A nerve ticked under her eye. She slammed her pen down on the table. "C'mon. Get up."

"Why?"

"You want to see what real life is like? What kind of job you can get without a diploma? Follow me."

He followed as she rounded the counter and pushed through the swinging door to the kitchen. Daniel and her father were busy preparing for the dinner crowd, chopping vegetables and meat.

"Hey, Tiff." Her brother grinned. "This must be Simon."

Tiffany introduced them briefly. "Dad, would you mind if Simon and I give you a hand?"

"Mind? Of course not." He waved them in. "Come, come, grab an apron, hairnet, wash your hands. You can start with the broccoli."

"You're putting me to work?"

"You want to see what real life is like for a kid with no education?"

"Hey!" Daniel protested indignantly.

With a look, Tiffany warned him to shut up and play along. She didn't want to explain to Simon why Daniel's MBA and her dad's engineering degree had still landed them in a kitchen. Not when she was trying to make a point.

"This *must* be illegal," Simon said.

"Only if we paid you. But then, if you didn't have your high school diploma, you might not know that. In fact, you probably wouldn't argue if your employer decided to pay you less than minimum wage under the table because, hell, who else is going to hire you?"

He folded his arms in front of him. "I am not doing this."

"You afraid of a little hard work?" she taunted.

That got him. He screwed up his face and snatched the apron from her hand. "This isn't hard work. Try digging a post hole for a fence. *That's* hard work."

Tiffany showed him how to clean and cut the broccoli into florets, then got him working on chopping cabbage, carrots, celery and onions. He did it all with intense concentration, and while he didn't work very fast, he was stubborn about it.

Cutting up vegetables was nothing, though, compared to what she could be putting him through. If it had been dinnertime, she'd have him begging for mercy after ten minutes of busing tables and washing dishes. Tiffany decided to step up her campaign. "If you like chicken balls so much, you should see how they're made."

She took him into the walk-in freezer where she pulled out

a plastic-lined box containing the garbage-bag-size pouch of frozen chicken balls.

"Whoa. I thought you guys made these."

"Chicken balls are about as American as pizza," she said, grimacing at the icy battered spheres. "*Real* Chinese restaurants don't serve these."

"But everyone loves them," Tony said from across the room. "That's all that matters."

She dropped the chicken balls into the fryer basket and showed Simon how the machine worked, then got him to gently place the heavy wire basket into the oil. She made him stand by the machine and watch as the chicken balls browned. If that didn't gross him out, the smells that would stick to his clothes would.

"Be careful when you dump the basket into the pan," she said. "Don't splatter any oil on yourself."

He did as instructed. "Cool. What's next?"

What's next? He was supposed to be hating this, not asking for more.

"He's doing a good job, eh?" Tony said, grinning hugely. "You want to volunteer here?"

"Dad, he's still in school."

"Volunteering is good for your résumé. You should do more of that, *Ah-Teen.*"

She was about to remind him that she was not a teenager when Daniel stuck his head in from the dining room and interrupted. "Mom's asking for you out front."

"I'll be right back," she told Simon. She checked her watch and groaned. It was almost six. She'd wasted a two-hour session making Simon work at the Good Fortune. She couldn't charge Chris for this day in good conscience, and she needed the money, dammit.

She went to the front, where her mother was seating an

older couple in a corner table. "Whatever it is, Mom, I can't do it right now. I have to drive Simon home."

"Why is he back there anyhow?"

"It's…a lesson. Sort of." One that didn't seem to be working, unfortunately. Then again, Simon was more engaged than she'd ever seen him. Perhaps what he really needed was a part-time job instead of a tutor. If college was beyond his means…well, someone had to flip the burgers.

"You go and drop him off at home, but come back right after. I've got a reservation for ten people tonight and Cindy called in sick. I need help."

Tiff was about to protest when she heard a shout and a noisy clatter. Her heart leaped into her throat as she sprinted into the kitchen. Simon was clutching his arm, whimpering. Daniel turned on the tap and ushered him toward the sink.

"What happened?" Nausea gripped her at the sight of the angry red marks seared into Simon's pale skin.

"I think the fryer basket slipped and splashed him." He jammed Simon's arm under the cold water, and Simon moaned in pain.

"It hurts," he sobbed. His face was red and streaked with tears. Right before her eyes, huge white blisters formed in a hideous pattern across his right hand and forearm.

Daniel swore. "We need to get him to the hospital."

CHRIS'S TIRES SQUEALED as he parked his truck in the hospital lot and ran for the entrance to the E.R. Tiffany's panicked call hadn't made sense. She'd babbled something about oil and chicken balls. All he'd understood was that Simon was hurt.

His heart hammered in his chest. After his dad's accident, he hadn't rushed nearly as quickly, assuming that the injury had been minor. But when he'd reached the E.R., he'd been informed that his father had been critical, and that he was being taken in for an emergency amputation.

He'd never dallied at an emergency again after that.

The nurse directed him to the appropriate cubicle. Simon sat on the edge of a gurney as a woman in blue scrubs gently wrapped a light gauze bandage around his oozing, blistered forearm. His stomach turned at the sight. His son wore a brave face, but he was pale, his expression pinched, and he kept his eyes averted from the procedure. In the far corner, Tiffany stood by watching, hugging herself, a fist pressed against her mouth.

"Simon," he said hoarsely. "My God, are you all right?"

Simon nodded slowly, blinking sleepily.

"I've given him some painkillers, so he might be a bit punchy. He sustained second-degree oil burns to his arm," the doctor said after introducing herself. "It's not as serious as it sounds, and as long as he follows my instructions, it'll heal up fine."

"How did this happen?"

"It's my fault," Tiffany blurted. "I made him work in the kitchen at the diner. He was using the deep fryer and the oil splashed on him."

Chris turned toward her, confused. "Why was he working at your parents' diner? What happened to tutoring?"

Tiffany opened her mouth, closed it and shook her head. "Let's talk outside."

Chris followed her, each step ratcheting up his fury. Outside the E.R. waiting room in the cooling evening, he took a deep breath and said, "Tell me everything from the beginning."

"Simon wasn't cooperating. I was really worried he didn't get how important his studies were. So...I tried to give him a life lesson."

"Life lesson?" It came out on a hiss.

"I wanted to show him... He needs to learn that education

can get him far. That without it, he can get stuck in a terrible job. Like being a short-order cook or something."

Chris stared at her, his breathing rasping hotly through his lungs. "So...you put him to work in your parents' diner. Without training. Without safety equipment. Without even asking me?"

"If I thought for a minute he was in danger, I wouldn't have brought him back there."

"Of course he was in danger. What the hell is wrong with you? He's fifteen." He raked his hands through his hair.

"I've been working there since I was eleven." It came out a weak protest.

"That's beside the point. The fact is, Simon got hurt. You didn't think about his well-being at all." It was a good thing he had health insurance to cover emergencies like this. "You're lucky if I don't sue you and your parents."

She flinched and backed away from him. Her eyes brimmed with tears, but anger burned there, too. "I didn't plan for any of this to happen." Her chin drooped. "I'm sorry."

Sorry wasn't going to heal the scars Simon might have for the rest of his life. "I paid you to tutor him in English, not life. You don't have the right— That's *my* job, not yours," he sputtered as he tripped over his words. This was exactly like the fights he had with Dad. William was constantly interfering, trying to steer his grandson toward a future in farming, trying to stuff him into a mold even Chris couldn't fully fill. His hands tightened into fists.

"I was only trying to help."

"By doing what? Telling him he'll be nothing more than a fry cook for the rest of his life?" His blood pumped so hard, his vision hazed over as he realized that was *exactly* what she'd been trying to do. That settling for a job that paid the bills was only for dropouts. "Believe it or not, Tiffany, some people do choose and enjoy that work. A formal education is not the be-all and end-all of life."

Her face grew pale. "You think I don't know that? You think I really believe school is all that matters? I did nothing but school for more than two-thirds of my life, and look where it's got me."

Her declaration rang out like the ominous toll of a bell. Tiffany's measure of success had always been rooted in grades and academics. Now, the broken girl behind the woman with all the ambition and skills and none of the luck stood naked and ashamed before him.

Look where she was. Look where *they* were.

Chris was too mad to feel sorry for her, though. He'd made peace with his choices. Only one thing truly mattered to him now, and he'd do whatever it took to protect him.

He pushed past her and said over his shoulder, "I think it would be best if you stopped working with my son."

CHAPTER EIGHT

"WHERE'S TIFFANY?" Simon asked when Chris returned to his bedside.

"She had to leave." He sounded as though he were chewing rocks. He looked away, not wanting his son to see how upset he was. It was as if someone had pushed every single one of his buttons, and every muscle in his body was ratcheted tight.

"Where'd she go?"

"Listen. I fired her, Simon. You won't see her again."

"What? Why? Because of this?" He motioned with his arm and winced.

"She shouldn't have made you work in that kitchen."

"She didn't force me." Simon sat forward on the bed, fully alert. "I was goofing around and dropped the basket in the oil by accident. She was just showing me how things worked there."

Chris settled a hand on his shoulders. "Simon, you don't need to defend her. She's the adult. You were her responsibility, and she couldn't keep you safe."

"I'm not a little kid anymore, Dad." He yanked out of his hold. "This is *my* fault. I didn't listen to her, and I got hurt."

Chris blinked. This was the first time in his memory that his son had taken responsibility for his own actions and the consequences. "What are you saying exactly?"

His lips pursed into a thin line. "She gets me, okay?" His glare hardened. "Which is more than I can say about you."

"What's that supposed to mean?"

"You keep talking about college and careers, and I can barely stay awake at school. You have this crazy idea that I'm going to get a job saving the world. Well, I can't, okay? I don't know what I want to do. I'm just trying to survive, but you keep pushing and pushing like it'll be the end of the world if I don't go to college. You're as bad as Grandpa."

The remark hit him like a backhanded slap. Had he really been pushing Simon that hard?

The teen deflated, his spine slinking back into its natural slouch. "Tiffany *gets* me," he said more quietly, plucking at the sheet. "This wasn't her fault, okay? Don't punish her 'cause of something I did."

CHRIS WAS STILL STUNNED on the drive home. All of Simon's admissions bore into him. He didn't realize he'd been putting that kind of pressure on his son. He wanted what all parents wanted for their children—a stable future, a good job and happiness. Someone had to want them for him: his mother had barely made the effort, and his grandfather was only concerned about the future of the farm.

At a stop light, he glanced over at Simon. Poor kid had passed out the minute they'd hit the highway. Thinking back, Chris realized that whenever they had a chance to talk, he and Simon only ever talked about school, about the things he was doing in class and whether any of it interested him as a field of study. It would have come across as a constant inquisition. Chris would have resented the hell out of it, too. Those dinner conversations were the only real quality time they spent together; how else would Simon have perceived a never-ending barrage of questions about his future?

He drummed his fingers against the wheel, irritated at himself. No wonder Simon tuned him out and avoided his company. Chris forked a hand through his hair and peered at his son, the snowy-white bandage around his right arm glowing in the darkness.

At home, Simon blearily said hello to his grandfather as he shuffled up the stairs to his room. William's glance flickered from the bandage to his son, standing in the doorway. Simon's bedroom door closed quietly.

"Will he be able to do his chores?" his father asked brusquely.

Chris slapped his keys down on the console table. "Do you even care that he was hurt? Or how?"

William changed the channel disinterestedly. "You're gonna tell me. Why waste my breath asking?"

His father's utter lack of concern shouldn't have surprised him. William was not one to worry about minor injuries or trips to the E.R. "He burned himself with fryer oil at the Cheungs' restaurant."

One eyebrow shot up. "How?"

"Tiffany wanted to…teach him about the restaurant business." He didn't know why he wanted to keep her role in this accident to a minimum. It was her fault, after all.

William turned in his seat to face him fully. "Are you paying that woman to make your son into some kind of white slave?"

"No, Dad—"

But his father had heard enough. He tossed the remote aside. "See? That's what you get for trusting her. I told you he didn't need her." He pushed up out of his seat, grabbed his crutches and followed him to the kitchen. "I hope you fired her."

"I did…but I'm going to get her back." He'd made the decision on the drive home. She'd connected with Simon in a way he hadn't, even if she didn't know it yet. If there was one thing his son needed right now, it was guidance, an ally. "Simon still needs a tutor. She's the best there is."

"Not this again…." He planted his crutch firmly in front of him. "Listen to me. He shouldn't be wasting any more time with this college nonsense. It'll distract him from what he actually needs to know. Do you have any idea how hard it is to keep up with things around here and turn a profit? If he doesn't step up soon, this whole place could fall apart."

Chris's blood boiled. And what, exactly, did his father think he'd been doing these past fifteen years? When he'd first taken over and looked at the books, the farm had been on the brink of financial ruin. He'd turned that around and made the failing Jamieson farm into a solid business all on his own. He'd poured everything he had into it. And William treated him as if he'd brought the ten plagues upon the land.

"You can't force Simon into taking over," he told his father.

"This farm is his legacy. It's in his blood."

Legacy. As if a fancy word would sway him. "Farming is *not* in his blood."

"How do you know that? You said the same thing about yourself right up to the moment you came back here, hat in hand, wanting a job and a place to raise your child. You always thought you were better than your old man, but I'm the one who raised you, gave you and the boy a place to call home. I'm the one who pulled you through after Daphne left your sorry ass. If you'd been anywhere as committed to the farm as you were to Simon—"

He clenched his fists. "I *am* committed. I dug you out of the financial rut you were spinning your wheels in. If I hadn't come back—" He stopped and paced back and forth.

"Go on. Say what you need to," William urged with sarcastic magnanimity. "You want to tell your old man he's nowhere near as smart as you? Go ahead, I know you think it."

Chris inhaled deeply and forced patience into his tone. "I

won't be goaded into saying something I'll regret. It's been a long day and I haven't had dinner."

"Coward." His father made a noise of disgust. "Heat it up yourself." He stumped out.

TIFFANY LAY ON HER BED, staring up at the ceiling, thoroughly miserable. The horrible burn scars on Simon's arms were seared into her mind, and that miserable whimpering... She was sick to her stomach that she'd caused him that kind of pain. He must really hate her now. On top of all that, Chris had threatened a lawsuit. The fierce look burning in his blue eyes struck her again. He'd been more than disappointed— he'd been enraged. How could things have gone wrong so quickly? Hot tears pooled in her eyes and throat.

Someone knocked on her bedroom door.

"What?"

Daniel poked his head in. "I just finished talking to Chris." He stepped into the room. "He isn't going to pursue a lawsuit."

The fist around her gut unclenched and she exhaled a long breath. "I'm so stupid."

"Hey, Dad and I were there, too. We should have stopped him, but we weren't thinking." He sat in her creaking desk chair. "We took his safety for granted. I should have been watching him more closely."

"I shouldn't have brought him back there. I just wanted him to care about his studies." She sat up and shook her head, forced to face the shameful truth. "No. That's not true. I wanted to show him how much working as a line cook would suck."

"At least you're man enough to admit it." Daniel leaned forward. "You were trying to give him the old 'someone has to flip the burgers' lesson. You had his best interests at heart. That's nothing to be ashamed of."

But she *was* ashamed. Not only because things had gone

so badly, but also because she'd absolutely believed it was the right thing to do.

And wasn't that the story of her life? She'd alienated nearly everyone because she was used to doing things her way by herself. No one had ever stepped up to help her, defend her, give her encouragement or offer advice. She was expected to do it on her own, to be fully capable, and no one ever questioned her methods because she always got the job done. Thinking back, her boss had gently mentioned that her ability to work as an individual overshadowed all her other assets. In other words, "doesn't play well with others."

She sank deeper into depression. No wonder she'd been fired. No wonder she'd been turned away from so many doorsteps after she'd been evicted.

"You don't just flip burgers," she said. Daniel watched her with interest. "You and Dad. You're not McFlippers." The expression had come from a hard-ass high school counselor, Mr. Murray, whose mandate was to scare kids into preparing for the real world. She thought of his favourite saying—*You're not above flipping burgers to pay the rent*.

Tiffany looked at her brother. "I know you work hard. I'm sorry if I offended you and Dad."

"As long as you're not judging us by what we do rather than who we are, you can think whatever you want."

She admitted she was guilty of doing that. She'd never been able to get over her brother's wasted education, or how her father had abandoned his job at that architectural firm in Brooklyn for a small-town Chinese restaurant business in the middle of upstate New York. But then, who was she to judge? Jobless, homeless, carless and up to her eyeballs in debt was not exactly a stellar way to live.

"I can't believe I've been fired from two jobs now in under a month." Tiffany pressed a pillow against her face.

"It's just a setback. Some things aren't meant to be. But

you'll pick yourself up and keep moving forward, right? You know that old proverb of *Kung-kung*'s—ride the horse, but if it goes lame, find a cow. If the cow dies, start walking."

"Am I supposed to be the cow in this story?"

"Don't be a bitch. I'm trying to help you out."

She knew that, but she couldn't help her rising resentment. It was a prideful, knee-jerk reaction to criticism and meddling from her family. "Are Mom and Dad mad?"

He hesitated. "Not at you."

Which meant they were fighting again, probably blaming each other for Simon's injuries, fearing the Jamiesons would sue them or start telling everyone in town what had happened so they'd lose business. It didn't matter if it was true—they would find something to blame each other for. That was how it'd always been. Why they hadn't divorced years ago Tiffany didn't understand.

Daniel picked up on her mood. "Listen, tomorrow, you'll get a fresh start. I'll make some calls, see if any of my friends in the city know of any openings...."

"No." Tiffany sat up. "Don't do that. I'm going to find a job on my own."

"But—"

"I have to do this on my own." She regretted her biting tone instantly. Daniel was only trying to help, but she couldn't lean on her family any more than she already was. She had to show them she'd earned every ounce of her professional success on her own merits. That her choices were good ones.

Confusion and disbelief warred on her brother's face. He raised his hands uselessly and dropped them to his sides. "Fine. Suit yourself."

DANIEL HAD DONE his brotherly duty. He'd offered to help, but Tiff had refused. Fine. He couldn't change his sister's pissy attitude, and he had no intention of trying. He had his own problems to deal with.

He texted Selena to say he was feeling a little under the weather and was going to bed early, so wouldn't be calling tonight. A minute later, she sent him a picture of her puckered lips and wrote, Get well soon, honey bear! XXX.

His spirits sank. He was a liar and a coward. He'd made excuses to cut their conversations short the past few nights, especially when she'd started talking about her upcoming visit and meeting his parents. Now he was outright avoiding her.

The thing was, he didn't know how he could, in good conscience, deepen or continue their relationship when he had no idea how their future would look. Selena made a whole lot more money than he did, which, now that he thought about it, bothered him. Call him old-fashioned, but he'd always pictured himself as the breadwinner, and when they had kids, he wanted his wife to stay home to care for them. In all their talk about children, Selena had never once said she'd become a stay-at-home mom.

And why would she? She was a doctor with her own practice. What did he have to offer her? A toehold in his parents' business, a few tidy investments and a well-padded savings account? Selena probably made ten times what he did, plus she came from a fairly well-off family. She owned a condo in Manhattan, for Christ's sake.

That only led to more questions. Where would they live? Who would be the one to pick up and move? Logically, it should be him, but he had difficulty imagining himself living apart from his parents, not because he didn't know how to take care of himself, but because someone had to watch over *them*. He didn't want his grandmother to spend the remainder of her years stuck in the middle of his parents' bickering. And a retirement residence was out of the question. According to his parents, Chinese families simply did not send their elderly to an institution full of strangers. His father frequently threatened to disown him if he ever considered putting him in a home.

No, Daniel couldn't leave Everville—for his parents' and his grandmother's sake. He owed them too much to abandon them. They'd paid for his education, food and housing. Besides, a condo in the city was no place to raise a family. He and Selena could get a big, roomy house in Everville with a yard for a fraction of the price of real estate in New York. In fact, there was a beautiful old cottage he'd had his eye on that had been on the market the past couple of months. Maybe he should look into making an offer on it....

And then what? Do you really think Selena will pick up and leave so she can be a housewife to a glorified short-order cook?

He might not be a McFlipper, but he wasn't earning a six-figure salary, either. What he earned was more of an honorarium than a salary. He'd never asked for more—it simply wasn't done. After all, he was living under his parents' roof, eating their food. Sure, he helped around the house when needed, but he couldn't demand a raise.

Not couldn't. Wouldn't. He closed his eyes at the bald truth. He was making excuses. His intentions might have been good, but the moment he thought about telling his parents he was off to find a job in the big city, he cringed at their imagined frowns, the disappointment in their expressions and the browbeating he'd receive.

Moh gwai young. Useless.

Depressed, he went to the living room. His mother and grandmother were watching a rerun of *CSI* with the closed captioning on since *Poh-poh's* English wasn't very good.

"Come sit and watch," *Poh-poh* invited in Cantonese. She offered him a plate of orange slices. "Try these. I got them at the market today. Very sweet."

This was the after-dinner custom in their household—TV and fruit. He knew Selena preferred richer desserts, but cake and pie weren't typical in Chinese home fare. What would they eat when they lived together? Who would do the cooking? Would Selena want to learn how to make *Poh-poh*'s healing soups? Would she even believe in their medicinal effects?

"Why aren't you talking to your girlfriend?" his mother asked.

"She's working tonight." Another lie.

"Are we ever going to meet her? I wonder some days if she's even real. We haven't even seen a picture of her." She smiled crookedly. "You didn't make her up, did you?"

"I don't own a picture of her." Not one he'd show anyhow. Most of them were of her in various stages of undress. The ones that weren't…

He sat back in shock. Oh, God. He had plenty of pictures that would have been fine, but he *hadn't* shown his parents. It'd been a conscious decision with an unconscious reason.

Tiffany was right. If race didn't matter, then why wouldn't he show them a picture of Selena? Was he simply afraid of what his parents would think? Was that why he was telling himself he wasn't good enough for her?

"The kids these days," *Poh-poh* said with a snort. "They don't do any of those things anymore. They don't know the value of these small things. Back when *Kung-kung* was courting me, I had to save up a lot of money so I could have a nice picture taken to give to him." Sadness crept into her eyes as she nodded toward the photo on the mantel. "I never got one of him when he was young. He was saving to bring us here, instead."

"You should ask Selena for a photo," his mother told him, her admonishing tone sharpening his guilt. "What's the matter with her? Is she ugly?"

"I don't have one printed out. They're all on the computer."

That should keep her quiet. His mother wasn't fond of technology and didn't even like sitting in front of a computer monitor if she could help it.

"Well, no matter. When we meet her, I'm sure she'll be everything you say she is. She doesn't have to be perfect— just a good Chinese girl. That's all we want." She patted his knee and smiled so benignly up at him, the only thing he could do was smile back.

CHAPTER NINE

TIFFANY TOOK A deep breath as she faced the Jamieson house once more, book bag clutched to her chest. She had barely believed it yesterday when Chris had called, and in a terse tone, asked her to come back. She'd readily agreed, apologizing profusely, practically groveling for forgiveness. She wasn't sure, exactly, that she'd gotten it, but she was here now, which had to mean something.

She watched Chris as he walked out onto the veranda, thumbs hooked in his back pockets, his expression unreadable as he squinted against the blazing sun. She was mad at herself for still being so drawn to him despite everything that had happened. She understood that he only wanted what was best for his son. She wasn't sure how Simon would react to his father's hovering, though. On top of that, if Chris was going to watch her tutor his son, she'd need to step up her game. No more terrible translations. She had to get serious with Simon.

"Thanks for coming," he said as she approached. "Before you go in, can we talk?"

She swallowed dryly. "Of course."

A wet breeze gusted, sweeping tendrils of hair out of her loosely tied ponytail and into her face. She'd dressed more conservatively today. The three-quarter-length-sleeved white collared shirt and knee-length brown pencil skirt made her look like the bookworm she'd been as a teenager, but she would put on her old Coke-bottle glasses if it would convince Chris she meant business.

He was silent on the short walk to the fence surrounding the paddock. A big chestnut mare plodded toward them. Tiffany stepped back as the horse nosed at her arm.

"Don't worry. She won't bite. She's just seeing if you have any treats."

She didn't want to think about the dirt the animal was leaving all over her freshly ironed shirt, but she didn't want to act like a prissy sissy, either. She held still and studied the musculature and fine red-brown coloring to distract herself from the mare's snuffling probe. As much as she was fascinated by the creatures, she didn't like the thought of those big teeth chomping on her. Chris pulled a carrot stump from his pocket, and the horse turned her enormous head and lipped up the proffered treat, slobbering all over his hand.

"Simon and I have a…difficult relationship." He patted the horse's neck. She trudged away once she'd ascertained there were no more treats. "Actually, I'm pretty sure he hates my guts right now. I've tried my best to understand who he is, who he's becoming. But we're not there yet."

Tiffany waited for him to say more. She wasn't sure where he was going with this.

"He insisted I not blame you for what happened," he said. "He accepted full responsibility for his actions. He doesn't do that a lot."

She was surprised and warmed by the thought of Simon defending her. At the same time, she hated that she'd come between father and son. Chris studied her face, searching for the secret to earning his son's esteem.

"Anyhow," he went on, "I wanted to get that out. You have a…hold on him that I don't. But I guess you've always been able to wrangle us Jamieson men that way."

Feeling undeservedly relieved and flattered, she asked, "Is he still working on *The Tempest?*"

"Far as I know." He scratched his nose and his brow furrowed. "Actually, I'm not sure."

"If you want, I can give you a daily update on his progress. Let you know where he's at in the class, what he's studying."

"Yeah. That'd be good."

She hesitated, unsure of how to approach the next question. "Are...*we* good?" she asked in a small voice.

He met her gaze shrugging slightly. "I guess so."

Well, that was something. She hoped she'd win back his appreciation with time. She'd never thought about how frail that kind of personal esteem was—and she'd shattered it so easily.

At the house, she found Simon sitting at the dining-room table, a three-ring binder open in front of him. He was doodling on a lined page with his right hand. The white bandage was already fraying and stained with a splotch of mustard.

"That's cool," she said as she put her bag down. Upon closer inspection, the geometric shapes really were quite beautiful, a mixture of art deco and Celtic patterns he'd made into knots and borders all over the page. "I take this to mean you can write okay?"

"It stings a little, but yeah, I can use my hand." He flexed it to demonstrate, lips tight.

"Simon." She waited till his eyes met hers. "I want to say again how sorry I am about putting you in that situation and getting you hurt. I shouldn't have done so."

"It's okay. But whatever, you know?" He picked up *The Tempest*. "Can we get started?"

Chris loomed in the doorway behind his son. Her eyes met his over Simon's head, and he lifted his eyebrows.

"So, where did you last leave off? Do you need me to help you understand any of the text? We can go through it if you like."

"Actually...can we not do that line-by-line stuff? I do have some questions, though."

Tiffany almost jumped for joy. Finally.

She caught Chris's half smile as he went into the kitchen.

CHRIS DID HIS BEST to stay quiet and unobtrusive, catching the little bits of conversation they were having while he poured himself a coffee and studied some pamphlets about a water reclamation system he wanted to install. Simon asked why he was hanging around the house when there was so much to be done on the farm, but Chris simply said he was waiting for Grandpa to finish with some numbers, which wasn't untrue—William was working on a new budgeting scheme he'd insisted on trying out. Chris wasn't about to tell his son he was hanging around to make sure things went smoothly between him and Tiff. Or that he just wanted to be around.

About an hour later, he heard William leave his office. Simon said hello as he pounded up the stairs for a bathroom break. "Well, look who's come back," Chris heard his father say. "You taking over my dining room again?"

"Hello, Mr. Jamieson," Tiffany said. "Yes, I'm still working with Simon on his English course."

"As if it'll do him any good. We should all be learning Chinese for when you people take over."

Chris's jaw dropped. He couldn't find a single word to rebuke him as his father headed out the front door. He looked at Tiffany, who'd focused back on the book in front of her.

"I'm so sorry. That was…uncalled for," Chris said quickly, hating himself the moment the words were out of his mouth. He raked his fingers through his hair. "No. That wasn't just uncalled for, it was plain rude and…and…" *Ignorant. Racist. Rednecked. Xenophobic.* All those words and more surfaced in his mind, and while his dad could be a real bastard, he'd never thought he was this special brand of backwater asshole. Anger twisted through him. "I'll get him to apologize." He started for the door, utterly humiliated.

"Chris, forget it. *Stop.*" She'd shot out of her seat, and her hard-edged command made him halt, one hand on the door-knob. She gestured wearily with one hand. "Leave it alone. I've heard worse."

Cold trickled down his spine. "He's said more, hasn't he?"

"It doesn't matter." She returned to her seat and made a show of flipping through her notes.

Intense heat rippled through him, stretching up and out-ward from his heaving chest. He wanted to go after his father and beat an apology out of him, but Tiffany's glare stayed him. She'd let his father's words bounce off her like glanc-ing blows, and yet remained resolved, jaw set as if ready to take another verbal beating.

Dear God, if he let this go, what would Tiffany think of him?

"Forget about it, Chris." She gave him such a tired, wintry look, he froze. Old pain burned in her eyes. A horrible sense of déjà vu flowed through him as he realized the frowning teen she'd been stared back, her remote silence and aloofness suddenly magnified by his father's words.

It wasn't only what his dad had said that had put that look there.

He suddenly remembered something Daphne had said when he'd told her Tiffany would be tutoring him. He'd wanted to be certain Daph didn't get any crazy ideas, and strangely enough, she hadn't.

"I'm glad she's your tutor. Those people are smart. I never see them do anything but study. But I guess that's how they're like."

They. Not *she,* but *they,* as though Tiffany were part of a horde rather than an individual.

He hadn't thought anything about the comment then—he'd just been glad Daphne hadn't flown into a jealous rage.

Bile rose in his throat. What else had he heard and sup-pressed from all those years ago? What jokes had he laughed along with, let slip by? It was no secret that the Cheungs were the only Asian family in the area, and he was certain they'd been the subject of plenty of crude comments. He remembered how Daniel had fought his way out of being a regular punching bag and only made friends after bagging that double to win the baseball team's championship. But what about Tiffany? She'd never escaped the quiet, studious loner stereotype. He couldn't remember ever seeing her eating lunch with anyone. He couldn't even name a single person she was good friends with.

Chris cringed inwardly as the past washed over him. He couldn't help staring at her as she sat at the dining table, her face a mask of concentration, shutting out everything around her. A minute later, Simon rejoined them, blissfully unaware of the tension in the room. Tiffany gave him an encouraging smile and went straight back to her lesson with renewed energy.

Everything she'd been through, everything he had dumped on her…and she was still here, helping his son.

His stomach lurched. He couldn't stand being there a moment longer. "I'll see you—" Later would be too late, so he said, "Soon."

"Sure." She didn't even look up.

He headed for the greenhouse, his head full of fog. He was trying to recall every word he'd ever said to Tiffany, worrying he'd offended her without knowing it, wondering how stupid and ignorant he might have sounded. He couldn't honestly say he'd ever sat down with her and consciously noted their differences—it hadn't crossed his mind. She'd simply been the smart girl who had tutored him.

The smart girl. *That* smart girl. *That smart Chinese girl.*

He'd singled her out back in high school when he'd needed help. What if she'd taken it the wrong way? Yes, she was smart, but did she think he thought she was smart because she was Chinese? Did she think he'd only asked her to tutor Simon for the same reason? He could have asked anyone.

He paced. He was overthinking this. Yes, he could have asked anyone to tutor Simon, but he'd asked Tiffany. She was highly qualified, had a proven record of success, and she'd needed the money. She was the right person for the job, period.

But he acknowledged he'd never really thought about the girl—or the woman—Tiffany was. He'd never made the effort to get to know her—not seriously. She'd simply been a means to an end, an appointment to keep on Thursdays after football practice. He'd told her he appreciated her for all she'd done for him. But he'd never truly appreciated *her* for who she was.

Tiffany wasn't just a tutor. She wasn't just "that Chinese girl" who lived in Everville.

What was her favorite color? What was her favorite book? Movie? Band? Considering all the time they'd spent together, he should have known these trivial facts.

Now he'd been given a second chance to find out…and make things right.

DANIEL CLOSED HIS BEDROOM DOOR and booted up the computer, his blood lurching through his heart like molten lead. A jumble of words kept stringing themselves together in his mind, but they were like beads on an untied string that kept sliding off the other end and scattering across the floor. Nothing he could say sounded intelligent, much less intelligible. This was going to be a disaster.

He loaded up Skype and checked himself in the mirror briefly. His hands were shaking, and his eyes looked a little wild. An alert chimed and he clicked the icon to load the chat.

Selena appeared in the window. She glowed beneath soft lamplight from a nearby fixture. She usually wore her long, dark curls pinned up while working, but they hung around her thin shoulders now. She had her glasses on, though he knew she wore contacts during the day. She looked relaxed in a light T-shirt, a cup of instant noodles visible in the webcam's view off to one side.

"Hey, honey bear," she said with a huge grin. "I'm so happy you got the camera working."

"I had to get a new one," he lied. He'd had this one for months; he simply hadn't had the balls to hook it up. "How's the image coming through over there?"

"Not bad, though I might be able to tell better if you took off your shirt." She waggled her eyebrows. He chuckled, forgetting for a blissful moment that their relationship was doomed.

"Are you blushing?" she asked, leaning forward, her dark eyes looking down and not quite meeting the camera's view. It felt like she was staring through his heart, trying to understand the muddiness there. "What's wrong, Daniel? Are you really that embarrassed?"

"Well…" He didn't want to admit it to her. "I don't want to be interrupted again and have anyone see you. Or me. You know. Naked."

"It's more than that, though, isn't it?" She peered into the screen. "Tell me what's wrong."

Oh, boy. "I've been thinking about you coming up here," he started slowly. "I don't know if you're going to be comfortable staying in the house for two weeks."

She tilted her head. "If you think it's going to be a problem, I can get a room at a hotel instead."

"There's only one motel on the edge of town, but I'd rather you not stay there. It's kind of sketchy."

"How about a B and B?"

"I'll have to look into it. I'd rather you stay with me, of course, but…"

"But you don't know if your parents will accept that?" The corner of her mouth twitched.

"Among other things." His eyes bulged. He hadn't meant to say that out loud.

Selena's eyebrows furrowed together. "What do you mean?"

He took a deep breath, the air burning his lungs. "I haven't told them about you being…you know."

"A gorgeous catch? Allergic to dogs? Web-footed? Help me out, here, honey bear." Her weak laughter missed the mark.

"Not…Chinese." He cringed.

She sat back, eyes wide. She blinked rapidly and glanced away. "Oh."

"I don't know how they're going to react," he explained. "My grandmother is from an older generation, and she raised my mom with certain beliefs, and my dad… Well, don't get me started…."

"You really think it's a problem, don't you?" Her eyes grew flinty as she scrutinized him. And then she couldn't look at him at all. Her hands folded and unfolded then hid from the camera's view beneath the table. "I don't understand why this hasn't come up before. I'd think the name *Dr. Selena Worthington* would be a dead giveaway. What have you been telling them about me?"

He struggled to explain. "I told them you're a doctor. I told them I met you online." He rubbed his jaw. "Look, my parents are old school. They have certain ideas about who I should be with—"

"You know," she interrupted, her tone rising from resigned to irked, "I've been dicked around by enough guys with commitment problems to know when they wanted out, and then gave me plenty of crazy reasons why they couldn't be with me. But this has to be one of the top three bullshit excuses I've ever heard."

This was spinning out of control. "It's not you, it's me."

Jeez, that sounded like a cliché. "I can't control what my parents think. I don't want things to get awkward—"

"For me or for you?" Selena pushed away from the desk and crossed her arms over her chest, fingers digging into her arms. She bounced her knee impatiently. "Let me ask you this. Does it matter to *you* that I'm white?"

He opened his mouth to say no, but nothing came out. He couldn't put the words together to tell her what his real insecurities were. "My parents aren't racist," he said miserably.

Her features twisted with disgust. "Grow a spine, Daniel. Call me when you figure out what your real problem is." She slapped a hand over the webcam and a second later, disconnected.

CHAPTER TEN

TIFFANY PACKED HER THINGS, rolling her stiff neck after a grueling session with Simon. She was looking forward to next week when they'd start *Animal Farm*. As much as she loved Shakespeare, she'd forgotten how much work it was to teach. On top of that, it was hard to keep Simon focused. The weather outside was bright and hot, and being cooped up indoors was doing little for his patience.

The clomp of heavy boots on the veranda heralding Chris's arrival made her heart stutter. He strode in, a little out of breath.

"I'm glad I caught you before you left." He was covered in bits of hay and grass, and his jeans were smeared with dirt, but Tiffany's heart couldn't stop pitter-pattering. Every time he rushed to see her, she had to stifle the smile threatening to stretch her face into a goofy grin.

"Is something wrong?" Her voice sounded a little raspy to her ears, but that was probably because Chris had pulled up the hem of his T-shirt to wipe his face. She was beginning to think he did that on purpose when she was around.

"I was wondering…" He hesitated, pulling off his hat and running his fingers through his sweat-slicked hair. "I wanted to know if you're free for dinner tomorrow night."

The words seeped through her muddled brain. "Dinner?"

"I want to talk about—" he glanced around, lowered his voice "—Simon. I have some questions and I was hoping we could discuss a few things."

She straightened, scolding herself for imagining his interest was in anything more than his son's welfare. "That would be fine," she said coolly, wincing inwardly at her all-business tone. Why couldn't she loosen up now and again and at least pretend she was used to having guys ask her out?

"Perfect. There's this great new place that's opened up in Kielsburg. I think you'll really like it. I'll drive us both there after you're done with Simon."

Later, Tiffany pondered the exact reasons for this get-together. Perhaps he wanted to talk about college options. While Simon was making progress, she couldn't guarantee scholarship-worthy marks. When it came to essay writing and reading, he wasn't as sure of himself as he was with hands-on tasks. He simply didn't have the confidence.

There was also the matter of William. She knew it wasn't her business, but the old man wasn't particularly encouraging. On two separate occasions, he'd called his grandson "a dummy" in that nasty half-joking way she couldn't really decipher as being a dig or an actual joke. But she knew it bothered Simon—he lost focus when his grandfather was around. She didn't want to interfere in their family matters again, but she couldn't let this slide. If nothing else, William was starting to piss *her* off.

THE FOLLOWING DAY BEFORE TUTORING, Daniel walked into the diner looking low and exhausted. Dark bags hung beneath his eyes, and his expression strained, as if he were holding back a scream. He'd been working nonstop, either at the diner or with his driving students, and it was obviously taking its toll. He hadn't been eating much, prompting *Poh-poh* to boil up some pungent concoction of herbs in case he was coming down with something. He'd been like this all week. When Tiffany asked him about it, he shook his head and went back into the kitchen.

Her conscience niggled at her. He hadn't been the same since their talk about his relationship with Selena. She'd been too cruel, too realistic, too *Tiffany-headed*. She should have known better than to think Daniel wouldn't listen when she was being mean.

Something had happened, and it wasn't good. Unfortunately, engaging him—or anyone in their family—in conversation about personal matters was like trying to pull teeth from a crocodile, so she came up with a new tack. "Hey, Daniel. I have a question for you."

He looked up at her balefully.

"Do you think you and Dad could use another hand back here?"

"We could always use help," he said with a slight shrug. "Why? Is there someone you have in mind?"

"Actually, yeah. Simon Jamieson."

He shook his head. "Tiff…"

"It's just an idea. The kid needs something to build up his confidence, and he seemed to like working here. I know things didn't go well the last time, but I think it'd work out with the proper training."

He scratched the thin stubble on his chin. He'd always been meticulous about his shaving habits and she was bothered by the sight of that scruffy shadow. "I'll have to talk to Dad. We have the funds but…well, you know how cheap he is."

"Thanks. I'd appreciate that." She sobered. Asking about a part-time job for Simon had only been an excuse to make her brother open up. "So…do you want to talk about whatever's bugging you?"

"My college reunion is coming up. I'm trying to figure out whether I'm going to go."

She didn't believe he could possibly be brooding that much over a reunion. She went straight for the kill. "How's Selena doing?"

A momentary flash of anger was quickly blotted out by sadness in his dark, bloodshot eyes. He let out a long breath. "I've gotta get this going." He turned back to the bowl of chicken marinating on the counter, staring at it as if he had no idea what to do next.

Tiff left for the Jamieson farm shortly after that, her worry for Daniel slowly giving way to thoughts about the lesson ahead. She was determined not to think about Chris and their "date" tonight. She didn't want to build up any expectations or anticipation for the evening. She had to take it minute by minute. It was a lovely day, clear and hot, a few puffy clouds in the sky. The evening forecast would be equally clear and warm. It was the perfect weather to go for a long stroll…if they were going on a date. Which they weren't.

Uttering a short curse, she realized she'd forgotten to change her clothes in her rush to leave the diner. It'd taken her all morning to choose an outfit that could do triple duty at the Good Fortune, tutoring and dinner. The problem was that she didn't want to smell like fryer oil when she sat down with Chris—it didn't matter so much with Simon. So, she'd brought a top to change into—a pretty, light pink cowl-necked thing with a few sequins that looked punky and flirty all at once.

It would be too obvious if she switched outfits in the Jamiesons' bathroom. Simon would notice her costume change for sure, and might get ideas. And she was adamant that no one got ideas of any kind, herself included. This was simply a meeting to discuss Simon's future. She wanted to look clean and smell fresh. That was all.

She pulled onto the shoulder and parked next to a wooded area. She changed quickly, praying no one would saunter up to the car while she was undressed. She took another minute to freshen her makeup. Then, because she was worried she'd put her shirt on inside out or left something untucked or unzipped, she got out of the car to check her reflection in the glass.

Shirt—neat. Hair—brushed. Teeth—no food bits.

She breathed deeply, trying to master the nerves fluttering in her tummy. There was no reason for her to be nervous. None at all. This wasn't a date. But she still needed a plan, a way to deal with Chris. She would be forced to engage in real, adult conversation with him during their meal, and there was no way they would discuss Shakespeare for two hours. She wasn't tutoring him anymore.

As long as they talked about Simon, they wouldn't lapse into awkward silence, she reasoned. She paced outside of the car and began categorizing all the things she wanted to discuss with Chris, giving herself a bunch of cues on where to continue conversation. Good segues in conversation, she reminded herself, used the words *by the way, speaking of,* and *I recently read/heard about.* She could only hope that what followed was equally as smooth and brilliant.

Finally ready to face Chris, she went to open her car door. It was locked.

She reached for her keys. The sickening plunge of her stomach occurred half a second before she realized she'd left them dangling from the ignition. Her purse sat on the passenger seat. Her cell phone was zipped inside the bag.

"No. Oh, no, no, no." She gently thumped her forehead against the roof of the car. She refused to let panic take over, but her heart had started a hard hammering inside her chest.

She couldn't be late. She was *never* late.

Maybe she should break a window and unlock the doors. But this was Daniel's car, and she did not want to lose another vehicle. She could just imagine what her parents would say.

She checked her watch. She still had time to get to the Jamieson farm. She could walk to the nearest farmhouse and call Daniel or someone else to deliver an extra set of keys. She knew there were a few homes along this stretch of road, but couldn't quite remember where she'd stopped on her journey. Things looked different standing on the shoulder.

Well, there was no use staying here. *When the horse dies, find a cow,* she told herself in *Poh-poh's* sage voice. She pointed herself toward the Jamieson farm and started walking.

It was after five when Chris walked into the house to grab a shower before his dinner date with Tiffany. He'd found himself whistling as he mounted the porch steps. He was looking forward to tonight. It had been a long time since he'd been out with other adults who weren't members of his staff or family.

When he entered the dining room, all was silent—there was no sign of either Simon or his tutor. He asked his father if he'd seen or heard them come or go, but William merely shrugged, testily adding he didn't come out of his office when "that woman" came over.

His father had been sulky ever since Chris had lectured him about his comments to Tiffany. William had insisted he'd been joking, and simply wouldn't acknowledge how offensive he'd been.

"It's not personal," he'd argued. "And it's not like I called her some of the things people used to call them. I was being downright friendly."

"Dad, I don't care. There's a standard of behavior I expect from every member of my family and my staff, and I will not have that kind of willful ignorance influence my son."

"So, I'm part of your staff now, am I? Why don't you fire me, then?"

They'd left it at that. His father was too stubborn to ever apologize. He didn't want to hear that he was wrong.

Chris left the house and found his son in the barn loft. The kittens swarmed around his lap as he scooped each one up in turn and set them on his shoulder, or rubbed his cheek against their purring, wriggling bodies. He smiled and made his way up the ladder. Simon glanced up.

"Where's Tiffany?"

"She didn't show." He set the kitten down, and it scampered to where Shadow lay watching from the straw.

"Did you try calling her?"

Simon shot him a *duh* look. "Three times. There was no answer."

Chris was immediately alarmed. "She's over an hour late and you didn't think to tell me?" A lot of things could happen on that long stretch of highway between here and town, and considering that wreck in Frank's shop....

No, he was not about to think the worst.

Simon looked worried now, too. "Sorry, Dad. I just thought she was late. Maybe she's still at the diner and forgot." He sucked in a lip. "Do you think something happened?"

"I'm sure she's fine," he replied, trying to keep the worry out of his voice. "Hey, how was your midterm?"

"It went okay. I'll tell you about it later." He'd sensed his father's anxiety and urged him on with a nod.

Chris left the barn and dialed the Good Fortune on his cell. Perhaps she'd simply forgotten the time, or was bogged down at the diner, but that wasn't likely. She always called if she thought she might be late, which she never was. By the time Daniel picked up, he was certain something had happened.

"Chris Jamieson here. We haven't heard from Tiffany. Is she there?"

The long pause at the other end of the line had Chris's heart racing. "She left over two hours ago."

"Okay." Blood pounded through his temples and cold fear raced through his system. He knew he was getting worked up, but he couldn't help it. He pictured her bloodied by the side of the road and his skin prickled. "I'm going to drive out along Route 28. That's the way she usually comes. She might have gotten a flat tire or something. My son tried to call her cell, but she's not picking up. The battery could be dead." His throat stuck on the last word.

"Let me know as soon as you hear anything. I can grab my dad's van and meet you." Daniel sounded as calm as a stone.

"All right. Keep your cell on." He hung up and headed to his truck. Simon ran up to the driver's-side window as he started the engine.

"What's going on? Did you find her?"

"I'm going to see if she's somewhere along the road. Her car might have had troubles."

"You want me to come?" He looked anxious.

"No, stay here. Wait and see if she turns up or calls. Grandpa might not hear the phone." Or he might ignore it. He screened his calls all the time. "I'll call you as soon as I find her."

Chris drove the route slowly, scanning the landscape for any sign of life. There were long stretches of road bordered on either side by tall, thick grasses, cornfields that could swallow cars and boggy, marshy ponds that could suck a man under without leaving a trace. Farther along, the dikes were steep enough that a car could roll down them. And there were all kinds of wildlife that could walk onto the road and startle drivers.

She didn't get scared by a sleepy raccoon, he told himself. People drove along this road all the time. If something had happened, she could wave someone down....

Which only opened his imagination to all the other unsavory possibilities.

He'd been driving for ten minutes with a hitchhiking serial killer starring in his waking nightmare when he spotted a lone figure walking along the unpaved shoulder. The figure paused, then started waving frantically with both arms. Her calves, bare beneath her modest gray skirt, and sandals were splattered with mud. Long strands of dark hair had escaped her ponytail, framing her reddened face. It must have been nearly ninety-five in this sun, and here she was walking without a hat or water or anything.

Chris pulled over, the tires sending up a spray of gravel, and he jumped out.

"Are you all right?" He ran to her, and before he even knew what he was doing, had thrown his arms around her, pulling her into his chest.

She smelled like sweat and cooking oil mixed with coconut butter. Her dark, shiny hair was warm from the sun, and he automatically turned his nose into it, inhaling. She was small and firm and hot all over. His hands flexed and trailed along her sides.

She stiffened and jerked against him. "I'm fine." Her sharp words were like a splash of cold water. He stepped away from her hastily as the fog lifted from his brain. The heat from her body clung to him tenaciously, and her cheeks were crimson-red. She was roasting out here.

"C'mon, get out of this sun. I have water in my truck." He steered her toward the passenger-side door. Her steps faltered a little, and she stumbled before he caught her and practically carried her to the truck. Poor girl must be dehydrated. Only after she was in the shade and he'd opened a bottle of water for her from a case he kept in the backseat did he ask, "What happened? Where's your car?"

"I stopped by the side of the road somewhere that way and got locked out." She gestured vaguely behind her. She sipped the water slowly, eyes glazed and darting. "I thought I'd find a phone at one of the houses along the way. I didn't realize those buildings were abandoned."

"If you're talking about the Guntersons' farm, their house is way farther up the hill. The buildings nearer the road are storage houses."

She nodded. "I started walking through their field, but I couldn't find the farmhouse. Once I got back on the road, I figured it'd probably be easier to walk the rest of the way to your place." She swiped at the dirt smudged over her legs, pursed her lips and sent him an arch look. "You live damn far. Has anyone ever told you that?"

"And here I thought New Yorkers walked everywhere." He laughed weakly, still feeling giddy and light-headed with relief. "It doesn't seem that far driving, but I wouldn't try walking to town."

"At least in New York, you can stop in a Starbucks for an iced tea every three blocks." She squinted at the sun-drenched landscape. "There are also things we call sidewalks." She looked down at her ruined sandals.

After a few minutes, her color had gone back to normal and her eyes cleared. "Let's go see if we can do something about the car." They got into his truck, and he started up the engine, blasting the air conditioner for Tiffany's comfort. "What made you get out, anyhow? Flat tire? Bathroom emergency?"

"Nothing like that." Her cheeks tinted pink, but she didn't explain further.

She directed him to Daniel's car, which she'd parked on the wide shoulder. He swung the truck around and pulled up behind it. There were no signs of any kind of accident. The keys were in the ignition, her purse on the seat.

He surveyed the car, hands on his hips. Tiffany was worrying her lower lip, drumming her fingers as she hugged her elbows. A slow, wry smile curved his lips as his gaze traveled from the car door to the girl who'd won the award for highest academic achievement in her class.

"I don't suppose you know how to jimmy a car lock?" she asked hopefully.

"No." He went to the rear passenger side door and opened

it. "But I do know how to check all my doors before assuming I'm locked out."

Tiffany stared. And stared. Slowly, her hands went to her face and she made a long, low moan.

CHAPTER ELEVEN

By the time they got back to the farm, there wasn't much time to do any tutoring. Simon didn't mind—he was simply glad she was all right. She called to assure Daniel that both she and his car were fine, then cleaned herself up in the bathroom. Chris gave her a towel so she could wash and dry her legs. She patted cold water on her flame-hot cheeks and touched up her makeup.

Perhaps it was simply embarrassment at her idiotic mistake that had her so flustered, but she knew all this flushing and stammering was her stupid body doing its best to get Chris's attention.

She could still feel his steel-cable arms around her. He'd squeezed her so tight, it felt as if his heart had banged against her chest. She still smelled the earth and grass and his antiperspirant clinging to his skin. But instead of melting and leaning into his embrace, she'd frozen. She'd been so startled, all she could think at the time was that he needed to step away before she did something truly foolish…like fling her arms around him and cover him in kisses.

She glanced at Chris, relaxed and wearing a half smile as he pointed the 4x4 toward the restaurant. He was probably still chuckling at her mishap. That hug hadn't meant anything to him, she told herself firmly. He'd showered and changed into a navy blue short-sleeve polo top and clean jeans, and his dark gold hair had been slicked away from his face. She kind of missed the hat, though.

"So, where is this place we're going?" she asked.

"It's a new restaurant, actually," he said. "A buffet."

Scratch that romantic candlelit dinner, she thought despondently.

"I hope you don't mind, but I know you like having choices."

"What's that supposed to mean?"

"It's something I noticed about you—how you like to give everyone around you choices." He grinned. "I still remember how back in high school you used to talk about how much better Starbucks was compared to the old coffee shop that used to be on Main Street because of the way you could customize everything. Remember that argument we had? It was right after one of those university tours you went on in New York."

His memory for these little details was supernatural, she thought, turning the AC vent to blow directly into her hot face.

Fifteen minutes later, they pulled into a big shopping plaza on the edge of the county that housed a big-box hardware store, a few outlet shops and a handful of restaurants. The parking lot was quite full, with most of the cars clustered near a newer-looking establishment. Tiffany's heart sank.

The restaurant was called Eastern Delights, and the sign touted Over 300 Items for the Low, Low Price of $14.99 Per Person.

"This place got great reviews," Chris said as he guided her toward the door. She doubted Zagat or Michelin was giving those ratings, but she kept her smile fixed. "I've been meaning to try it, but Dad cooks all the meals, and I don't get out of eating them often."

It was the least intimate setting Tiffany could possibly imagine for a date. Throngs of noisy, hungry patrons circled the long steam counters like pilot fish around a stainless-steel whale. Children high on unlimited ice cream chased each other, zigzagging through tables and dodging waiters who gathered plates, some still full of uneaten food. Considering Chris's rants as a teen about the obesity epidemic, she was surprised this was where he'd chosen to eat.

Perusing the steam tables, she couldn't help comparing the food to what the Good Fortune served. The sweet-and-sour pork looked heavily breaded, the sauce thin; the vegetables in black-bean sauce looked pale and flaccid instead of crispy. She cringed at the pools of oil sitting on the bottom of the trays of spring rolls. Making up for the marked difference in quality was the fact that the buffet did have a wide variety of dishes, many of them "authentic" even if they looked unappetizing. An assortment of international foods rounded out the menu, including a sushi bar, a pasta station and an array of North American classics like pizza and baked potatoes.

Tiffany went to the salad bar, loading up on cocktail shrimp, beets, bean salad and coleslaw. In the corner, she spotted a man carving up a huge slab of roast beef, and made a beeline for the station.

When she returned to the table, a waiter had delivered the bottle of wine Chris had ordered. She looked at Chris's plate as he sat and found rice, noodles, stir-fried vegetables, hoisin beef, stewed shiitake mushrooms and pieces of roast duck all piled on his plate. She looked at her own mounds of mashed potatoes and gravy, brussels sprouts, rare roast beef with horseradish, and her salad bar selections. She laughed. "Should we trade meals?" she asked wryly.

He looked at their plates and chuckled. "I think I chose the right place to eat. Though, if you'd had a hankering for beef, I could've barbecued a steak at home."

"And if you'd wanted Chinese, we could've gone to my parents'," she shot back.

"Ah, but I bet they can't grill a porterhouse like I can. I make a mean gravy, too."

"Careful, or I'll have to invite myself over one day so you can prove it."

"Challenge accepted." He winked.

Had she actually managed to flirt? Her head spun, and she took a bracing gulp of the bold Shiraz. It sent a pleasant warmth through her bones.

Even though there was a fork, knife and spoon on his place mat, Chris extracted the disposable chopsticks from the paper wrapper and without fumbling or fuss, expertly picked up a piece of beef and ate it.

"You have perfect chopstick form," she marveled.

He glanced at his chopstick hand and shrugged, sheepish. "It's all the chicken balls I buy for Simon. You should see him. He can use them with both his left and right hands."

They ate in silence. Tiffany struggled not to simply stuff her face the way she usually did. She wanted to prove to herself she could have a polite, adult conversation with her old crush. Now was the perfect time to employ her list of conversational cues. "Speaking of Simon—"

"Did you know shiitake mushrooms have been cultivated for over a thousand years?" Chris said at the same time. He held out the slimy-looking sauce-covered black fungus toward her.

She looked between the man and the mushroom, blinking. "I...did not know that."

"I've been doing research into new crops. They're getting quite popular with a lot of restaurants." He bit into the mushroom. His eyes bulged, and his chewing slowed. "Now I'm not sure why," he said as he swallowed, then sipped his wine liberally.

She smiled. He probably hadn't been prepared for the strong woody flavor of the shiitake.

"I saw the Shanghai bok choy in your display at the grocery store. Are you trying to get into the Asian vegetable market?"

"There's a huge demand for bok choy, and it's a crop with a long growing season and a big yield—a lot of chefs like to use it as a side dish instead of the usual frozen vegetable medley."

She'd noticed that even in fancy restaurants in the city. "Daniel mentioned something about you starting the 100-mile program, as well."

"It was mostly to raise awareness and cultivate business contacts," he admitted as he attacked his noodles with aplomb. "I wanted to get people eating locally grown stuff instead of going for the cheapest imports all the time. But I couldn't get everyone fully on board, considering things like coffee and sugar can't be produced here. Folks aren't likely to give up their daily joe, and I didn't want to put any of the restaurants or cafés out of business. The point was made, though, and all things considered, it's working pretty well."

"That's cool." Which was an understatement. It was amazing he'd moved the town to do anything. Everville hadn't grown or changed in the years she'd lived there. They went through the same cycle of fairs and festivals every year, never got new businesses in, didn't build anything new. The town had gone stagnant, and no one was moving in.

Chris explained, "Ever since Bob Fordingham left the mayor's office and his cronies started retiring, we've seen a lot more progress. The new mayor, Cheyenne Welks, is finally putting the city's money to good use, replacing the old water mains, tearing down the eyesores and building new infrastructure and housing. That's why you're seeing so many new businesses popping up along Main Street. The new members on council are really receptive of any ideas, too."

"You sound like you could run for mayor yourself."

He laughed. "I wouldn't have the time, though I've served on a couple of environmental committees. There's only so much I can do, but you know what Ghandi says. 'Be the change you want to see.' Converting the farm to a certified organic one was my first big project, and that was tough. But once we got on our feet, I started lobbying for greener energy alternatives in the area. The wind turbines went up a couple of years ago, but they're only part of a test project. It'll be a long time before we get a full wind farm, and that's going to take a lot more lobbying. I'd like to get the town to look into municipal composting, too, but no one really wants to pay more taxes for waste diversion."

She couldn't stop the smile breaking on her face. Chris was still trying to save the world. The intellectual she'd admired was still there, hiding beneath all those muscled layers of farmer.

"I'm finished bragging now," he joked. "Nothing I've done can be half as interesting as what you've been up to. Tell me about your life in New York. What happened to you in college and afterward?"

She shifted in her seat and played with her mashed potatoes. "What's there to tell? I went to school, got a degree, got a job."

He chuckled. "There's gotta be more to it than that. I want to know more about you. You barely talk about yourself. I know more about your brother than I do you, and considering how much time we spent together in high school, I feel like I should know you better."

Her heart thumped hard and she took another gulp of her wine.

He's not actually interested in you. He's just making conversation.

Not that it would hurt to oblige him. She blew out a breath, searching for those elusive details that would make her story more interesting. "Well, I guess the first thing you should know, then, is that I applied to NYU for an English degree against my parents' wishes. I told them I was applying for premed."

He cocked an eyebrow. "I could have sworn I saw you fill out applications for premed."

"I did. But I never sent them in."

He grinned. "Rebel."

"That wasn't the word my parents used," she said, and sipped. "When I got accepted and told them, they flipped out. But they couldn't stop me from leaving because I'd received a full scholarship, so they wouldn't have to pay a cent. They almost didn't come to our grad ceremony."

She didn't mention they hadn't bothered to make it to her college graduation.

"So, you worked your ass off and got a full scholarship, but they weren't happy?" Chris looked disturbed. "I'm starting to see your parents in a new light."

"Don't. I mean, I did lie to them, after all. I had to. They got over it eventually. Mostly." She chuckled without humor. "I think grad's one of those moments parents look forward to for seventeen years, that day they can stand up and cheer and be proud their kid made it. So, when their kid doesn't live up to that fantasy..." She shrugged.

He cleared his throat and chased a piece of food around his plate, and she regretted her sentiment. She didn't know exactly what kind of expectations he had for Simon, and she didn't want to sound like she was lecturing him for being a parent. It seemed she never stopped meddling when it came to his family.

"Did the scholarship cover housing?" he asked, giving her something else to focus on.

"Barely. But Daniel had helped me invest my savings in some bonds that helped with that. And my grandmother sent me a lot of care packages. There were plenty of nights of instant noodles," she added hastily at Chris's look of awe, "and I did manage to get a bursary here and there, but I did okay."

"I'm impressed you did it all on your own."

"It's what I wanted." It'd been everything she'd wanted— being away from Everville, away from her parents, living in the big city. "So I got my degree in English literature and then I interned for a magazine publishing company as an admin assistant, then as a marketing assistant in another firm, and then as a junior assistant to the publisher at a custom publishing firm."

"Not that I'm making fun of you, but I have to ask…what do you do with an English degree?"

"Lots. I want to be a book editor," she said. "I want to find the next J. K. Rowling or discover the new *Da Vinci Code.* I want to help good writers get gooder." She grinned wickedly.

Chris laughed. "You'd make a great editor. I still remembered how you used a red pen to mark up all my essays. I'm sure that kind of instinct and brutal honesty will get you where you want to be."

She toyed with her wineglass. "Except, of course, that I got laid off."

"You'll get where you want to go eventually." As Chris topped off her wine, a funny pang wormed through her. Yes, she was certain she would make it eventually. She wouldn't allow herself to fail. But all that mattered was the present, this moment she was sharing with the man who made her feel like the schoolgirl she'd never allowed herself to be. She'd given up a lot for the future she wanted—it was time she enjoyed the here and now.

"So, where in the city did you live?" Chris asked.

"I had an apartment in Chinatown. I lived there after my third year of college and stayed right up to the day I was evicted. It was a one-bedroom with a tiny bathroom and a

galley kitchen. But it was enough." She really couldn't think
of anything else to recommend her former tenancy.

"That's a nice area, though, isn't it?"

"It was a roof over my head." In fact, the cramped apartment above a Chinese herb store had smelled like pungent
dried roots all the time, and was full of roaches, but it had
been all she could afford in Manhattan. She added deter-
minedly, "I didn't need much."

"It must have been great having the city outside your door.
I can't imagine the convenience of walking to a corner store
for milk. You must have loved living there."

"I did. I *do,*" she corrected. "I love all the different neigh-
borhoods, all the things to see and do. Even if I spent every
waking minute wandering the streets, I could never see it all."
Her chest constricted, homesick for the sounds and smells,
the throngs of people, the variety, the sheer verve that pulsed
along the city streets.

"You miss it?"

"Immensely. But I'll be back there soon enough." She said
it with conviction, attacking her slab of roast beef with renewed vigor. "As soon as I can pay off the car repairs and
find a job, I'm outta here." She took a bite of her roast beef
and chewed. It was tough and the gravy was way too salty.
She made a face, but didn't think it'd be polite to spit it out.
She hated wasting food.

"You hate it here, don't you." Chris's quiet statement had
her looking up from her plate.

She didn't want to seem ungrateful. "Well, the food's not
five-star but—"

"I mean, you hate being back in Everville."

"What makes you say that?" she asked uneasily. *Hate* was a
pretty strong word. *Loathed* and *dreaded* were probably more
accurate ways to describe her feelings for her hometown, but

it had more to do with her family and present situation than the town itself. Or so she told herself.

"It was bad in high school for you, wasn't it?" His voice was soft, full of regret. "People didn't treat you very well."

Her stomach cinched tight, and her appetite fled. "It was high school. No one treats each other very well."

"Were you bullied?"

"Not the way some kids were." She stabbed at the meat, but made no more effort to eat it. His long, hard gaze made her set her utensils down. "People are stupid sometimes. They say stuff they don't fully understand, or they say it because they want to take their problems out on others. Sometimes, they're just plain terrible people, but I try not to let them get to me." She gave him a lopsided smile. "I can say that now as an adult looking back. Hindsight's twenty-twenty, after all."

Chris reached across the table, letting his hands settle between their plates, palms down. "For what it's worth, I'm sorry."

"Sorry for what? You never said anything nasty to me." He'd been her one friend. The one person she could count on spending time with who wouldn't mock her ruthlessly for being different. It was no wonder she'd harbored her crush for so long.

"I didn't speak up when other people talked about you. I might even have laughed. That makes me as bad as them."

She wasn't sure why *he* was so upset. Sure, it made her mad and sad thinking about how she and Daniel had been treated, not just by students but by teachers who'd told them to deal with it and ignore the taunts. But who didn't have problems? High school sucked for everyone. Chris alone could not have changed that.

"You didn't know any better back then. Or maybe it was self-preservation. That's normal for teens."

He shook his head. "Don't make excuses for me. I *did* know

better. I had plenty of opportunities to call people on their behavior." He closed his eyes. "People say stuff, and it's funny when you're a kid, I guess…" He said quietly, "I wonder if I somehow learned it from my father."

So, that was what this was about. "You have nothing to apologize for. Not to me, anyhow. I appreciate that you're trying to say sorry for William, but his opinions aren't your responsibility. Neither are the things anyone in high school ever said about anyone else." When he didn't look like he was going to accept her explanations, she sighed. "If it matters that much to you, I forgive you." It was William who'd been the idiot. But she wasn't about to stir that pot. "Anyhow, I don't let other people's opinions define me."

But as she looked around the restaurant, she knew that was a lie. Realizing she was the only Asian person in the room, she grew uncomfortable, convinced everyone was watching and whispering and wondering what she was doing with a guy like Chris. Not even the servers were Asian.

Of course the things people said had shaped her. Why else would she have stopped using chopsticks and refused to order Chinese takeout when she'd lived in the city? She stared at her roast beef dinner and pushed her plate aside.

"At least the wine is passable," Chris commented as he tipped the last of the bottle into her glass. It seemed he'd moved on in their conversation, noticing her barely touched meal. She drained her glass, belatedly wondering how much he'd drunk, since he was driving.

Not as much as me, came the sinking realization when she tried to lever herself out of her seat to go to the ladies' room.

"I think I'm done here. Do you want to get a coffee?" he asked tentatively. "The night's still young."

"We should," she said as solemnly as she could manage. "We still haven't talked about Simon."

His lips quirked into a smile. "We don't have to talk about my son exclusively, you know. We are friends."

Friends? Was that what they were? And then she realized she'd spoken her thoughts aloud. Chris gave her a puzzled look. "Of course we are," he said.

Friends. She grinned widely and giggled. In the back of her mind, she was kicking herself for acting so foolishly— she was supposed to be a sophisticated New Yorker, not this bubbleheaded ditz. But she was feeling warm and giddy and Chris was just so wonderfully big and broad, and that smile… If someone could bottle that smile, they'd make a killing. She'd drink ten of those a day if she could.

Chris paid the bill and guided her out of the restaurant, his hand pressing gently on her lower back and sending a sizzle along her spine. She leaned into his touch, resting her temple against his shoulder.

He didn't try to push her off.

IN THE TRUCK, Tiffany babbled about the food they'd eaten and her fears that their "authenticity" might mean their chicken balls were literal. He laughed along: maybe it was the wine talking, but she sure had loosened up. All that bubbly train-of-thought chattering was kind of funny, but soothing, too. Entirely out of character, but he couldn't help but be intrigued by her loss of control. What would Tiffany be like if she let herself go completely? If she let herself laugh and relax instead of trying to steer every aspect of her life toward her career goals?

What would she be like in bed?

He nearly stomped on the brake as his mind ground to a halt. No way. He could not be thinking those kinds of thoughts. Not about Tiffany. For starters, she was not his type—small, serious and city chic. She obviously preferred life in the big city—something she and his ex had in common.

He was not looking for any kind of relationship right now—dealing with his father and son was plenty enough distraction. To top it off, she wasn't here permanently. There was no point in thinking about any kind of involvement with her.

He glanced over. The lights from the road curved softly around her face, and his heart tweaked. She was a beautiful woman. One he was seeing less and less as his old tutor and more as a woman he could have inappropriate dreams about. She glanced up and caught him staring, and he returned his eyes to the road.

To her utter delight, they went to a Starbucks that had recently opened a couple of plazas over. She insisted on paying for the coffee since he'd gotten dinner, and he let her. But there weren't any seats available, so they went back to the truck.

"It's a nice night," he said, rolling down the windows. "How about a walk? I mean, you've already walked a lot today…." He suddenly remembered the way he'd hugged her earlier, right in the middle of the road, and he shifted uncomfortably in his seat.

"I don't mind." She was practically snuggling the drink, hands cupped around the venti cup, inhaling the rich smell from the hole in the lid. "I have my extrahot, half-sweet, double-shot soy latte now. I'm a happy camper. Anyhow, a little extra exercise after that meal wouldn't hurt."

"You're not one of those city girls who's always trying to make herself stick-thin, are you?"

"Not any more than country girls or town girls or desert girls or igloo girls or whatever. Or boys, for that matter." She appraised him crookedly. "Don't tell me you haven't stood in front of a mirror and pinched your belly once or twice and told yourself five fewer pounds would make you perfect."

"I don't know. I haven't had an objective opinion lately. Want to give me a pinch and tell me what you think?"

Even though it was dark, he could see her blush to the roots of her hair. He laughed, and to ease her embarrassment, said, "I'm kidding. I already know I'm gorgeous."

Just like you. He almost said it, but something stopped him.

They drove to Osprey Peak, a lookout point high above the township. The Peak, as it was called, was a well-known spot where teenagers went to make out. Not that he was entertaining those thoughts about Tiffany. Adults went there all the time for the view. At least, they did in the daytime.

They ambled side by side along the path in comfortable silence. She walked in a perfectly straight line and didn't lean on him the way she had as they'd exited the restaurant, which was kind of a shame. The effects of the wine must have worn off. He couldn't help but remember all the times in high school he'd had to carry Daphne home from house parties, and how in their later years together, he'd sometimes find her lying on the bed, claiming a headache, an empty wine bottle on the nightstand, while Simon cried in his crib.

"Hello? Did you hear me?" Tiffany waved a hand in front of his face.

"I'm sorry?"

"I was asking about Daphne. Simon's mother." She hesitated. "Not that it's any of my business, in case you were trying to ignore me…." Her eyebrows knitted as she waved a hand. "Never mind. It was too personal. I didn't mean to—"

"It's okay." He kicked a pinecone into the underbrush and paused to collect his thoughts. "After Simon was born, she got…I don't know. Jealous, maybe, of all the attention the baby was getting. I thought it was postpartum depression, but she wouldn't see a specialist about it. She was sick all the time. At least, she claimed she was sick."

"You were living at the farm with your father, right?"

He nodded. "He did his fair share of raising Simon, especially when Daphne was having a spell. It was…difficult.

They didn't get along." To put it mildly. His father had been disgusted by how lazy Daphne was. She'd expected Chris to be the breadwinner, and had no intention of getting a job or helping out on the farm. Her job, she'd told them, was to take care of Simon. Which she barely did, even between migraines.

"Does Simon get to see her often?"

"She makes promises, but hasn't kept one for years. She'll invite him to stay with her for a couple of weeks in the summer, but then she'll call and say something else has come up, or her husband has to entertain colleagues, so they can't have him around. Last year, she called the night before he was going to see her and told him not to come because she had a migraine coming on." He shook his head in disgust.

"The last time he saw her was on his twelfth birthday. She flew up from California—that's where she is now—and we drove out to meet her in the city. She gave him his gift and we took him to a ball game. But she didn't stay for more than a night. She said the air quality was hurting her sinuses, and she flew home the next day. I've never seen Simon so disappointed in all my life."

"I've known other people with killer migraines like that. She must have been going through hell." To Chris's surprise, she said it without a trace of sarcasm.

He laughed, low and flat. "I was kind of hoping you'd come out and say what I won't."

"Well, I was trying to be sympathetic, but all right. She's a selfish bitch and you and Simon deserve better."

Coffee nearly spewed through his nose. "And you didn't even blink," he gasped out as he recovered from laughing.

"I have issues with parents who don't take responsibility," Tiffany said without a trace of remorse. "If she'd really cared, she would have seen him anyhow. Or gotten help. Or done something. Migraines don't last two weeks, or for that matter, three years." She gazed off into the distance. "My mom and dad probably wouldn't ever win the award for best parents, but at least they never made flimsy excuses for not treating us well. They did a lot for us. They actually cared."

He studied the proud line of her shoulders, the stubborn set of her jaw. "You surprise me more and more."

"How's that?"

"After everything you've told me, I didn't think you'd ever say a good word about your parents. I got the impression you didn't get along when you were growing up."

She toyed with her cup. "I resented the way they treated me for a long time. I still do, at times. Still—" she dug a toe into the gravel and ground a divot into the path "—they took good care of me. They cared about what I did, and made me care about my achievements. In college, I met people who assumed since their parents were paying for their education, they didn't need to worry about failing grades. There were kids who'd never cooked for themselves or done their own laundry. That's when I realized how lucky I was. My parents raised me to be self-sufficient and appreciate the opportunities and advantages I was given." She glanced around quickly. "Don't tell them I said any of that, though."

He zipped and locked his upturned lips.

The path opened up onto the bluff, and a stiff breeze whipped through his hair. The lookout was well lit by a few lampposts and small solar-powered LED lights embedded into the ground along the edge of the path. Benches scarred with years of lovers' initials—some *4eva,* some not so much—faced the cliff edge, along with a couple of battered coin-operated binoculars. They walked up to the sturdy wrought-iron railing and peered down. The town spread out below them, twilight casting everything in a sea of shadows flecked with twinkling lights. "Ooh, pretty," Tiffany said. "Wish I had my camera. I'd love to paint this."

"You still painting?"

"A little. I spent weekends in Central Park painting some-times, but it was mostly to relax."

"Do you still have your paintings? I'd love to see them."

"I had to leave them behind when I got kicked out," she said on a sigh. "They weren't any good, anyhow."

Somehow, Chris doubted that. She was good at anything she applied herself to. "If I recall correctly, you used to be really good in art class."

She tilted her chin. "You weren't in my art class, were you?"

"No," he admitted, "but a friend of mine was. He really liked your work. John Abrams. Do you remember him?"

"Vaguely."

"He's getting married soon, actually. In Vegas."

"That's nice."

The conversation petered out. Chris searched his brain for something interesting to talk about. It had been a long time since he'd had difficulty chatting up a woman. But Tiffany had more depth than most of the women he'd dated, and he didn't want to bore her with talk about the weather or the lat-est articles he'd read on commercial solar panels.

The last light of the sun faded. A cloud of bugs swarmed the blue-white light of the lamppost above their heads. As si-lence stretched between them, Chris itched to say something that wouldn't make him sound ridiculous.

"Can I ask you something?" Tiffany leaned her hip against the railing. He was grateful she'd been the one to speak. "When you found out about Daphne being pregnant…why did you come back?"

He drew back and looked at her. "How could I not?"

"Not every man would. You had your whole life ahead of you and…" She trailed off, and her lips pinched together. "I'm just not sure I would've done the same thing in your shoes. Not that Simon isn't a great kid," she added hastily.

"Wow, you really don't pull your punches, do you?" At her puzzled look, he said, "Since dinner, it's been one heavy soul-searching question after another."

"Sorry. I guess…you got me thinking about the past."

He hadn't wanted to bring up old wounds and make her brood over things they couldn't change. He was supposed to get to know her better by asking her the trivial stuff. Instead, he'd stirred up the past.

"Okay," he said decisively. "I'm putting a moratorium on serious topics from here on in. No more talk about the past or about our families."

"But…what are we supposed to talk about?"

"Anything. Everything. For instance, tell me about the last three books you read." When she stared at him blankly, he said, "C'mon. You worked in the publishing industry. You do read, right?"

"I just don't think you'd be interested in hearing about the books I read."

Maybe she read erotic romance or something…which would have made interesting but awkward conversation, he supposed. "Okay, then, let's try something easier. How about movies? What's your all-time favorite movie?"

"Why do you want to know?" She looked genuinely nonplussed.

"Because." He laughed, feeling just as stumped as he had at seventeen when she'd stonewalled him. "I'm interested in you."

She reminded him of a flower wilting in a time-lapse video as she shrank away from him. "Don't say that."

"What? That I want to get to know you better? I don't know anything about you. I must have spent a hundred hours with you tutoring, but I don't know when your birthday is, or what kind of ice cream you like or which Beatles song is your favorite."

"No one's ever asked me that."

"What? About the ice cream, or the Beatles?"

"About my birthday." Her lips pursed. "No one's ever asked me that on a first date." Her face froze. "I mean... on an outing...like this...um..." She spun away, and Chris stood stunned.

Was this a date? He'd invited her out with honest intentions. He was sure he had. He'd wanted to get to know her. He'd wanted to make amends for his foolish youth. He'd wanted...

He'd wanted to go on a date with her.

How else did he explain all the visits to the Good Fortune? The way he'd drop whatever he was doing to hurry to the house whenever she was tutoring? He'd been denying he had any interest in her, but if that was true, why was he even out here, at an infamous make-out spot, trying to get her to open up to him?

STUPID, STUPID, *STUPID.*

Tiffany stewed in agonizing silence on the ride home. She leaned against the glass, murmuring an excuse about how tired she was when all she wanted was to let out a long, Charlie-Brown-esque "Auuuuugh!"

She could have blamed the wine, but she'd sobered up somewhere between leaving the restaurant and that second gulp of latte, which wasn't sitting so well now. No wonder she had such a hard time dating.

Dating. What a stupid thing to say. This wasn't a date. He'd wanted to talk about his son—though she supposed he'd wanted to talk about other things, too. But she shouldn't have assumed that meant he was interested in her in that way. He was only trying to be friendly.

She was almost relieved when Everville's town limits came into view. Chris pointed the truck toward the main part of town.

"My car's still at the farm."

"It's late, and I'd rather you not drive home in the dark. I'll have Jane drop your car off tomorrow morning."

She was going to argue, but she caught the dogged glint in his eye and kept her mouth shut. It would have added an extra fifty minutes to her ride home if they went to the farm first, and she wasn't sure she could stand the tension.

Minutes later, he turned down her street, pulled up to the curb and shut off the motor. She opened the door before she'd even popped the seat belt off. He got out with her. "Is there something you need to talk to Daniel about?" she asked, hesitating.

"I'm walking you to your door."

"Oh." Was that a thing people did still? She glanced up at the house—the light was off in the living room. Everyone must have had retired for the night. They'd left the porch light on for her, though. "You really don't have to."

He folded his arms over his chest and waited expectantly. *Oookay.* With quick small strides, she went up the short walkway and climbed the three steps, feeling Chris at her back. Was he going to kiss her good-night? A tremor rippled from the base of her skull all the way down to her belly. Even a friendly peck on the cheek would probably make her pass out. She couldn't let him tease her like that, but she couldn't let him know she was affected by him, either. She didn't want things to be more awkward than they already were. God, what if he kissed her out of pity or something?

At the door, she took out her keys, then stopped. "Thank you for dinner."

"You barely ate."

She lifted a shoulder. "Then thank you for finding the Starbucks."

"This night didn't turn out the way I wanted it to," he admitted, scratching the back of his neck. "I'll take you somewhere nicer next time."

"You don't have to," she said hastily. She didn't want him making promises, giving her false hope. "We had fun." She thought they had, at least, even if she had mucked things up. Now she had to say good-night before she absolutely ruined the evening. She straightened her spine, recovering some of her cool dignity. "It was fine. Good night." She put her keys in the lock, turning away from him as she opened the door.

"Wait." His hand clamped over her upper arm. She turned and jerked the door closed as he stepped closer.

His face hovered an inch away from hers, eyes lowered to her mouth. She could smell the rich aroma of coffee on his breath, his spicy aftershave and the barest hint of freshly cut grass. Her eyes fluttered close, and she swayed forward, pulled inexorably toward him.

Their lips met on a surprised half gasp, half moan, and she wasn't sure which of them had made that sound. Her skin prickled all over as he tasted her, probing until he gained entrance. His mouth was sweet with that splash of bold dark Verona coffee. Her hands slipped around his neck and he pressed forward, backing her against the door as the kiss deepened.

He leaned into her, and the unmistakable hardness of his arousal pushed against her belly. She wasn't a virgin, but she'd never felt like this—skin too tight as blood rushed to all the places on her body she wanted him to touch.

This was no high school crush. What she wanted was decidedly adult.

Boldly, she ran the tip of her tongue across his, and he groaned. Her nails raked the soft fabric of his shirt. She could feel the way he was flexing his hips, wanting to get closer. She arched her body toward his—

Chris yanked back as if she'd shocked him, and she stumbled against the doorjamb.

"I—I…" Chris searched the porch, flustered. "Good night." He turned, strode quickly to his truck and got in. He didn't pull away immediately, though. He sat watching her in the driver's seat, both hands wrapped tightly around the wheel. He was waiting for her to go inside.

She opened the door, but paused and looked over her shoulder. Still there.

She smiled. Waved. Then closed the door.

It was a solid five minutes before she heard the engine start up.

CHAPTER TWELVE

THE FOLLOWING AFTERNOON, Tiffany darted into the consignment shop and quickly pulled the door closed behind her. Her father had been standing outside the Good Fortune, hands on hips and staring up at the sky as though searching for portents for the day's business. She wasn't sure he'd seen her, but she couldn't press her luck.

Last night, he'd caught her sneaking up the stairs after her passionate clinch with Chris on the front porch. Before he could ask any questions, she'd said good-night and shut herself in her room, hoping her wet, swollen lips and mussed hair hadn't given anything away.

That kiss… She'd replayed it over and over in her head, experienced that same wicked thrill pulse through her at the memory. But the way he'd recoiled, leaving her standing there like an idiot…

"Hey, Tiffany. You okay?"

She spun around. "Oh, Maya. Hi. Sorry." The shopkeeper wore a leopard-print jumpsuit today and black patent-leather heels. A big black bow nestled in her short-cropped hair. She glanced back at the door. "I was lost in thought."

"I was about to call and tell you a bunch of your stuff sold this past weekend."

"Really?" She clapped her hands together. "That's great. If you want, I've got more clothes I can bring in." Tiff rifled through her mental closet. She was happy to part with anything that could get her some quick cash.

Maya gave her the paperwork and handed over a tidy sum of money. It wasn't a fortune by any means, but it was promising. "So…" Maya gave her an expectant smile. "How are *things?*"

"Things?"

Maya grinned. "Rumor has it you were out with Christopher Jamieson last night."

Tiff's face exploded in flame. She ducked her head, ears so hot they stung.

"Where did you go? What did you do?" She gave her a sly look. "Did things go *well?*"

Her instinct was to simply say it wasn't anyone's business what had happened, but as she turned to snap it out, she blurted, "I don't know."

It came out a broken whimper. Maya's smile became uncertain. "Tiff, are you okay?"

She shook her head silently, frustration and bewilderment mounting. She wasn't going to have a breakdown, was she? She didn't quite feel like crying, but the laughter jammed in her throat. She was confused and besotted and ecstatic and terrified all at once, and she didn't know what to do about it.

"Wait." Maya snatched up a purse and tugged her toward the door. "Let's go for that coffee."

"But…your store…"

"The great thing about owning a business is that you make your own hours."

That was the exact opposite of what her parents had always said: when you own your own business, you can't afford to stop working. She followed the shopkeeper out, taking a quick peek first to make sure her dad wasn't outside the diner.

They walked a few doors down to the Grindery. Tiffany insisted on a table in the back away from the window, just in case a member of her family walked by. Maya brought them each a cup of coffee, sat and folded her hands in front of her. "So? What happened?"

Tiffany didn't know Maya, and yet somehow it was much easier to relate the past evening's events to her than it would have been to anyone else. The story poured out of her, starting with what had happened when she'd locked herself out of the car and Chris had rescued and hugged her, and ending with the kiss on her porch. Maya only stopped her to ask a few clarifying questions. When she'd finally ended her tale with her going up to her bedroom to a sleepless night, Maya nodded, then broke into a grin.

"I always wondered if there was anything going on between you guys in high school," she said, dimples deepening as she flashed her white teeth. "He was with Daphne and all that, and everyone knew how crazy she was, so if she wasn't freaking out nothing underhanded could've been going on. But now…"

"I'm sorry I barf-talked all over you," Tiff said, embarrassed she'd dragged this poor woman through her problems. She'd never blabbed like this to someone who wasn't in her family and even then, she never talked about anything personal. No one in the house needed to hear about her boy troubles.

Maya propped up her chin. "So, from the way you're describing dinner, it wasn't great?"

"I wouldn't call it date-worthy, no," she admitted with a shake of her head, "but I might be a snob when it comes to food."

"No, I'd definitely say a buffet is not on any approved list of first-date restaurants. Driving out to Osprey Peak tells me something else, though. But you said nothing happened out there?"

Tiff shook her head. "We just talked."

"Talk about mixed messages." She tapped her black-tipped

nails on the table. "So, are you going on a second date with him?"

"I don't know."

Maya studied her, confused. "Maybe I'm asking the wrong questions. Do you want to go on a second date?"

Tiff shrugged. "I'm really not the one to determine that."

"Why not? Nothing in the rule book says you can't ask him out. What you need to ask yourself is, what do you want this thing between you to be?"

"Over." She rubbed her temples. "I can't ask him out. We have different lives now. I have a career path I have to follow. A life in the city. I'm not sticking around here, and I don't need *this* to complicate things." No matter how much she wanted a complication like Chris.

"'The lady doth protest too much, methinks,'" Maya quipped, and Tiffany chuckled dryly. Great, more Shakespeare. When it came to her love life, though, things usually ended in tragedy.

"Look, you guys have a history. It could be that there was always friction between you, and now that you're adults and both available, you can explore those feelings. But you're also his son's tutor. He's paying you to help Simon, and that kind of employer-employee relationship can get sticky. Anyhow, it wasn't as if he was going to push you into your parents' house and ravage you on the dining-room table, right?" She sat back, and a sly look crossed her face. "Maybe you're simply in lust with him."

"What?" Tiff sat back hard, startled.

"Chris is a good-looking guy. Half the girls were in love with him. You're here temporarily. It's summertime. Why not have a fling? Get him out of your system, make a few good memories to take with you."

"I…I…" She'd never considered a fling because…well, it had never crossed her mind. Being with Chris had simply never been a real possibility before—only a fantasy daydream. The idea that she could indulge herself and say good-bye when things had run their course was too tempting, and deliciously simple. And she liked simple.

A guy like Chris could get sex however and whenever he wanted, but he'd shown an unmistakable interest in *her*. Tiffany would be too happy to oblige him. And then, before he got bored, she'd say goodbye and head back to New York.

The more she thought about it, the more it made perfect sense.

CHRIS'S TURBULENT THOUGHTS were as mercurial as the mid-July weather. Neither could decide on one mood. Most days dawned with the golden haze of promise and desire, but by midmorning, a warm, heavy rain of regret would drench him, and by late afternoon, he'd be wallowing beneath hot, sticky, oppressive self-loathing.

He shouldn't have kissed Tiffany. That much he knew for sure. Apart from the fact she was Simon's tutor and on his payroll, he knew they couldn't start anything and hope for it to last. The moment she'd secured a job, she was going back to New York. She'd made that abundantly clear.

But damn. If he'd known she kissed like that, well... He didn't know what. He wasn't even sure what was going on in his head when he'd walked her to the door. He'd thought, at most, it would be a friendly peck on the cheek good-night. Another hug, perhaps. Tiffany had never struck him as all that touchy-feely. Okay, so he'd acknowledged that spark of interest that had been smoldering since he'd first heard she'd come back to Everville. And he'd admitted on the drive back home that he'd always been more than a little curious. But as he'd stood there, watching her open the door, something in his chest had balled up tight as she turned away from him. In that brief, insane moment, he hadn't wanted to let her go. He'd stopped her bodily, and what happened after that still made him uncomfortable in ways that thrilled and frightened him.

He set down his toolbox and gulped tepid water from his sport bottle, trying to quench a thirst he hadn't been able to slake all week. He'd been tinkering with this irrigation pump for way too long. It'd been fixed an hour ago, but he'd been stalling, knowing the rest of his chores were in and around the barn, within sight of the house and of Tiffany. All week, he'd stayed as far away from her as possible, even if it meant he was out in the fields during the stickiest part of the day. He didn't want to fight with the temptation to go up and say hello.

The sound of an approaching ATV made him look up. "You planning on digging a new dike out here or something?" Jane called as she slowed. "You've been out here for nearly three hours. I swear you're staring at the ground, hoping it'll dig itself or something."

"Just lost in thought."

"Should I be worried? Last time you started thinking, we ended up with a dozen windmills on county land. I don't need to remind you how many people we made mad about it."

"They haven't complained since." He dusted off his hands, unsure of what to do with them. "I was thinking about that compost program…."

Jane interrupted with a snort. "Now, there's a load of crap, pardon my pun. You have something on your mind, that's for sure, but it's not fertilizer. How come you haven't gone up to the house while Tiffany's been around? Things get awkward between you on your date?"

Damned gossip mill. He kept his expression carefully neutral. "It wasn't a date."

Jane chuckled. "Whatever it was, it's keeping you out here, baking under the sun in ninety-degree heat. You wanna tell me why a tiny, pretty girl like her is scaring you off?"

"It's not like that." He refused to meet her eyes. Jane could read lies on a statue's face and wasn't afraid of calling "liar, liar" on anyone.

She turned off the ATV's engine and leaned casually against the handlebars. "Look, I know how hard it is to get back on the dating wagon after a bad breakup. I don't pretend to know what was between you and Daphne, but no matter how the divorce went, it can sting, even years later." She picked up the Grindery coffee cup from the cup holder attached to the handlebars and tipped it at him. "From what I've seen, though, you could do a lot worse than that young lady. She'd make a good match for you and a fine stepmom for your son."

He tried to laugh her off. "She's not really my type." *Liar, liar...* "I prefer hometown girls. Ones with more meat on their bones. Ones that are stacked like layer cakes and have a little more boom and ba-da, if you know what I mean." He traced the air with a crude hourglass outline.

Jane sent him a flat look, clearly unimpressed by his act. *Pants on fire.*

He sighed in defeat. "Look, it's complicated. I'm Daniel's friend, for one, and I don't want him coming after me for going out with his sister." Though he was certain that Tiffany's brother would do no such thing. "And she's too much like Daphne. She's used to finer things. She's a city girl at heart. She likes variety and five-dollar coffees and designer labels. There's nothing here for her. Anyhow, as soon as she gets a job, she'll head back to New York. She won't stick around."

"She might with the right incentive. Don't sell yourself short, Chris. She could do a lot worse than you, too."

Jane was crazy. A little chemistry and a shared past didn't translate into wedding bells and forever love. He'd had much more with Daphne, and he'd once believed he was in love with her. Some happily-ever-after that turned out to be. One kiss didn't mean anything, no matter how hot those sparks had been.

And he had to think about Simon. His son had faced enough rejection and disappointment in life. He couldn't pretend that he could work something out with Tiffany when he could barely manage to provide for his own family. It was better to go back to the way things were. Tiffany was Simon's tutor. And they were…friends. He should treat her accordingly.

"You need to get out of this sun," Jane said, squinting up at the sky. "That's an order. I don't want to be hauling you to the hospital 'cause you were too stubborn and stupid to avoid heatstroke."

"Thanks, *Mom*."

She swatted his backside with her trucker cap as he loaded his toolbox onto the rear of the ATV and hopped on. When they arrived at the barn, he headed to the tack room to put his tools away. He unlatched and slid the big barn door open.

"Close the door!"

He slipped in past the crack before quickly pulling it shut. Simon peeked down from the loft. "What are you doing here? Aren't you supposed to be with Tiffany?" Chris asked.

"I'm right here." Her head popped up next to Simon's, and she smiled at him.

Blood rushed southward at the sight of her. He made a pretense of setting his tools down while he readjusted himself.

"Awfully hot in here to be studying, isn't it?"

"We needed a break, and Simon said he had to check on the kittens." The mewls of the quickly growing kittens chorused together and she said, "No, not that way, little guy."

"You two be careful up there." He fought the urge to climb up and join them, but he didn't want to look like he was *trying* to avoid her, either. He ended up dawdling on the ground level, pacing and looking for something to keep him occupied.

"Jeez, Dad, lighten up. I promise I won't throw any tools down or nothing."

"How did your quiz go?" he asked.

"Okay. *Animal Farm* is a lot more interesting than *The Tempest*."

Tiffany popped up holding a black kitten. "'Four legs good, two legs bad,'" she bleated, waving the kitten's feet in the air.

Simon laughed, picked up his own kitten and countered, "'Four legs good, two legs better.'" They dueled with the two kittens and their extended paws.

Chris laughed. He climbed the ladder and found the rest of the kittens frolicking around the seated pair, sniffing their visitors and nipping at their heels. Shadow was probably off stalking a mouse somewhere.

Tiffany was wearing a sky-blue cotton T-shirt and khaki shorts with roman sandals. Her hair had been tied back into a ponytail. A black kitten nestled in her lap. It yawned and snuggled deeper as she rubbed its belly. Damn lucky animal.

"I think he likes you," Simon said.

Chris whipped his head around. Was he that obvious? He realized then that his son had meant the cat.

"He's such a sweetie," Tiffany cooed, stroking the little guy's head. "He's so gentle, too."

"He's in need of a home," Chris said, looking to Simon for confirmation. "You could adopt him, Tiffany."

Simon nodded eagerly. "Yeah, that would be cool. We're going to have to give these guys away...." He rubbed a gray tabby under his chin and laughed as the kitten chirruped and purred.

"Well, not all of them," Chris said. "You've done a really good job with them, Simon. They all made it, they all look healthy and you kept the loft clean, too. I said I'd let you keep one. Shadow could use some help keeping the mice out of the barn." His son's face lit up. "Take your pick."

"This one," he said without hesitation as he snuggled the tabby closer. "I'll name her Clover, like the horse in *Animal Farm*." He grinned up at his father. "Have you read it? It's a great book."

Chris could have sworn he heard the "Hallelujah" chorus. He never thought he'd hear those words out of his son's mouth. "It's been a while. I'll have to see if I can find my old copy."

Tiffany met his eyes, smiling with pride.

"So, what do you think, Tiff? That little guy there is yours if you want him," he told her. "I know you'd take good care of him."

Her smile softened. "I can't." She lifted the bundle out of her lap, hugging it and then setting it back down. The kitten tried to climb back into her lap but Tiffany stood and swept the straw from her shorts. "I can't take him to my parents' house. My mother's allergic to animal fur. And I won't be able to bring him back to New York with me." The kitten butted his head against her ankle and meowed in protest. She smiled ruefully at him. "It'll be hard for me to find a place that'll accept pets. And even then, he won't have a place like this. He'll have four walls and if he's lucky, a window where he can watch a brick wall age. It wouldn't be fair."

She was being practical, he knew, and he expected practical from Tiffany. As he watched regret and longing play across her face, he'd never realized how easy, in fact, she was to read. He'd always thought of her as being stony and stoic. But there were tiny tells. When had he started to see them?

Or was he seeing something he wished he could?

"Well, if you change your mind…"

"I won't." She glanced at her watch. "It's getting late. I promised my grandmother I'd help with dinner tonight, so I better get back. Good work today, Simon."

"Thanks. See you tomorrow." He picked up Clover and

waved goodbye with her tiny paw as the kitten meowed her own farewell.

Chris watched her cross the loft, her steps slower than usual and…was she swaying her hips? She climbed down the ladder and got as far as the bottom rung when he hurried after her.

"Wait." He clambered down, then gestured toward the door. They exited together. "We can work something out if you really want him."

Her eyes locked with his. A flush rushed into her cheeks and she glanced up…at his lips? He licked them, throat suddenly dry. "Of course I want him." The words came out a little breathy.

A surge of lust kicked Chris in the abdomen. She went on forlornly, "I've always wanted a cat. But I can't make that commitment. I can't take him with me."

"Cats can have very fulfilling lives indoors." Though he had a hard time imagining any of the barn cats being cooped up inside some tiny apartment.

"I wouldn't want Simon to know Mack's stuck inside all day. And then there're all the food and vet bills…" She shook her head. "It's more trouble than it's worth. I really, really like him, but I can't keep him."

"Mack?"

She lifted a shoulder. "He plowed straight into my ankle like a little truck and nearly knocked me over. The name stuck."

"Well, that's a sign if ever I've seen one. Naming an animal you're going to give away? You two were meant to be."

"I can't." She pouted, making Chris want to kiss her frown away.

"That's too bad. He would have been good company." Tiffany could use an animal companion in her life. Someone

she could lavish her affection upon, who'd love her back un-
conditionally and not judge her. She needed that in her life.

"Do you think…" she said. "Would it be okay if I came
over to play?"

Trapped in her softly imploring gaze, Chris stared as her
lush lips parted slightly and she tucked a strand of hair behind her ear, fingertips tracing down her neck.

Were they still talking about the cat? Something weird was
happening inside him. A spring coiled in his abdomen. But
this was way stronger than simple lust. He swallowed hard,
trying to push down the feeling.

"Chris?" She tilted her chin. "What do you think?"

"Of course," he replied a little too brightly, a little too
loudly. He shoved his trembling hands into his pockets to keep
from reaching out and hauling her into his arms. "Anytime.
Come play with us. Him." He bit his tongue as he blurted,
"The kitten. Come and play with the kitten anytime you like."

Her smile was wide and sly, and she lowered her eyes.
"Thank you." She reached out and touched him, her fingertips lightly sliding along his forearm, electrifying his bare
skin. "I love how soft he is. I don't know if I can help myself
if I start stroking him. I can't wait to come again."

She turned and walked away then—no, more like prowled—
with only the briefest glance over her shoulder as she said,
"'Bye."

Chris couldn't move. He was afraid if he did, he'd trip on
his hanging jaw.

CHAPTER THIRTEEN

"Danny boy!"

Daniel looked around at the sea of faces in the arrivals area at Grand Central Station. It took him a moment, but he finally recognized his old college roommate. "Isaac, my God, man. You've lost weight."

"It's the rat race that keeps me thin," he said with a hearty laugh. They clapped each other on the back. "C'mon, my car's this way."

"Thanks for putting me up for the weekend," Daniel said as they made their way out of the station. He knew he needed to get away from his thoughts about Selena, and his class reunion was a good enough excuse to take a few days off from the diner. Although, in hindsight, coming to the city she lived in was probably a poorly thought-out strategy.

"Hey, I've been waiting to christen that guest bed for months, and you've turned down all my invitations to hang out so far. I wasn't even sure if you were coming to the reunion."

Daniel grimaced guiltily. He hadn't kept up with his friend nearly enough. "I wasn't sure I could get away."

"You must have one hell of a restaurant empire for you to be so busy."

Daniel felt small. "Just the one restaurant, actually. Family owned and operated."

"Must be doing well." Isaac didn't hold it against him one way or another.

"Oh, it is."

"You could open a second one here in Manhattan, start a franchise. I saw this property for lease in Nolita that would be perfect."

That was Isaac, always looking to grow, to expand. He lived large, dreamed big and never went halfway with anything. "The cost and competition would be too high here."

"Well, if you change your mind, let me know. I helped open a small chain of roti restaurants in Brooklyn. They're taking off. Here's my car." He hit the automatic lock button on his key chain and the late-model Mercedes blinked and bleeped as the alarm disabled.

"Nice. You lease?"

"Comped. Lot of perks for working at Halo." It was one of the largest marketing and PR firms in the country, and had been built up from a grassroots organization that had made its money helping small businesses become big ones. "I keep telling you to come back to the city."

Daniel shrugged. "I'm not sure it's for me."

"You won't know till you try it. Did I mention I get a bonus for hiring on anyone who stays with the company for more than six months?" He flashed a wide grin. "I wouldn't mind making it to Maui before I turn thirty-five."

They pulled out of the station and into city traffic. It was a nice car, sure, but Daniel wondered whether it was worth owning a vehicle in Manhattan. They caught up along the way, talking about old times, old friends. Isaac announced he'd taken the whole weekend off to host his old roommate. Daniel's guilt tripled—he'd barely made time for a drink the last time he was here. Mostly because he'd been visiting Selena.

"So, are you still dating that doctor?" Isaac asked on cue.

It took a moment for Daniel to get his throat working.

"No. Not really. We're kind of in the middle of… No," he finally admitted.

"Aww, man. Sorry to hear that. Was it recent?"

"Last Monday."

"Ouch. What happened?"

"It just didn't work." He didn't want to hash it all out in the car. This weekend was supposed to be about forgetting Selena and rediscovering himself. He'd decided moping wouldn't help him get over her. Coming to the city, reconnecting with his college chums and finding a decent hookup was exactly what he needed.

Isaac must have sensed the direction of his thoughts because he knew exactly what to say. "Some of the old gang are meeting up at a pub down in midtown tonight. We'll get some food, then head out for some drinks. Sound good?"

"Sounds perfect."

They dropped off Daniel's stuff at Isaac's swank condo, went to their favorite deli from their college years, then hit the pub.

A few of the guys were already there and well into their cups. Daniel nursed his whiskey and soda slowly as he listened to the guys tell stories about their jobs, their families, their various sexual conquests. More people showed up and their party grew until their graduating class had commandeered a quarter of the pub's seats. Many of the guys had brought their significant others to the city, but had left them at their respective hotels. This night was about getting the old boys together.

The drinks flowed freely. People exchanged whiskey for martinis, martinis for beer, beer for shots. The waitresses came around frequently, smiling and flirting. Guys in nice dress shirts and well-tailored pants were where the tips were at.

By ten-thirty, Daniel was starting to get a little tired. "I think I'm going to go," he told Isaac.

"What? So early?"

"You stay. I can get your key and leave it with the concierge."

"Danny boy, don't do this to me. I finally get you back in the city and you're already crying off like you have to go study. You never have any fun, man." Isaac slid an arm around his shoulder and squeezed. "You're always leaving early to do some work, going home to your parents, acting all responsible. I've never even seen you drunk."

"That's 'cause you always pass out before I do," he countered. "Remember that one time after finals at Carl's place? I was the only one left standing."

"So you claim."

"Well, I was the only one who still made it to the bathroom before the tequila came up." He'd also been the only one sober enough to make sure no one was drowning in their own vomit. It was one of the many reasons why he didn't drink like that anymore.

Isaac ignored his arguments and turned to address the whole table. "Guys, guys—is Daniel too serious?"

A chorus of *yes*es and *hell, yes*es came back.

His friend fixed him with an arch look. "Look, man. I don't want you hanging out all alone in my big, empty apartment nursing a broken heart. You need to be out here. You need to loosen up, drown your sorrows, find a soft bosom to smother them in. Besides—" he grabbed Daniel's chin and pointed his face toward a group of young ladies watching them from the corner "—I need a wing man for those fine Asian honeys."

"You are such a rice king." Daniel pushed him off. The girls giggled and waved them over. Isaac made a whimpering sound and gave him big, pleading puppy-dog eyes. "Fine. I'll stay for one more drink."

"One more drink!" Isaac hollered, and the guys at the

table all cheered. He pushed Daniel onto a stool and a line of shot glasses full of clear liquid appeared. With a shrug, he picked one up, toasted to his memory of Selena and downed the tequila.

IF HE FOCUSED HARD ENOUGH, Daniel was certain he could regain control of the ship he was sailing and ride through smoother waters.

Or was he on a plane? That dippy up-and-down feeling in his stomach suggested he was, but maybe the boat was crashing through some waves.

The world weaved and blurred before him. Helluva storm. He kept on swimming—flying?—though, and knew he'd get to where he needed to be soon. He could never forget this street, never forget her. She was his true north, his guiding star....

The stoop was solid beneath the soles of his shoes. He climbed to the top, experiencing a tremendous sense of achievement when he managed to find the right buzzer and push it. It was a miracle he could even hold his finger on the button the way the boat was rocking.

"Who is this?" a voice rough with sleep snapped.

"Hey, babe. Open the door. It's me."

A long pause. "Daniel?"

"I...I came to talk to you...." He leaned his forehead against the blessedly cool metal plate of the intercom speaker. Selena's voice buzzing through the perforated surface was like the softest kiss. He smiled and mashed his face harder against the speaker.

"What the hell? It's three in the morning. Are you drunk?"

"Don't be silly. I've got the constitution of a horse. A sea horse. Neeiigh." He belched, tasting the deli sandwich he'd had at dinner.

"Goddammit, Daniel..."

"Listen, listen, listen…I came to New York to find my-self and…and I couldn't. I'm lost, Selena. Lost without you."

"For God's sake…hold on." The intercom went abruptly silent. Daniel leaned harder on it, wishing Selena was still bussing him on the cheek. He missed her.

The door opened and someone clamped a strong hand over his arm and hauled him inside. He tripped over his own feet as Selena pulled him up the stairs, landing hard on his butt on the third step.

"Don't you make me carry your ass up," she hissed. "And don't make me yell at you in the middle of the hallway, either. People are trying to sleep."

He put his finger to his lips, giggling, sealing his promise to shut up and behave. He dutifully got to his feet, grabbed the banister and climbed the stairs to Dr. Selena Worthington's apartment.

Even tipsy, Daniel remembered every inch of this place. Mostly because they'd made love across every inch of it. Right here in the doorway, he'd pressed her up against the wall as they'd stripped each other naked. They'd barely been able to pull their shoes off. They'd taken it from there to the living room couch, then the floor, then the bedroom, bath-room, kitchen…

As soon as she'd shut the door behind them, she glared at him, arms folded across her chest. Her wavy dark brown hair was a mess, but her eyes flashed with fire. A short black satin bathrobe was wrapped tightly around her, but he could see her bare legs. He'd forgotten she liked to sleep nude.

"Why are you here?"

He tried to recall, but then it came back in a sobering rush. "I came to tell you…I'm sorry. I'm not worth it, and I should have seen it earlier."

The lines between her eyebrows deepened. "You came to tell me this at three in the morning?"

"I don't have a watch." He pointed at his wrist, but then saw that he was, in fact, wearing a watch. "Oh."

"You're drunk," she observed stonily.

"I only had a few drinks. Wee little ones like this." He pinched the air. "Great stuff. Grows hair on your chest, see?" He pulled at his collar, trying to show her, but his fingers caught on the button and it popped out and hit her in the face. Uh-oh.

Selena huffed and pushed him toward the couch. "Sit. Or lie down, I don't care. But if you're going to vomit, you get to the bathroom, you hear? I don't want stains on my sofa or carpet."

"You never worried about stains before."

Her cheeks tinted pink and she spun away and headed for the kitchen. She came back shortly with a tall glass of water and a sleeve of saltines. "Here."

His stomach revolted at the thought of drinking any more liquid. There was enough buoying the boat-plane he was riding. "I don't need any more to drink tonight."

"Drink it." Her directive could not be ignored. Daniel gulped the water down, popped a few saltines under her watchful eye then finished the water. His stomach churned, but the fog in his head wasn't quite as thick as before. And the boat didn't rock quite so much.

"What are you doing in town?" she asked.

"Reunion. I'm staying over at Isaac's."

"And he's...where?"

Daniel thought hard. "I don't know. He was talking to some girls at a table." He concentrated, but couldn't remember what had happened after his seventh shot of tequila. Or was it ninth? All he did remember for certain was the boat and the stoop and beautiful, angelic Selena glaring at him.

"Look, you got his number or something? I don't want him worrying about you."

Daniel fumbled for his cell phone. She snatched it out of his hand, scrolled through his contacts and dialed. She left the room as she started talking.

He wasn't sure why, but he was getting this strange sinking feeling that he was in trouble, like the days when he'd come home from school after a fight, trying to hide the fact from his parents. They always yelled at him, as if getting picked on was his fault. If he did what he was supposed to and kept his nose clean, he wouldn't be a target. Why couldn't he be more like his sister? She never got in trouble or got picked on the way he did. Obviously he was doing something to make the kids not like him.

"I'm not," he said out loud. Why was the boat spinning? Oh, no, it must have gotten sucked into one of those whatchamacallits...whirlpools. He was going to get sucked in if he didn't do something.

Maybe if he lay down and braced the boat, it wouldn't slide into that blackness....

But it was no use. He went under, drowning in darkness. Sweet, deep, blissful abyss...

DANIEL WOKE SUDDENLY. A faint bluish light that might as well have been the brightness of a billion suns pierced through the swollen, heavy weights blanketing his eyes. His limbs were like lead, and the contents of his stomach floated freely inside his chest cavity like blobs of oil in a lava lamp.

He pushed a scratchy wool blanket off his chest and tried to settle his mind. Flashes of memory and nonsense assaulted him. His head felt as if it'd been stuffed with birdseed and a thousand chickens were pecking and scratching at his brain.

Crackers. A slice of lemon and salt. Isaac trying out his god-awful Mandarin on the ladies in that corner booth. And a whole lot of tequila.

At that moment, his bladder and stomach both indicated

they needed emptying, followed by the equally clear voice in his head warning him there'd be dire consequences if he did it here. He hurtled toward the bathroom.

His messy business complete, he took note of his surroundings, the fact he'd known where the washroom was, and that particular way all those pill bottles were lined up on the shelf above the sink.

The sick feeling came oozing back and his head pounded. What had he been thinking? Why hadn't Isaac stopped him? How had he made it all the way here?

No, wait, the pub hadn't been far from Selena's. He'd known the moment the cab had entered the neighborhood and dropped them off. He'd looked down the block and noted exactly how close they were. And he'd thought about calling, visiting, talking....

And he had. Drunk.

Daniel cradled his throbbing head.

It was barely six in the morning. He peeked out of the bathroom. Selena's bedroom door was closed, and he could hear her snoring. She sounded like a jet engine when she was really out. He thought it was adorable.

He had no right to think that about her anymore. Especially not after this. She deserved someone more like Isaac, who lived in the city and had ambitions and a great job that comped fancy cars....

Daniel found his cell phone on the coffee table. She'd thoughtfully removed his shoes and put them by the door. As quietly as he could, he left the apartment, slipped on his shoes in the hallway and walked down the stairs. He wished he'd thought to take a couple of Tylenol, but he'd imposed on her too much already.

The street was quiet, though a few cabs patrolled the roads, stalking disheveled denizens doing the walk of shame. The faint odor of urine and something spicy made him gag, and he stood bent over a sewer grate for a few minutes until the feeling passed. He hadn't missed the myriad smells the city offered, that was for sure.

He headed north for Central Park, seeking fresher air. He needed quiet and solitude before heading back to Isaac's. His friend probably wasn't in any better shape than he was. Or maybe he had hooked up with one of those girls....

The bench he claimed was along a path frequented by early-morning joggers who paid him no heed. *Just another loser,* he imagined them thinking. Exhausted, he leaned his head against the back of the bench and closed his eyes. The sunlight pierced his eyelids, sending blades of pain through his skull, but he was too weary to move from the warm spot. A breeze ruffled his hair, carrying with it the smells of a nearby bakery and a trickle of nostalgia.

Kung-kung used to walk through Central Park every Saturday morning. His grandfather would catch the bus, get a paper and sit and read on a bench like this one. Sometimes he'd take *Poh-poh* and his grandchildren along, and they'd go to the Museum of Natural History to look at the dinosaurs. Afterward, they'd get ice cream from a truck. His grandfather always got butterscotch dip.

Daniel had just turned eight when he'd tried to go to the museum by himself. He'd always hated how long it took his grandparents to walk around, and they never got to see everything. When his parents had finally found him, they'd dragged him back to the apartment and screamed at him until they were hoarse. But Daniel had stubbornly refused to admit he'd done anything wrong. Going to the museum by himself meant he'd saved everyone the hassle—why didn't anyone else get that?

They'd spanked him with the bamboo handle of a feather duster until Tiffany had screamed in distress. His parents had stormed out of the room, telling him they didn't want a naughty boy like him anymore. Daniel had gone crying to *Kung-kung* for solace.

"Your parents love you very much," he'd said to his angry, tearful grandson. "They were worried about you. You scared them and you disobeyed them."

"They said I was *moh gwai young.* They like to hit me and yell at me. I hate them!"

"Don't say that. It's not true. They only punished you because you were being naughty. You stole money from them and tried to run away. Your father had to leave work to find you, and you know how stressful his job is." *Kung-kung* had gripped his shoulder. "Daniel, you have to be good and listen to your parents. If you don't, bad things will happen."

His grandfather had taken his parents' side. He'd been abandoned. *Kung-kung* went out for his walk after that and left his grandson alone at home with his wicked family. The betrayal stung almost as much as his backside.

Well, if no one wanted him, fine. He would go and live in the park like he'd seen bums do, sleeping in cardboard boxes eating junk food. He would live like a king.

But then the police came. How had they known he was going to run away? He ran and hid in his grandparents' closet. He didn't want to go to jail. He'd apologize to everyone. He didn't want to leave, really.

A wail pierced his ears. At first he thought it was Tiffany crying. But then there were more raised voices. Another scream—his mother's. Daniel stumbled out of the closet. The police must be hurting his family because they couldn't find him. Bad people on TV did that.

He steeled himself and marched down the hall, ready to give himself up to the authorities. In the living room, his grandmother and mother huddled together, sobbing, while his father held a whimpering Tiffany. Two uniformed officers stood with their caps off, faces sad. They looked up as he walked in, and their eyes somehow told him everything.

Kung-kung was dead. He'd been stabbed by a mugger in Central Park.

Daniel opened his heavy eyes now, surfacing from the dark dream. He wiped at his wet cheeks. It had been a long time since he'd thought about his grandfather, about the night that changed everything.

They'd move out of the city a few months later. His parents were convinced it was too dangerous to raise their kids there. The apartment was small and crowded, the air foul and dirty. His dad had hated his job, and his mom was miserable, too. They left in the middle of the school year, left all of Daniel's friends behind. Tiffany had taken the move especially hard. For weeks, all she wanted was to go home to be with *Kung-kung,* and her whining had grated on their parents' nerves. They were all trying to adjust to their new lives and the strain of running a diner in a small town. The long hours started to take their toll, and then the arguments started.

And it was all Daniel's fault. If he hadn't delayed his grandfather with his sniveling, *Kung-kung* might not have encountered that mugger. If Daniel had simply been the good boy he was expected to be…

He blinked up at the sky, wondering if *Kung-kung* were looking down on him now and shaking his head. He'd thought he'd done everything he could to keep his parents happy, keep the family together. So, why did he feel like he was still being punished?

CHAPTER FOURTEEN

TIFFANY USUALLY DIDN'T TUTOR on a Sunday, but she needed an excuse to get away from her parents. They'd been snapping at each other like feuding teenagers passing in the halls between classes since Daniel had left for his reunion. She was so anxious, her gut burned whenever they were within sight of each other. Seeking sanctuary, she'd called Chris and asked if she could come by to play with the kittens. "Of course," he'd said, though his tone was unsure.

As she drove away from the diner, butterflies replaced the lead sitting in her stomach. Her flirting techniques hadn't been terribly subtle, but she was certain Chris had gotten the message. All she needed now was the right moment to make her indecent proposal.

She drove up to the house and decided to check in with Simon first to see if he needed any help with homework. As she got out of the car, the front door flung open and Simon rushed out. "Tiffany, I need help."

"What's wrong?"

"Grandpa fell. He's awake but he's breathing really hard and he won't let me help him up or call Dad."

She hurried to the house. "In the kitchen," Simon said tensely.

William was lying on his right side on the cold tile, half-curled and shaking. His face was pale and dotted with sweat. He clutched his stomach, hugging himself. "I told you not to call your father," he rasped, pain making his voice tight.

Tiffany knelt and reached for him. "It's me, Mr. Jamieson. Let me help you up."

"Don't touch me," he snarled, and she withdrew her hands as if he might try to bite her. "I don't need *you*."

Patiently, she asked, "Do you want me to call an ambulance?"

"I'm fine. Just mind your own business." He shrank away, tucking his chin as he bore down, making a strangled gurgling noise. Okay, now she was really worried. Did heart attacks happen like this? Or maybe it was his appendix or something. He was sweating profusely, and his face had gone green-gray. "Bucket," he mumbled. She didn't understand. He snapped his fingers at the mop and bucket standing in one corner. She brought it to him just in time. He vomited into it.

This wasn't good. Getting an ambulance out here would only waste time. "Simon, get your father."

"No." William struggled to a sitting position. "I'm fine, goddammit. It was just something I ate. If you call him in here, I swear I will expire on the spot to spite the lot of you. I will not let him see me like this. I am not some invalid old man."

He might as well have been throwing a full-on tantrum, pounding his fists on the floor, but the vigor in his protest was a good sign. Ornery was better than quiet. Making a decision, she ushered Simon to the doorway. "Call Dr. van Vierzen here right away. Tell him what's happened, but do it where your grandfather can't hear you."

"Is he okay?"

She couldn't say for sure, but she'd done enough first-aid classes to know she couldn't take any chances. "He seems to be better after throwing up. But let's get the doc here, just in case."

Simon nodded and dialed for the doctor on his cell phone. He walked a little away from the house as he spoke.

Tiffany returned to the old man's side. Will sat there, massaging the center of his chest, breathing deeply in and out. "Well, we're not calling the ambulance, and we're not calling Chris. Now, are you going to let me help you up or do you want to keep sitting on the cold hard floor?"

He gave her a mutinous look. She took his silence as a yes.

She slid a chair next to him then grabbed him under the arms and hauled him bodily into the seat. Then she brought him a glass of water and nudged the bucket over. "Here. Rinse your mouth."

He glared. "Gimme a whiskey."

"I don't think that's a good idea."

"It helps with the digestion. That's all this is. A bad turn. Probably that deli meat from the grocery store." He clutched his stomach and closed his eyes as another wave of pain burned through him.

Tiff looked around for clues as to what else he might have eaten. The Jamieson men seemed to live off a steady diet of white bread and red meat, and from the smell of the place, a lot of deep fried meals.

"How'd you fall?" She glanced around. "Where are your crutches?"

"I told you, it's none of your damn business."

"Did you hurt yourself?" He could've bruised something, might even have broken a rib. Something told her he wouldn't admit it if he had, though.

"I said I'm fine. Get me my crutches. I'm going out to talk to my son."

She had to make him stay put until the doctor arrived. "I thought you didn't want him to see you like this."

William eyed her suspiciously and tried to sit a little straighter. "It's passed now. It's normal. I need to get to Chris before he does something stupid. He's out rounding up the pigs right now without me. I can only imagine the fool things he'll do."

"I'm sure he'll be fine."

"What do you know? You weren't here when he started tearing apart everything I've built. He's turned the place upside down for his hippie dippy experiments."

"You mean going organic? I thought organic methods of farming were closer to what your father would have—"

"Shut up," he shouted, and she flinched. Color returned to his cheeks with a vengeance. "You don't know anything about my father. You don't know my family."

"All I meant was—"

"Why are you just standing there? I need my crutches. Simon!" he shouted. "Where's that useless boy?"

Something inside her cracked, and angry heat boiled through the fissures in her careful facade. "Simon is *not* useless. Don't you dare call him names and put him down."

He looked like she'd struck him. His milky blue eyes narrowed. "You don't have the right to tell me what to do or what to think. You think I don't see what you're trying to do? I know green-card-seeking, gold-digging hussies like you."

She tried to reconstruct her careful composure. Reacting would achieve nothing. She imagined an iceberg standing between them, that impenetrable wall of ice being hammered away at by his words.

"You want to get in here and strip this place bare. You don't care about farming or family. All you people do is come here and take over like locusts."

"Grandpa." Simon's low rasp made them both turn.

He stood in the doorway, fists at his sides. His eyes burned beneath his bangs as he inserted himself in front of Tiffany. "What the hell is wrong with you? Tiffany's done nothing but be nice to you and help me with school, and you're acting like some ignorant redneck." The words tumbled out of him louder and louder like the approach of a train, his tirade gathering steam.

The last thing Tiffany had wanted was for Simon to get in between her and his grandfather's hate. "Simon…" She placed a hand on his shoulder, tried to draw him back, but he pulled away.

William struggled to stand but Simon advanced, making him stumble backward. "Don't you—"

"You're such a hypocrite. You keep telling me to treat people with respect. To treat *you* with respect. But I don't see respect from *you*. Not for Tiffany, not for Dad and not for me.

"You treat me like I'm some kind of stupid kid. I'm not five anymore. You and Dad don't get to live my life for me, so stop acting like whatever I do has to be for you two. I'm sick of it. I never want to be a farmer. Not if I turn into a bitter, racist asshole like you."

Tiffany gasped.

William gaped, sputtering. "You're out of line. And if you knew anything—"

"I know a lot, including how to treat people with respect, and that's because of Dad, not you. Don't dump your bullshit on Tiffany or her family or anyone else just because you lost your leg." He stormed out, slamming the door behind him.

The tension in the kitchen could have sliced a ripe tomato. William turned pale once more. His hands flexed and clenched in his lap. Tiffany felt a brief pang of pity for him.

"I'm American," she finally said quietly.

He glanced up blearily. "What?"

"I don't need a green card. I was born in New York City, and both my parents and my grandmother are naturalized citizens."

He blinked slowly, and his face drooped. "Yes. I know."

Of course he did. You didn't make your home in Everville

and not know about the history and lives of every single resident. "So why did you say it?"

"I don't know." His voice was rough like sandpaper. "I guess I was mad. It wasn't personal."

"That's not true." She knew it, deep down. "Why have you been treating me like this, Mr. Jamieson?"

William wiped a palm down his face. "Ever since you came here, it's like I was losing another piece of my family, like when Daphne lived here. You'd think having a woman around the house would make a happier home, but that girl was like a vacuum. She sucked up every bit of energy in the room. It was always take, take, take. Nothing was good enough for her. That's why she left."

Tiffany didn't say anything. She had *nothing* in common with Daphne Blaine, and it bothered her that William would compare her to Chris's ex—the woman who'd abandoned Simon.

He rubbed his hands up and down his thighs. "He knew I was joking, didn't he? About you people? I suppose it's not flattering, but it's kind of true, right?"

Kind of true? Her nails dug into her palms. "That I'm like a locust or that I don't care about my family?"

He had the decency to look ashamed. "I don't mean half the things I say."

"And exactly which half was Simon supposed to believe?" Her personal feelings weren't as important as the chasm that had opened between Simon and his grandfather, and she felt responsible to the teen's feelings first.

"He really thinks I meant all those things about him being stupid?"

"Don't you?"

"Of course not. He's lazy, not an idiot."

Well, she supposed that was some progress, but jeez, did he ever need an attitude adjustment. She dragged a chair over and sat next to him. He wasn't clutching his stomach anymore. This drama had probably diverted his attention from the pain. She glanced at the clock on the wall, hoping the doctor would arrive soon.

"He's really mad at me, isn't he?" William said.

"I don't presume to know what his feelings are. But at a guess…" She looked out the storm door, hanging open after Simon's abrupt departure. "Yeah, he's pissed off."

"But why? It's not as if I said anything that offended you."

"Of course you offended me," she exploded, nearly making her chair rock. "And, to tell you the truth, you've been offending me for years."

Surprise sprang into his aged features. "But…you never reacted. You never even frowned when I said something funny. Your family knows I'm joking. They think I'm funny."

"No. They don't."

"Yes, they do. They always laugh." He licked his lips, eyes shifting, sounding less certain with each word he spoke. He rubbed his palm hard against his thigh above the stump as if he'd worry a revelation out of it.

She waited, everything in her wound up to pounce. The years of hurt this man had inflicted upon her and her family sat heavily on her shoulders. And yet, a sliver of sympathy kept her from jumping all over him and telling him what she *really* thought.

"I never meant anything personally," he said. "Your people are good people. You're a hardworking, stoic bunch. You never let anything faze you. I always admired that about the Orientals."

She pinched the bridge of her nose. Good Lord, the man really didn't know. And Tiffany wasn't sure where to begin the monumental task of educating him.

"First off," she said slowly, releasing the words like a hiss of steam from a pressure cooker, "it's not PC anymore to say *Oriental* unless it's referring to a rug or a salad. Second, third, fourth and fifth…"

NEARLY AN HOUR LATER, Tiffany's throat was sore, her nerves were shot and she needed a stiff drink. It would have to wait, though. She found Simon in the tack room in the barn with the kittens. He was slouched in one corner with Clover curled up on his stomach. He glanced up as she approached.

"Sorry I walked out like that and left you alone." He sullenly focused back on the kitten. "Are you okay?"

"I'm fine. I'm more worried about your grandfather. The doctor's checking him over right now."

The teen stuck his jaw out. "Whatever. I don't care."

"Of course you care."

"Did he apologize to you?"

"Yes." No need to repeat the whole conversation. She'd made him listen while she enumerated his insults over the years. He seemed genuinely surprised by the things he'd said and done to anger her. Apparently, no one had ever called him out on his behavior. "We talked mostly about you, actually."

"I meant every word," he told her bluntly. "I don't want to be like him. I don't want to be a farmer."

"You don't have to be," she said, plopping down on a bale of straw. "There's no reason you won't get into the college program of your choice if you work for it."

"But that's the problem. I don't know *what* I want to do."

"You don't need to know definitively right now. I know people in their fifties who are still trying to figure it out. Your education doesn't necessarily mean you'll have a straight-and-narrow career path."

And hadn't it taken right up to this moment for her to realize it? Tiffany cocked her head, surprised by this minor epiphany. All those years in high school with all that focus pointing toward college… And then that focus had gone to graduating and getting a job in publishing…but she hadn't found that perfect fit yet. It could take her another fifteen years before she did.

Simon's head fell back against the bale of straw. "It's just that…Dad really wants me to go to college. I get it's a living-vicariously-through-me thing. But he thinks I'm going to do all those things he didn't get to do, travel the world and stuff. I've never even left the country." The kitten mewed plaintively as Simon shifted and pushed his bangs out of his eyes. "I can't do all those things he wants. I don't even think I want to."

She chuckled. "I know exactly what you mean. My parents have always had these insane expectations of me, but success has always been on their terms." She shook her head. She didn't want to bring up her own problems. "If you don't want to become a farmer or go to law school or become a…I don't know, a circus clown, you have to say so. You need to speak up for yourself. Otherwise, all kinds of people are going to get in your face and try to shape you."

"Yeah, I wish they'd lay off."

"Your dad and grandfather are only doing it because they love you. They want you to have a good future and they have different ideas about what that means. You know that, right?"

He lifted a shoulder. "Yeah, I guess."

"They want what's best for you, but you're the only person who knows what that is, even if it's not clear right now. There's lots of time to figure it out, though, so don't stress about it. If you want help, we can look at your options together. Maybe we can find an internship or apprenticeship somewhere and see how that works out for you.…"

She trailed off as she realized what she was promising. She could be heading off to a new job any day now. But she was sure they had time. The summer stretched ahead of them, and anyone who'd be hiring would call in September, after all the summer interns went back to school.

Simon peeked up at her skeptically. "You think that's going to help?"

"Simon, let me tell you the truth. You're a smart kid, a lot smarter than everyone takes you for." At that, he smiled bashfully. "But you're also too young to know what you really want, which is why you need to stay in school. I know it seems like it's going to take forever, and that it all sucks, but I promise you, as long as you work hard, you'll figure it out. We'll figure it out together."

He nodded slowly. "Okay."

It was a minor triumph that he hadn't dismissed her with "Whatever." She just hoped Chris wouldn't object. After all, it was supposed to be his job to guide him through these kinds of decisions. But she couldn't help sticking her nose in his son's business. She cared about what would happen to him. He was a bright kid who could get things done when he applied himself. She'd hate to see him waste his smarts.

She stilled and frowned. Was that what her parents thought about her when she was Simon's age?

Tiffany shook herself and came back to the present. "Listen, your grandfather was really upset after you walked out. If you want people to respect you and your decisions, you have to stand up for yourself and tell him how you feel without throwing accusations. Man up about it, you know?"

His eyes traveled to the house. "You think he's okay?" He might have been angry, but he was still worried for the old man.

"Let's go find out. Dr. van Vierzen should still be around."

They went back to the house together. In the living room, William sat on the couch buttoning up his shirt, a sour expression creasing his features. Dr. van Vierzen turned and smiled. He'd been the Cheungs' family doctor since they'd moved to Everville, and despite the passage of time, his age only showed in the slight graying at his temples and the fine lines around his eyes. He still looked like Gregory Peck to Tiff.

"How is he?" she asked, darting a look at William.

"He's a little banged up. Nothing's broken from the fall. But I can't tell what else is going on until he comes to my office for a few more tests."

"I'll tell Dad. He'll make him go," Simon said.

"Actually, your grandfather's already agreed. Readily, in fact. It makes me a little suspicious."

"There's nothing wrong with my hearing, you know. Don't talk about me like I'm not in the room."

"Sorry, Bill." The doctor grinned wryly. "It was good catching up with you. Lucky thing I was in the neighborhood when this happened, eh?" He winked at Simon discreetly. "Try to lay off fatty foods for now. It might simply be a case of indigestion, but if it's a gallstone or something worse, I'd rather you not have another attack. You could stand to lose a few pounds anyhow."

"You gonna air my health issues to the whole county? What happened to doctor-patient confidentiality?"

"I'm not here as a doctor, I'm here as your friend. Otherwise, I'd be charging you an arm and your other leg for a house call."

William snorted. "Get out of here before I decide to sue your ass for malpractice."

"Nice to see you, too, Bill." He clapped him on the shoulder and nodded to Tiffany and Simon on the way out.

"So…" The elderly Jamieson folded his hands over his lap. "You have something else you want to say?"

Simon shuffled in place. "I'm sorry I yelled at you," he said. "I was mad and I went off. I didn't mean it."

"Of course you meant it," William said matter-of-factly. "You meant every word. And if I knew that sooner…" He eased forward, rubbing his hand up and down his truncated thigh. "Look, Simon, I didn't mean anything by my words. And...I realize now that some of the things I've been saying are plain wrong. Not just about you, but about Tiffany, her family...a lot of things. I guess I took it for granted that you'd know I didn't really feel that way about anyone."

Simon watched him warily. He looked like he was waiting for a *but*. Tiff knew what that was like.

"I'm going to try harder," William said. "I need to...think before I open my mouth and not...how was it you put it? 'Dump my bullshit' on everyone?"

Simon's mouth twitched, and he stuffed his hands into his pockets.

William gave a dry chuckle. "Sorry, I guess I'm too old to be using language like that. Actually, there are a lot of words I should probably cut from my vocabulary. Your tutor gave me a lesson in that." He shot her a look. "Not that she needs to be smug about it or anything."

"Me? Smug? I thought we were all stoic to you."

He harrumphed. "I take it all back. You, young lady, are an uppity, meddling, precocious know-it-all."

She smirked. "Finally, an insult I can live with."

She startled a smile out of William. His chuckle became a laugh that turned into a hoot. Tiffany couldn't help but laugh along. It was contagious and soon, all three of them were laughing.

After the day they'd had, it was exactly what they needed.

WHEN CHRIS SAW Micah van Vierzen's car parked in the driveway, he dropped his tools and ran toward the house, heart banging in his throat. Who was hurt? Why hadn't anyone called him in from the field?

The doctor was stepping out of the house when he got there.

"Doc," he gasped out. "What is it? What's happened?"

Micah smiled reassuringly. "Your father had a little fall. Simon called me down to check on him. He's all right."

He gave Chris a brief rundown, told him William had agreed to a checkup. If the doctor didn't look worried, Chris supposed he had nothing to be afraid of. Micah drove off, and Chris hastened into the house. Simon would probably be shaken up. Tiffany had now seen more medical emergencies in the past few weeks than Chris had seen over the past five years. And who knew what kind of mood his dad was in.

He walked in through the kitchen door to a peculiar sound: laughter. Simon, his father and Tiffany were sitting in the living room with mugs of coffee. His father looked quite relaxed on the couch, a throw over his lap. Chris never realized how old he looked.

He hovered in the doorway, listening as William told some story from his youth. His dad's eyes shone the way they had when Simon was a baby and William would cradle him.

Tiffany glanced Chris's way, giving him an easy smile. Longing filled him. The scene looked so natural, it was as if he were finally coming home.

It was as if she belonged there.

CHAPTER FIFTEEN

THE FOLLOWING SUNDAY, Chris asked Tiffany to drive out so he could discuss something with her. She puzzled over what was so important that he couldn't have sent her an email or phoned. She was happy to have an excuse to see him, and to get away from her parents. Daniel could deal with them, since he was back from his reunion.

When she pulled into the farm's driveway, Chris strode out of the house. He wore jeans and a clean blue T-shirt that showed off his muscled arms. He carried a small cooler in one hand and a stuffed backpack in the other.

"Headed somewhere?" she asked as she got out of the car.

"I'm taking you out." He ushered her toward his truck, and tossed the bag and cooler into the back of the cab. "We're going on a grand nostalgia trip of Everville."

"A what?"

"C'mon." He helped her into the passenger seat. "This is my personal guided tour, complete with a picnic lunch and visits to everything Everville, old and new."

"Why?"

The suspicion in her voice made him stop in his tracks, and she cringed at herself. He scratched his nose and gave a quirky smile. "Because why not? You've worked hard, and you and I both deserve a break. It'll be fun. You do know how to have fun, right?"

Tiffany was going to protest, tell him she really didn't need to revisit all the old haunts, bring up old, stale memories.

"Please," he said at her hesitation. He looked so excited, and he had gone to the trouble of packing a lunch. How could she refuse?

It was a gorgeous day for a drive, sunny and not too hot, a few fluffy white clouds in the sky. "First stop, Georgette's Bakery, now Georgette's Bakery and Books."

"She's still open? She must be in her eighties now."

"Eighty-two, and still waking up at four every morning. Actually, her grandson, Aaron, moved back to town to help her run the place. I don't know if you remember him—he was a year or two behind us in school. He was the one who opened the bookstore. I hear he's looking to expand the business even further."

"What did he do before that?"

"I think he was a lawyer or something. He lived in Boston before this."

Tiffany couldn't imagine why a man would leave a career in law to run his grandmother's bakery and bookstore all the way out here. But she was glad the woman famous all over the county for her treats was doing well.

It was a solid ten minutes to the roadside bakeshop and, sure enough, the tiny building had a new addition sporting a hand-lettered sign that read Georgette's Bakery and Books. The parking lot, expanded and newly paved, teemed with weekenders and locals alike.

The bakery was almost exactly as Tiffany remembered it, though the glaring fluorescent lights had been replaced with attractive halogen fixtures. Everything had a shiny new coat of paint, and there was a lot more on display. The rich smells of chocolate and baked goods mingled with fresh brewed coffee. The faintest hint of drywall plaster lingered in the air.

A pretty young woman served customers cheerily behind the counter. Her gold-brown hair was caught in two pigtails, but she had to be closer to thirty than twenty. It took a minute for Tiffany to recognize her. The girl had been a cheer-leader at their high school—one of the popular girls whose circle of friends was practically in another galaxy. Her name was Stephanie something or the other.

"Chris." She greeted him brightly over the counter. "How's it going?"

"Doing great, Steph. You remember Tiffany, don't you?"

Tiffany was caught off guard as he nudged her forward. Stephanie's eyes widened. "Omigosh, it's so good to see you." She ran out and threw her arms around her. Tiff squeaked as the former cheerleader's thick arms smooshed her against her ample bosom. "How have you been? I heard about the accident. Are you all right?"

"I'm fine." She regretted saying so when Stephanie squeezed her again, tighter this time. Why did people she barely knew keep hugging her? She sent a pleading look toward Chris, who smothered a laugh.

Steph finally let go and gave her an approving look. "Wow, look at you. You're gorgeous now. I mean, wow."

"Um, thanks."

"Listen, I've got to get back to work—" she glanced at the customers who'd walked in "—but promise me you'll call me up and we can go for coffee, okay?"

First Maya, now Stephanie. Hugging and coffee, appar-ently, was what people did in this town now. Why did every-one think she'd want to "catch up"? What would they catch up on? They'd never spoken to each other.

You're being pissy, she told herself. Just because Stepha-nie had been popular, didn't mean she was cruel. "Sure," she finally answered.

She was making way too many piecrust promises. Easily made, easily broken. But surely, no one would miss her once she was gone, so what could it hurt?

"Is Georgette around?" Chris asked. "I have a special order to pick up."

"She's working in the back with Aaron. Hang on. I'll let her know you're here."

Georgette Caruthers looked almost exactly as she had when Tiffany had last seen her. Her hair was silver with a few darker streaks of gunmetal-gray, but she'd maintained that slender almost ballerina-esque frame. How she stayed so slim while working with butter and sugar all day, Tiffany wanted to know.

"Hello, Chris." The woman came out from behind the counter and hugged him. She was still as graceful as ever, though she moved much more slowly. "You're here for your cake, I take it?"

"Is it ready?"

"I have it boxed up for you in the back." Her smiling eyes canted toward Tiffany. "Hello. You must be the special lady Chris had me make this for. You're a local, aren't you?"

"No. I mean, yes," she corrected, "but I haven't lived here in a while."

Georgette closed her eyes briefly, lids fluttering. "Pecan tart and orange soda. Saturdays or Sundays." She opened her eyes. "That's when you'd come in. You used to wear glasses. And there was usually paint on your jeans." She cocked her head to the side. "You won the blue ribbon one year for that gorgeous watercolor of Silver Lake."

"You remember all that?"

"I remember everyone who comes in, especially a pretty face like yours."

A tall man with neatly clipped brown hair and gray eyes brought out a small cake box tied with gold ribbons. Georgette introduced them, and Aaron Caruthers nodded to Chris and acknowledged Tiffany with a smile before heading to the bookshop portion of the store where a few customers lingered.

"I'm so glad he's come home," Georgette said. "So many of my grandkids left. I don't see much of my family anymore. But I guess that's how life is. I wish people would see how things are changing here and move back." Her eyes moved to Tiffany. She had the strangest sensation of a trap closing in around her.

Before they left, Georgette called, "Wait." She went behind the counter and put a pecan tart into a paper bag, pressing it into Tiffany's hands. "For you. For old times' sake."

"Oh, I couldn't possibly…"

The woman insisted. "Half the reason I keep this place going is to make people smile, and I think you have not done enough of that. And don't you dare try to pay me. Just promise you'll come back and visit again soon, won't you, dear?"

The wistful, forlorn note in her voice made Tiffany think of *Poh-poh*. She thanked Georgette as she clutched the bag.

The sweet scent of pastries clung to them as they climbed into the truck. Tiffany stuck her nose in the bag and inhaled deeply.

"That's a sound I'd like to hear more of," Chris murmured.

"Sorry?"

He froze. "I said that out loud, didn't I?" He chuckled nervously. "You were humming. *Hmm-mmm-mmm*," he mimicked her soft sigh, then cast her a grin. "I liked the way it sounded."

"You have to smell this. It must be fresh from the oven." She pushed the bag and he leaned over and sniffed, repeating her *hmm-mmm-mmm*. She didn't realize how sensual it'd sounded until he'd said it in those low, sultry tones. It made her very aware of their proximity and the fact she could no longer deny this was a date.

They swung east in the truck, heading back to town. Tiffany had driven these roads herself years ago while finding scenes to paint, though they looked different now. In places, the road had been widened, and previously unpaved or gravel roads now sported new black asphalt.

"Me and the guys used to race our bikes along this stretch, back when it was still mostly gravel," Chris said. "I took plenty of ugly spills on this road."

"Whatever happened to your motorcycle anyway?"

He shrugged. "Had to sell it when Simon was born. Turns out diapers cost money." His eyes grew distant. "I still remember the last time I rode the bike out to Merchant's Grove. A bunch of us got together and lit this bonfire that was so big, it melted the beer bottles we threw in. I think the glass is still there."

Tiffany nodded along. She didn't want to admit how alien Chris's youth was to her. Even if she'd been invited, her parents would never have allowed her to go to some clandestine party in the woods where people smoked and drank and broke laws.

They cut through the center of town, passing all the monuments to Everville's beginnings.

"To the left, you'll see the plaque commemorating the first settlers in Everville," Chris quipped in an overcheerful tour guide's voice. "To the right is Everville's oldest building, now the site of the Everville Tavern. Their menu's as old as the building, and the food smells that way, too." He smiled wryly. "Calvin's probably going to sell soon, though. He's getting too old to run the place."

"It'd be the perfect spot for a Starbucks," Tiffany said automatically. When her comment was met with silence, she looked over to see Chris's mouth pursed tightly. "Any café," she amended hastily. "Any new development is good, right?"

He pointed to the statue of the town's founder, Bernard Howlings Everett, and told her how he and two of his buddies had TP'd it one night and had been caught by the local sheriff. He gestured at a row of vacant storehouses and a dilapidated cinema that sat between a residential neighborhood and an old heavy machinery depot, and described some of the town's efforts at revitalizing the area. There was talk of turning the space into a farmers' market to draw more weekenders in, but rumor had it a condo developer was sniffing around the properties. Tiffany had a hard time picturing a monolithic condo tower in Everville.

At a roadside chip wagon, Chris ordered a massive pile of hand-cut fries and gravy. There, they bumped into a couple of high school classmates who'd married, settled down and had two young girls. Tiffany vaguely knew them. They greeted her warmly.

"It must be nice to come home after all this time," the woman, Annabelle, said. "Joe and I lived in the city for a while, too, but we couldn't take it. All the noise and pollution and crime…"

"It's not all that bad." Tiffany was compelled to defend the place she called home. Her *real* home.

"Well, sure, but it's no place to raise kids. When we heard how things were changing back here, we thought, heck, Joe can be an optometrist anywhere, so we decided to pick up and move. Anyhow, the housing prices in the city were ridiculous. It didn't make sense for us to be paying what we were in rent for a two-bedroom apartment when we could own a four-bedroom house and land out here for the same amount."

"As long as you're okay mowing farm-size lawns and shoveling snow off a runway-size driveway," she murmured.

Annabelle laughed. "Oh, it's worth it, believe me. There's nothing like coming home." She glanced between her and Chris speculatively. "You'll see, as soon as you start thinking about the future, you'll want the extra space to grow."

They parted ways shortly thereafter, and Tiffany was once again invited to share a coffee with a high school acquaintance she barely knew.

"You look confused," Chris remarked. "Are you starting to get overwhelmed?"

"I don't understand…." She trailed off, trying to articulate her thoughts without coming off as a complete loser. "I don't know any of these people. Stephanie was just some girl in my class. I know next to nothing about her. And all I remember about Annabelle was that she's been dating Joe forever. I never talked to her. Why would either of them want to have coffee with me?"

"You act like it never happens."

She shrugged. "I just don't see the point."

"They're being friendly. They're taking a genuine interest. They want to reconnect with their youth and find out where their classmates got to. Aren't you even a little curious about their lives?"

Tiffany honestly couldn't say she was, and for reasons she didn't fully understand, that fact made her feel bad. Frankly, part of her remained suspicious. Maybe those women were looking for fodder for the gossip mill. Maybe they wanted to find out what the smartest girl in school was doing with her life after her fall from grace….

Or maybe you're completely paranoid and simply never learned how to make friends.

She frowned. She didn't like this negative woman who constantly sought the backhanded insult behind an innocent remark. Growing up with her parents' philosophy of never praising their children meant she didn't trust any compliment.

She had to let go of these feelings of mistrust. She glanced over at Chris. She'd never mistrusted him. Well, she had when he'd first asked her to tutor him—she'd seen *Carrie,* after all, and hadn't wanted a bucket of pig's blood dumped on her. But once they'd started working together, she'd been… comfortable, sure of herself. She'd known where they stood, and she'd known he would never hurt her.

Mostly because she would never allow him to.

"Hey, why so quiet all of a sudden?" Chris prompted.

She yanked her gaze away from the scenery rushing past. "Just thinking."

A few minutes later, they pulled onto a familiar turnoff and drove down the short, gravel road that wound through the woods and ended in a currently unoccupied clearing that served as a parking lot. Chris cut the engine, and they got out. He grabbed the cooler and backpack while Tiff carried the cake and fries.

"I know a great spot," Chris began. "But it's a ten-minute hike from here and there's no path. Are you up to it?"

"Sure." She already had an idea of where he wanted to go.

Not many people knew about the spot. People who came to Silver Lake's shores were more likely to picnic or swim along one of the more accessible beaches on the north side. Tiffany had only found the swimming hole because she'd wanted a more interesting view of the lake for her paintings and to avoid curious onlookers.

She followed him through the underbrush. Luckily for them both, poison ivy didn't grow out here, and Chris was courteous enough to hold back any larger branches in their path. She was slightly sweaty by the time they exited the forest, but the view was worth the trek. The egg-shaped cove was ringed by smooth, flat rocks, and pinched off from the rest of the lake by a short spit of land and hidden by tall, thick pines. A sandbar farther out kept the water in the cove calm, and it was deep enough to dive from the embankment.

Chris spread out a blanket on a flat, grassy spot in the shade of a willow and invited her to sit. The sun had that syrupy gold quality, and burned through the swaying branches of the willow. A sweet breeze carried the scent of pine to Tiffany's nose.

She couldn't help but glance over to the far edge of the

cove to the spot where she'd once spent a whole weekend painting. It had been from that vantage point that she'd captured the magical spot, winning the five-hundred-dollar prize and a blue ribbon at the county fair that fall. Her eyes slid to Chris, crouched by the cooler as he unloaded it, and she allowed herself a private smile.

He glanced at her. "What?" The corners of his mouth turned up.

"Hmm?"

"Why are you looking at me like that?"

"It's been a nice day," she said, unable to meet his eyes.

"You're a really bad liar, you know that, right?"

"What? It *has* been a nice day."

"C'mon. I don't hear you sigh like that often, so it must be something. You can be honest with me."

Not with this she couldn't. But as his gaze lingered like a coaxing caress, she blurted, "I was thinking about how I once saw you naked here."

Omigod, did I say that out loud?

His jaw swung open, but he didn't look offended. "When was this, exactly?" he asked slowly, disbelieving laughter tugging at his question.

Tiffany cleared her throat, looked back toward the shaded spot on the far side as if she could run there and escape. Instead, she replied by calmly pointing. "I was over on that ledge there, painting one afternoon when I was sixteen. I wanted to paint the lake—it was for the fall fair contest, and it took me almost an hour to find the right vantage point. It was really hot out. I planned to stay the whole day until I had my notes and sketches done…. And then you showed up and started stripping." Her memory fired as she pictured his long, lean form glistening in the heat.

Chris's dark blond eyebrows climbed up his forehead to escape the fire flaming in his cheeks. He laughed, pushed his hand through his hair. "I take it this was that one time I didn't have my swim trunks on me and decided it was safe to go skinny-dipping."

Tiffany held back a giggle. "That would be the day."

"I thought I was alone."

"You were." She leaned back on her elbows on the blanket. "At least, you didn't act like you were with anyone worth being shy around."

"And it didn't occur to you to say anything?"

She slid him an innocent look. "After spending all that time looking for the perfect vantage point, I wasn't going to leave." Besides, the show had been terrific. She flashed back to that day, watching Chris's sinewy, golden body diving into the water like an arrow and resurfacing with equal grace. She'd been too far to see any details clearly, but what she had seen had been enough to make her want to strip down and dive in after him.

He tilted his head, still smiling broadly. "You won the blue ribbon prize with that painting. The Rotary Club sold it for charity." He chuckled weakly. "Please tell me there wasn't a little naked me in that picture."

Her lips pursed, she admitted, "You're in there. But you wouldn't know it unless you knew what you were looking at." It had been her secret, a special memory to commit to paper in watery shades of saffron and silvery blue, his body like a fish flashing in the dark water. Most people would have assumed it was a reflection.

He was giving her such an odd look now that her body heated up. Something pulsed between them, and the air grew thick. Determined, she met his eye unflinchingly, dared him to look away as she uncrossed her ankles and shimmied over to one side of the blanket. "There's room here for two," she invited, lowering her voice, her eyes and her defenses.

CHAPTER SIXTEEN

CHRIS WAS STRUCK DUMB at the same time a goofy grin froze to his face.

The idea that she'd been watching him, studying him, painting him while he'd been so vulnerable should have outraged or embarrassed him. Instead, he was flattered, intrigued... and fully turned on.

Easy, boy, he scolded himself as he lowered his body gingerly onto the old king-size duvet he and Daphne had used when they'd shared a bed. It left them plenty of space to sit without touching. A queen-size marriage bed would have sufficed, but Daphne had insisted on the upgrade. Thoughts of his ex-wife stopped the southbound blood flow, and he let out a breath as he regained his vision.

Tiffany and Chris ate their sandwiches as birdsong and lapping water filled the comfortable silence. A breeze slid through her hair, lifting its delicate scent to his nostrils. When the sun burst through the sparse cloud cover, she turned her face to the sky, exposing her slender, pale neck. His blood resumed its southbound course. He couldn't tear his eyes away. When had she become this lovely, sensual creature? When had the staid tutor in her buttoned-up shirts turned into this woman who made him think all these lurid thoughts?

He couldn't help imagining what might have happened if he'd known she'd been watching him skinny-dipping all those years ago. Probably nothing—he would have hastily gathered his clothing and slunk away, mortified. They would never have been able to meet each other's eyes again.

But this was not teenage Tiffany. And he was not that Chris anymore.

She picked at the fries and delicately sucked gravy from her fingertips. Watching her, he became light-headed. She caught his look and smiled, lashes lowered.

"You want?" She held out a fry.

"I thought I'd get more than a taste since I was buying."

And now he sounded like a douchebag. "Of the fries, I mean," he said quickly.

She grinned. Thank God. But as he was about to take a nibble of that French fry and suck it right down to her fingertips, she grabbed a huge honking handful dripping with gravy and held it out in challenge.

He smirked, assessed the mess and angled his head, taking a large bite out of the many-tentacled fry monster waggling in her hand. They laughed as she tried to stuff it into his mouth, and he snagged her wrist, holding her still, eating the fries in a messy, slobbering way.

"There's gravy running down my arm," she yelped as he held her hand higher.

"Don't worry." He'd swallowed down the last of the greasy potatoes and only had her hand left. Holding her gaze, he set himself to licking the salty drippings on her fingers.

Her cheeks turned scarlet, and her lashes fluttered like moth wings, but she held perfectly still. He lapped up the gravy greedily then traced the thin trail that had run down her forearm past her elbow. He didn't stop there. She tasted so sweet, and her skin was as soft as silk. He brushed kisses higher to her shoulder, her neck, heard the way she was whispering his name, half plea, half worship, as he pressed her down against the blanket. "Chris…"

His heart banged in his chest as he stared at her. Her long, dark hair flowed across the periwinkle-blue comforter.

"You're so beautiful," he said, marveling at the softness of her dark eyes, her radiant complexion. Her wide, warm smile was all the invitation he needed to lean in and kiss her fully.

Dear God, why had he denied himself these past weeks? He took his time licking the salt from the fries off her lips. She clung to him, and her soft moans whispered through his blood.

Her hips pulsed against his, coaxing, and he struggled for control. He wanted to be skin-to-skin, and the way she slid her hands up under his T-shirt to lightly scrape her nails across his back told him she was just as eager.

This was going to end too quickly if he didn't calm the hell down.

He sat up. Her expression hung somewhere between relaxed and curious. Whatever happened next, he wasn't sure he could forgive himself if he'd read her wrong. Taking the leap, he glanced around to make sure they were alone, then unsnapped the top button of his jeans.

She eyed him hungrily, saying nothing as he kicked off his shoes and socks then reached for the hem of his T-shirt. This was going to happen, even if it was out here in the wilderness instead of in a proper bed. It had to be here, he thought a little wryly—neither of them could have gotten away with it in either of their homes.

There was nothing shy about the way she watched him. He'd caught her staring more than once before—of course, it was possible he was being egotistic, but sultry looks had never made him feel self-conscious or objectified. No, he hadn't minded her looking one bit. Making sure she'd get a good show now, he slowly dragged the fabric up and pulled the shirt over his head.

Her eyes widened. She hummed, *"Hmm-mmm-mmm,"* and

the sound reverberated across his sensitized skin. He grinned
slyly and reached for his zipper.

"Me," she blurted, jolting upright as if volunteering for
a class assignment. He couldn't help himself as he laughed.

Her returned giggle was the most musical thing he'd ever
heard. On her knees, she maneuvered the zipper down, then
hooked her fingers around his waistband, snagging his boxer
briefs in the motion. Slowly, painfully, she pulled down. He
sprang free, and she made that enticing *hmm-mmm-mmm*
sound again.

"You have condoms?" she asked breathily, eyes fixed on
him.

"In my wallet." Call him an optimistic, opportunistic horn
dog, but he'd rather be prepared than disappointed.

She didn't move, though. Tiffany dug her fingers into the
curls around his shaft, grasping him before putting her mouth
over the head and taking him in.

Chris nearly collapsed at the slick, wet heat surrounding
him, the gentle, exploring pressure of her tongue. He groaned.
How long had it been? Too long, but that wasn't what made
it so good. He had to think about the latest baseball scores to
keep from exploding right then and there. He didn't want to
end it this way, with him stark naked and her fully clothed
on her knees.

He pulled away from her ruthlessly, holding her shoulders.
"I want you naked," he growled.

Her lips glistened. He helped her out of her shorts, then
unbuttoned her sleeveless top to bear small, ripe breasts in a
silky blush push-up bra. Her panties didn't match—they were
plain black cotton—but somehow, it fit with who she was.

Chris gathered her into his lap, kissing her, playing with
her breasts. He was hot and hungry and he couldn't get
enough. She gasped and writhed beneath his touch. How
he'd ever thought her cold and unresponsive he didn't know.

"Do you think anyone will see us here?" she murmured, arching against him as he nibbled her neck.

"No." But the slight shudder that went through her made him pause. "Do you want to stop?"

She shook her head.

He knew instinctively they'd be safe, unwatched and alone. He'd never brought anyone here—not even Daphne. It was where he'd gone to escape his father, the farm, the pressures of school, Daphne's dramas and his hectic social life. There'd never been any pressure to be anyone other than himself in this place. That Tiffany had secretly shared it with him all those years ago made this moment all the more wonderful.

He slipped off the last of her clothing and with it, her reserve dissolved. He eased her down and she splayed herself across the blanket enticingly. Her flawless, pale gold skin contrasted against his sun-burnished complexion. He trailed a light touch over her stomach, and she shivered and arched into his touch.

Oh, boy. He definitely wasn't going to last at this rate.

"Wanna go for a swim?" he asked.

A skeptical look wrinkled her brow as she glanced toward the water. Before she could reply, he scooped her up and walked down to the embankment. She shrieked. "Put me down!" He didn't listen. Instead, he waded in up to his stomach and set her gently into the warm water. He could have dropped her in with a big splash, but it didn't feel right. He wanted to treat her like a princess.

Her eyes never left his as she floated up to him, sliding her arms around his neck. He struggled not to moan as she pressed every inch of her body up against him.

"I've had fantasies about this," she whispered. Buoyed by the water, she wrapped her legs around his hips. His hands drifted down to cup her bottom. "Ever since I saw you here, I dreamed I'd come down to meet you and we'd..." She trailed off.

"We'd what?" He nudged his erection against her. She was so warm.

"We'd kiss. We'd make out. You'd touch me and I'd let you. I'd let you do anything to me...."

He stopped her with another kiss. He had to remember the condom was still in his pants on the shore. The throbbing impulse to join their bodies in the water and make love until they both dissolved hammered through him, but he knew not to make that mistake twice.

Steam must have been pouring off them by the time he picked her up and walked out of the water on shaky legs. Placing her gently back on the blanket, he fumbled for the condom and sheathed himself in record time. Her eyes were dark and hazy, her skin flushed. He bent to take her, but then she surprised him by wrapping her legs around his waist, forcing him to a sitting position. With more speed and finesse than he thought her capable of, she poised herself above him, then sank slowly down.

Chris buried his face against her neck, holding tight, fully enveloped. They stayed joined, breaths mingling as they both adjusted to the deep sensation. When she met his gaze, they started a slow and steady rhythm, and he struggled to hang on. His world narrowed to the taste of her lips, the smell of their mingled arousal, the friction and heat building between them. She whispered his name over and over, and she tightened with every gasp.

His control slipped at the same time he felt the first flutterings of her climax. Clutching, clinging, they both rode the urgent wave until it crested and crashed down in a shattering roar.

DANIEL WATCHED HIS SISTER hum her way through a lunch shift and knew something was up. He'd heard the rumors about her and Chris, of course, but wasn't about to put that much stock in the town gossip mill. Anyhow, he wasn't sure he wanted to think about *exactly* what had put that smile on her face. This was his sister, after all.

After the lunch rush was over, Tiffany speedily wiped everything down, bringing him the empty steam trays to be washed. "I'm heading over to the farm early," she told him. "Simon's exams are coming up and we need to do extra prep."

Daniel didn't point out that classes didn't end until after three, and it wasn't yet one-thirty. Compelled to say something—on Chris's behalf if not hers—he asked, "Are you sure you know what you're doing?"

"Of course I do. Once summer school is over and I start working on math with him, it'll be a little harder, but I'm up-to-date on my geometry. It took a couple of nights to review. Funny how quick it all comes back—"

He interrupted her nervous ramblings. "I meant with Chris."

Her expression shuttered briefly, but she brightened her smile, turning up the dimmer switch to full. "You don't need to worry about me, big brother. We have an understanding."

"Are you sure about that?" At her narrowed look, he said, "Look, Chris is my friend, and his ex really screwed him and Simon up. I don't want to see you doing the same to them."

She grabbed a dish towel and started wiping the already pristine counter once more. "I'm not going to screw them up. Chris and I are adults. And it's none of your business what we do together."

His jaw clenched. "You still planning on going back to New York?"

"Of course I am."

"And are you planning on a long-distance relationship with Chris?"

She darted a guilty look at him. "I don't see why you're

so worried. There's nothing serious going on." She took off her apron and folded it precisely.

Tiffany was not the sort to have a fling. Daniel was sure that hadn't changed in the fifteen years she'd been away. She thought she could get away scot-free without hurting anyone, but he knew better. She'd harbored this crush for nearly two decades. She put up a good front, but she was about as emotionally resilient as a jelly bean. It was plain to him his sister was in love.

It wasn't his place to judge or say anything, though. He had his own issues to work out, and was hardly qualified to tell her what not to do. All he could hope for was the best, and that his sister would be able to pick herself up after things went south.

"Listen." He stopped her before she left and lowered his voice. "I have something to tell you. I'm going away for a while. I haven't told Mom and Dad yet, but I thought you should know first."

"Going away? Where? You just got back."

"I don't know." He'd come to this decision after returning from New York. He'd actually stayed an extra day to see if there were any jobs open for a guy with an MBA and an honorary master's in slaving over a hot stove. But his job search had turned up nothing. He'd known the impulse had been sheer insanity based on his desire to be near Selena. But as soon as he realized that, he knew he had to get away, forget her, forget anything they'd ever shared. Until he figured out who he was, found his worth as a man on his own, he couldn't call on her ever again. "I'm going to need my car back, in any case."

"Wait...what?"

"I'll give you a loan to pay for the repairs to your car," he said placatingly. "You can pay me back later."

She balked, searching him for answers. She didn't look happy. "When are you leaving?"

"As soon as your car is out of the shop. I know Frank's been working on it, so it'll probably be sometime this week. I've already paid him for the work, so don't bother refusing."

"You're serious, aren't you? How long will you be gone?" Worry crowded her brow.

"I don't know."

She groaned. "Mom and Dad are going to flip out."

He nodded. They'd be mad, of course, and he'd have to leave right away or risk getting trapped by guilt and duty. *Poh-poh* would be the hardest to tell—she would probably cry and beg him to stay. He could never say no to his grandmother.

"I have to go. I need to find myself, figure out who I am, where I fit in this world."

Her expression blanked. She was probably trying to decide whether to be outraged or frightened, or perhaps even understanding. It hadn't been an easy decision. She'd told him about how much their parents had fought while he'd been away. But he couldn't be their referee for the rest of his life. He'd already stayed too long.

TIFFANY GRIPPED THE STEERING WHEEL HARD, wishing for once that the drive to Chris's was longer.

Thoughts ran circles through her brain. Daniel was leaving. Her brother was fleeing the nest, abandoning her here alone to fend for herself against her parents....

No, that wasn't what was really bothering her. This identity crisis had come about because of what she'd said. He'd been depressed since he'd returned from New York, and Tiffany was sure it was about Selena. She kicked herself for ever doubting his feelings and questioning his suitability. As strong-willed as he was, his self-confidence was surprisingly fragile. She'd acted like a superior bitch, and it was eating her from the inside out.

She thought about what he'd said about hurting Chris's feelings, but didn't want to dwell on why his remarks had bothered her. She and Chris had had great sex, but that was it. He knew she wasn't going to stay in Everville. A summer tryst was all they could ever have. And it wasn't as though he could live up to fifteen years of daydreams and fantasies. The scorching heat between them would flare and burn out quickly. Once they were out of each other's systems, they'd go back to their regular lives. An extended commitment would only suffocate them both.

They were already getting too comfy with each other as it was. She'd tried to limit her exposure, but the more she pulled away, the more she pined for him. If she didn't seek him out, he would find her. And he'd get her to follow him on some pretense to the barn, shed, greenhouse, tack room or whichever building was unoccupied. Then he'd quietly close the door, press her up against the wall and kiss her until her knees turned to butter.

It's just a fling. She repeated the cold mantra quietly even as warmth rushed between her legs. *All good flings must come to an end.*

The most dangerous thing was that part of her wished it could last. Chris was everything she'd always wanted in a man—strong but gentle, playful, and hot as hell. But she couldn't imagine a life here with him. The farm, his son, his father—none of that had ever figured in the life she'd pictured for herself. Her career—everything she'd studied for and worked for and sacrificed for—was going to be in the city. New York was the center of the publishing world, and the path to becoming an editor began and ended there. After all her hard work, she wasn't willing to settle for anything less. She wouldn't sacrifice her dreams to become a farmer's wife.

When she pulled up, Chris was waiting for her on the porch. He stood in one smooth motion, a lazy, suggestive smile on his face. All thoughts of Daniel and New York and the future fled as he strolled up to her car.

"Hey," he said as she got out. He slipped his callused hand over hers surreptitiously and squeezed. By silent agreement, they'd kept their relationship under wraps, which meant no public displays of affection. Even so, the space between them was kept at a minimum. "You're here early."

"And you were waiting. Don't you have a cow to milk or something?" she teased.

He moved closer, backing her up against the door, and his hips brushed against hers. "Something needs milking, all right." He lowered his mouth to her ear. "My father's out at a doctor's appointment. He'll be gone all afternoon."

A shiver of pleasure rippled over her skin as he trailed his fingertips up her arm, and she remembered the erotic way he'd licked the gravy off her. Without another word, he turned toward the house, and she followed like a besotted puppy dog.

CHAPTER SEVENTEEN

IN THE HOUSE, Chris pulled her into his arms and kissed her as if he hadn't seen her in months. He cupped her bottom, the same way he had at the swimming hole. She obligingly wrapped her legs around his hips, pressing the center of her need against his rock-hard heat. She flung her purse onto the dining-room table as he carried her up the stairs and into the bedroom, where he laid her on the bed. They wriggled out of their clothes quickly. With her naked skin sliding between the smooth, cool bedsheets and Chris's hot, hard body, she felt absolutely hedonistic.

She didn't question the rightness of the way he made love to her. He wasn't frantic or hurried in his ministrations, but the intensity in his kisses and caresses and long, hard strokes kept her riding the brittle edge between pleasure and ecstasy. The bed was soft and smelled faintly of sandalwood. The way the room glowed, as the afternoon sunlight slanted through the window, reminded her of a sepia-toned snapshot and made her long for more stolen moments like this. She closed her eyes to relish the delicious sensation of him moving over and inside her, clutching him close as they found their pleasure together. When they finally came, she whispered a secret wish to the sky, letting her heart soar with it.

Blood thrumming, she lay in his arms, head resting against his slightly damp chest. She listened to the hard drum of his heart slow to a strong, steady beat. He stroked her hair absently. Neither of them spoke as their breathing evened out.

Normally, she wasn't into the sticky business of cuddling, and had never really enjoyed her previous partners' heavy limbs trapping her in bed. But Chris was different. He held her as though she were precious.

She must have drifted off because all of a sudden, her eyes snapped open. Something had woken her. She sat up, disoriented.

"What time is it?" She nudged Chris as she fumbled for her panties.

He stirred and groped for the alarm clock on the nightstand. His hair was sticking out in all directions. "Almost four. Damn." He levered up and dragged his hands over his face. "I was hoping to get one more go in before Simon came home." He peeked up over his fingers with a smile.

It was meant to be a joke, but his words niggled. This had been a pleasant afternoon diversion—it was what she'd wanted and all she could expect. She shouldn't get huffy because she was a booty call.

"I'm going to clean up and head downstairs," she said. "Take your time in here."

In minutes, she'd dressed and brushed her hair out and re-tied it into a tidy, efficient ponytail. Her makeup was in her purse downstairs. She needed to touch up the lip gloss Chris had kissed off. She probably wouldn't need much else, though. She was rosy cheeked and bright-eyed, and a nice healthy glow radiated from her normally pale skin. Sex was the best makeover, it seemed. Unfortunately, she couldn't do anything about the stubble burn on her neck, and she didn't have time to shower and get Chris's earthy musk off her skin. She'd have to take those little souvenirs home and hope no one noticed.

She grinned to herself as she headed down to the dining room, but at the foot of the stairs she stopped cold.

Simon sat in the kitchen, a can of soda in hand. He took

her in from head to toe, and Tiffany knew by the glimmer in his eyes that she was well and truly busted.

"Hey," he greeted her, not taking his dark eyes off her as he took a long swig of his soda. His expression was unreadable, neither disappointed, happy or even speculative.

"When did you get home?" she asked, folding her hands in front of her to keep from tugging on her suddenly too-tight collar. "I was…in the bathroom. I didn't hear you come in."

"Half an hour ago. I got a ride home from a friend's mom."

"Oh." *Shit, shit, shit.* "Sorry. If I'd known you were here early—"

"Hey, Dad," Simon greeted over her shoulder.

She turned to face Chris, who'd halted halfway down the stairs. With his bare feet and sexily mussed hair, it was pretty clear he hadn't been working in the fields. Chagrined, she watched him slowly descend the rest of the way.

"Hey, Simon. How was school?" How he could sound so casual she had no idea.

"All right," Simon returned with equal coolness.

"I was just saying if I'd known he was home early that I would have been waiting for him down here instead of looking at the bathroom." Tiffany cringed. God, she *was* a terrible liar.

Chris nodded. "Yeah…I was thinking of renovating it. Getting some new tile in. You know. She's got a good eye for color, being a painter and all. Did you know that about her?"

"Sure, Dad," Simon said, and downed the rest of his cola. As he got up to pitch the can in the recycling bin, he nodded at his father. "Your T-shirt's inside out."

LATER THAT EVENING, Chris sat through dinner, feeling like he was sitting on a very high and narrow stool. The gravy-laden steak and mashed potatoes his father had prepared tasted like cardboard. He was nervous, though why that was, he couldn't say. He was a grown man, after all, and whatever questions his father and son had, he could deal with them. Dad and Simon were both watching him surreptitiously, glancing up now and again as if trying to work up the courage to say something. He wondered what his son had told his father.

He spooned out the pool of oil sitting in the caldera of his mashed potato volcano. "How much butter did you use, Dad? I thought the doctor said you were supposed to cut down on fatty foods."

"But I'm eating greens now, see?" He scooped up a forkful of peas dripping with yet more butter. "Nothing's wrong with a little butter."

"You know, Grandpa, I bet Tiffany would know of some healthy ways to cook vegetables," Simon suggested.

"I'm not fond of their food," he said. "Pardon me. Her food. Chinese food. You know I only ever go there for the Friday lasagna special."

"Well, her grandmother is over seventy and she's really healthy. I bet I could get Tiffany to give us some recipes for bok choy."

William grumbled, belligerently shoveling more peas into his mouth.

"Actually," Simon went on, "I was thinking about getting a job at the Cheungs' diner once summer school's over."

Chris raised an eyebrow. "You were?"

"I was talking to Theo, who's in my class. His sister Cindy works there as a waitress, and she said they needed someone to help with kitchen duties and stuff. I asked Tiffany about it, too, and she said she'd talk to her parents. She told me they were okay with it, so I phoned and asked Mrs. Cheung."

"I don't know, Simon…." He eyed the fresh bandages taped around his arm. Simon tugged his sleeve to cover it.

"Dad, it's fine. They'll train me and stuff. This was a stupid mistake and I won't make it again."

For whatever reason, Chris looked to his own father for guidance. William only shrugged in response. "How are you going to get to work? You don't drive."

"Mrs. Cheung said I could come in when Cindy did. She drives past here on the way to work, so she could pick me up. Once I get my license, it won't be an issue."

"What about school?"

"It'd only be two nights a week. They said they can't afford more right now, but Mrs. Cheung said she'd be happy to have me on."

"What about *Mr.* Cheung?" William asked. "You know those two fight like cats and dogs, don't you? From what I've heard, you can't get them to agree on anything."

"She said he'll be fine with it."

Chris preferred that his son focus on school, but he couldn't help remembering what Tiffany had said about his son needing something else in his life. He didn't want to say no right off the bat, and besides, he couldn't help but notice his father hadn't forbade him outright, either. "I'll think about it."

"You should talk to Tiffany," Simon suggested, eyes dancing. "She can tell you all about it tomorrow afternoon. I'm going to a study group after school. I'll be away until dinnertime. Better yet, I'll get dinner out." Brightly, he added, "Grandpa, you should come and pick me up and we can go to the tavern for dinner. It'll be fun."

"Now, why would I do a thing like that?" William groused. He stiffened suddenly and glowered at Simon. "Are you kicking my one good leg, boy?"

"*Grandpa.* Take me to dinner tomorrow. Please?"

"Why? Are you trying to hint at something? Speak straight to me. What are you— Is this about your father knocking boots with your tutor?"

Chris choked on his mouthful of potatoes. "Dad!"

Simon burst out laughing.

"What? You think no one notices the two of you sneaking around together? I'm crippled, not blind." He pushed his plate aside and folded his arms across his chest.

"You are pretty obvious," Simon agreed, scraping his plate clean.

"I'm sorry." Chris ran his hand over his face, humiliated. Time to come clean. "I won't deny that we're…involved. But it isn't anyone else's business, so I'd appreciate it if you'd both keep it to yourselves."

"I think it's cute," Simon said with a smug smile. "I like Tiff, you know? She's all right. It's a little weird, but I don't have any problems if you guys wanna date or…you know." He made a face and shuddered as he took the dinner plates to the sink and started to wash up.

Chris blinked back unexpected tears. His son's blessing wasn't something he'd sought, but now that he had it, it was like he'd been handed a check for a million dollars. He hadn't realized how important Simon's approval was to him. He'd dated on and off since the divorce, of course, and Simon had tolerated those women. Then again, none of them had lasted very long. His son was too old to need a stepmother, but he did need someone who cared about him.

After cleaning up, his father asked to talk to him on the porch. He sat in his rocking chair, smoking a slightly bent cigarette. He rarely smoked—it was only to "help his lungs" he insisted, despite all medical evidence to the contrary. Chris sat in a rickety wicker chair and leaned back. They listened to the cricket song as the summer sun swept low in the sky. He loved these long summer days. He knew they were coming to an end soon, but it only made them that much sweeter.

"I take exception to the fact that you're dating that woman," William proclaimed.

Chris stiffened as his blood went cold. "Are you saying you don't approve because she happens to be Chinese?"

"It's got little to do with where her folks come from or what she is," his father snapped. "My problem is with *who* she is."

Chris gripped his knees to keep from leaping out of his chair. He needed to hear the reason behind his father's objection before jumping to any conclusions.

William blew a cloud of smoke into the sky. "I'm not going to deny she's done a lot for Simon. And she's put up with me aplenty, God knows why. But I don't think you know what she can do to you. What she'll do to this family if you think you can hang on to her when you can't."

"You don't think she'd stick around for me?"

William's steady gaze was suffused with pity. "I'm saying that whatever happens, I don't want it affecting Simon. It was hard enough when his mother left, hard on all of us—you especially, even if you won't admit it to yourself." He extinguished the cigarette and pocketed the half-smoked stub. "Now, I'm not saying she's like Daphne—Lord knows Tiffany works ten times harder than that woman ever could. But Tiffany's got her sights set on bigger things than we can give her. I think you know that, too." He looked off toward the fiery horizon. "Life in Everville is simple like a ham sandwich, and a girl like her needs more than that to keep her satisfied. Now, you can dress up a ham sandwich all you want, but it is what it is. Eventually, she'll get sick of it and go looking for something else. And she'll hurt you and Simon when that time comes."

"She would never hurt Simon." Chris knew that for a fact. She cared about his son. He'd seen her dedication and concern for his well-being, treated him with care and respect.

"Maybe not intentionally. But it can't be helped. The boy's getting attached. She won't be here much longer, Christopher, and I know you don't want to hear it, but there's nothing you can do or say to keep her."

"You have no idea what you're talking about."

"It wasn't enough to keep you here," William went on relentlessly. "You're only here because you have to be. Do you expect her to make the same noble sacrifices for you as you did for Simon?"

"Go to hell." Chris stormed off. He was so sick of how his dad treated him, as if nothing he did would ever be good enough. Invoking Daphne's betrayal had hurt; labeling his son as an obligation was mean. But telling him he wasn't good enough for Tiffany—

He tamped down the molten fury rising in him. He had plenty to offer Tiffany—or any woman. They had chemistry. Common interests. A shared past. She was used to having a Starbucks on every corner and take-out food from every part of the world within walking distance, but things in town were changing and growing. She'd seen that for herself.

William was wrong: Everville was so much more than a ham sandwich. And even if it was, what was wrong with that? Life here was good. It was enough.

He kicked a stone so hard it went bouncing into the sunset. Dammit, he'd worked hard and had built a decent living here. Why *wouldn't* she want to be with him?

DANIEL STOOD IN THE DINER on Sunday afternoon after the lunch rush had cleared out, feeling as though he were before a firing squad.

"I'm leaving," he told his parents.

Their jaws dropped at the same time their faces alternately flushed and paled.

"What?"

"You can't."

"Where do you think you're going?"

"What's the matter with you?"

"Are you crazy?"

"No."

The admonitions came out in rapid-fire sequence, but it was that last simple "No" from his father that kept him standing tall.

"Yes, Dad. I'm leaving. I don't know for how long, but it's time for me to go find a real job."

His father paced, folding and unfolding his arms, while his mother slouched at a table, forehead resting in one hand, a deep frown lining her face. Daniel felt strangely disconnected from his body, as if watching himself from over his own shoulder. He'd practiced this speech a hundred times in his head. Perhaps he'd been subconsciously doing it all his life because he was unnaturally calm for a man who was betraying everything he'd been raised to believe.

The chimes by the door heralded Tiffany's arrival. She'd taken their grandmother to a doctor's appointment, so had been excused from lunch rush. Her gaze bounced among the three, but understanding lit her face when he met her eyes.

Dad gestured wildly. "Did you tell him to do this?" His accusation made Tiff flinch.

"Tiffany had nothing to do with it," Daniel said. "I already told you, I made this decision a while ago."

"You can't go. We need you here," Tony insisted. "Who is going to help me cook?"

"You'll figure it out. I'd start by seeing if Manny can come in full-time. Offer to pay him more—he deserves it after all these years. If he doesn't want the job, you'll have to hire someone."

"I don't understand," Rose said in exasperation, lapsing into Cantonese. "Weren't we paying you enough? We let you live in our house, eat our food, all so you could save up for a house."

"It's not about money. I have to go live *my* life. I have to find out who I am outside of the family business." It had taken all this time to realize how right his sister was. He'd never cut the apron strings, never lived a life that wasn't connected to his parents. His mom, his dad and *Poh-poh* had always been his first priority. He had always put his needs second.

"What's wrong with the family business?" Tony asked, throwing his arms wide. "This is good, honest work. Why would you throw it away?"

"I'm not throwing it away. I just need time to figure things out."

"How much time? A week? A month? You left us for all those days to go to your reunion and it was so busy, I could barely keep up."

Daniel pinched the bridge of his nose. "You're going to have to figure it out. I'm sure you can find kitchen help easily."

"I don't have time to train new people," Tony groaned.

"Well, you're going to have to make time," Daniel snapped, his patience thinning.

"I'll be here to help out," Tiffany offered.

Daniel turned to give her a grateful look. At least she was in his corner.

"You?" her father scoffed. "You can't help us."

"It's not as if you'll stay," Rose agreed. "We need someone we can rely on long-term."

Ouch. Tiff's face fell. Her hands curled into fists as she crossed her arms and glared back. Even if they were right, they didn't have to throw it in her face.

"Dad, Mom, I'm doing this. I don't expect any pay while I'm gone. You can hire a replacement. There's no reason you actually need me here."

Tony kicked a chair, toppling it. "You want to leave? Fine, leave. But don't come back here begging for your job. You're an ungrateful, selfish boy. I don't need you." He flung his stained apron on the floor and slammed into the kitchen. *"Moh gwai young."*

Pain as familiar as a well-used chef knife slid into Daniel's chest. He collapsed into a chair opposite his mother, and Tiffany joined them.

"Do you really have to go?" Rose asked quietly when the swinging door stopped flapping back and forth.

"Yes. Now more than ever."

She wouldn't meet his eyes. She kept shaking her head. "It's about Selena, isn't it?"

The mere mention of her name sent a sharp, cold sting through his chest. When he didn't answer, she said, "You haven't been yourself for a while. I guessed it was because something happened, but you never said anything."

Daniel leaned on his elbows, exhausted. "It's partly that. But there's more to it. I don't expect you to understand. I don't even expect you to forgive me."

"Forgive you?" She sent him a startled look. "Of course I forgive you. You want to do more with your life. You want to get a good job, have a family. That's nothing to be ashamed of. We raised both of you—" she addressed Tiffany "—to always do your best. You've outgrown your place here."

Rose got up slowly, her age suddenly showing as she went to the counter and started methodically wiping down the plastic-covered menus. "We would have liked you to stay, of course. We wanted you to carry on the business. We worked very hard to build it up, and…well, your father has a lot of pride." She grimaced toward the kitchen. "But I don't blame you for wanting to leave."

Hope flared. "So, you're not mad?"

"Mad? No. Disappointed, maybe, but mostly, I'm a little sad." She sighed. "You're both more American than Chinese, and your father forgets that sometimes. For our generation, we don't leave our family behind. We don't abandon and forget about our parents."

"We haven't abandoned you," Tiffany protested, but her mother only shook her head sadly.

"You'll have lives of your own, boyfriends and girlfriends, husbands, wives. One day, you'll have children, too. With everything else happening in the world, it becomes harder and harder to remember where you came from. That is why we raised you the way we did, to remember your heritage, your roots, your family. Family is what you have left when everything else is taken from you," she said, then smiled faintly. "Wherever either of you end up, always know you have a place here with us."

TIFFANY SNAPPED A MENTAL PHOTOGRAPH of the scene before her: her newly repaired Honda Civic hatchback was parked on the street right behind Daniel's Camry, while her dad's old minivan sat staidly on the driveway. If she were a better poet, she could write a few lines about that uncharacteristically crisp summer morning on the day her brother was finally leaving home. Maybe it was just the chill that had fallen between Tony and Daniel that made it feel so cool.

Daniel had told her there was no point delaying his departure. If he stuck around in some misguided effort to placate their father, he would end up staying. *Poh-poh* seemed more baffled than upset by his announcement, but with typical grandmotherly care, she gathered snacks for the car ride as if he were simply heading to the city for the day.

"Why all the books?" Tiff asked as he loaded two office boxes stuffed full of old tomes into the trunk. "They'll weigh you down and cost you more gas."

"You sound like Dad," Daniel said with a humorless chuckle, running a finger along the spines. It stopped over a copy of Kerouac's *On the Road,* and he pulled it out and set it on top. "I just want them with me."

He didn't sound like an excited boy heading toward adventure. He sounded…resigned. Tiffany's worry grew.

A heavy weight crept into her chest as he closed the trunk. She swallowed back burning tears and smiled hard to keep them from reaching her eyes.

"Well, don't look too happy to see me go," he said, punching her in the arm.

"What can I say? It'll be nice not to have you hogging the bathroom."

He glanced over her shoulder and up to the porch. Tony stood there watching him, his features stony. He curled his lip in disgust, turned stiffly and walked back into the house.

"'Bye, Dad," Daniel called softly.

"He'll get over it," Tiffany assured him, hiding her doubts beneath a pithy wave of her hand. "Dad'll probably hire some guy fresh off the boat and adopt him to replace his firstborn son. I bet he'll speak better Cantonese than you do, too."

"No doubt." He laughed weakly.

"So, know where you're headed?"

"I've always wanted to drive along the coast," he mused. "If I'm lucky, I'll end up in Florida before I get really homesick. I've always wanted to see Key West."

"Well, wherever you end up, make sure to email me. And do Mom and Dad a favor and call once in a while."

"So, now *you're* taking care of them?"

"One of us has to." As rough as things had been, she couldn't stand the thought of her family falling apart over Daniel's departure.

"Wait." Loud footsteps banged across the wood porch and down the stairs, house slippers slapping across the paved driveway. Rose pushed a plastic bag into Daniel's hands. "Map, compass and a GPS. Also, an emergency kit, flashlight and road map."

He peered dubiously into the bag. "Aren't these Dad's?"

"He won't miss them." Rose stepped back, smiling tightly. "You be safe. Be careful. Don't pick up hitchhikers, and make sure to lock your doors at night."

"I will, Mom."

"Okay." She stood, hands clasped tightly. When she didn't move toward him, Daniel sighed and hugged her. As if her hands and emotions had suddenly been unchained, she latched onto him tightly.

"I won't be away too long," he promised.

"I don't know what I'm going to do without you." Her sob shocked Tiffany, and a pang of empathy echoed through her. She knew her mom would get over it eventually, though. It wasn't as if they were saying goodbye forever.

"Ah-Day," Poh-poh said, pushing another plastic bag into his hands. "I steamed the last of the *cha siu bow* for you."

"Aw, I love barbecue pork buns." Tiffany stuck her lip out at him. "Still the family favorite, obviously."

"You'll have time to become the new favorite." He clapped her on the shoulder then pulled her in for a half hug. She surprised them both by wrapping her arms around him and squeezing tight.

"Go on, before things get really mushy," she said, giving him a light shove. "Drive safe."

"You, too." He grinned lopsidedly, got into his car and drove off. Tiffany stood with her mother and grandmother and watched until the car turned the corner.

"You all look stupid standing there staring." Tony scowled from the porch.

"Why didn't you come to say goodbye?" her mom demanded.

"What for? He'll be back before the end of the week is up. He knows he belongs here." He glared toward the end of the street where Daniel had turned, then made a pretense of looking at his watch. "Why are you still here? You should be opening the diner."

Rose snapped. She started in on him at the level of a shriek right there in the middle of the street. She berated him in a long string of throaty syllables, and he shouted back until the neighbors started peering out of their doors and windows.

Tiffany stared longingly down the road, then at her feuding parents. Her grandmother was pleading with them to go inside, and was quickly dissolving into tears.

Sudden, hot anger replaced her sadness.

"Hey!" Tiffany's shout silenced them momentarily. In very precise Cantonese, she said, *"Save face and take it inside."*

Hands trembling, she marched into the house.

CHAPTER EIGHTEEN

SUMMER SCHOOL WAS DONE.

Chris couldn't believe six weeks had flown by already. Simon looked so excited to be out of school finally. He'd worked his ass off, with Tiffany at his side drilling him about the plots and characters of the books he'd studied, staying extra hours that didn't add up on her time sheet.

Chris hadn't spent as much time with her since Simon had caught them at the house, but he knew that she'd been busy working at her parents' diner. It was probably a good thing since he had so much work to catch up on himself.

In the meantime, his son deserved a break. He wanted to reward Simon for his efforts, so he gave him a few days to himself—no chores except for the ones he did normally. Tiffany would start helping him brush up on his math skills after his hiatus. It would've been kinder to simply let Simon have the rest of the summer to himself, but then Tiffany wouldn't have a reason to visit.

She usually came to the farm between the lunch and dinner rush. Her parents had been fighting a lot since Daniel had left. Chris had heard rumors that passersby could hear pots and pans crashing around the place when there were no customers around. Tiffany wouldn't confirm or deny the gossip. She simply gave him a tired, defeated look and shook her head. That she wouldn't even talk about it worried him.

Today, as he went to the barn to put away some tools, he was glad to see her fully restored Civic hatchback tucked into the driveway. Frank had done a superb job on it. Chris found her in the barn with Simon, chasing the kittens around the space and putting them inside a large box.

"Hey, Dad." Simon waved. Tiffany turned and smiled wanly.

"We're taking the kittens to the vet," she said. "He said he'll give them a quick checkup and make sure they're okay for adoption." She scooped up the black kitten she called Mack. "We're gonna find them all good homes, aren't we?"

The kitten extended a paw and placed it on her nose, mewing. She buried her face into his belly fur. Her eyes grew moist. Chris's heart ached.

"Tiffany, if you want him—"

"No." She hugged the squirming bundle tight. "I wish I could, but I can't. Really." Resolved, she put the animal back into the box. Mack peered over the top, watching her with bright, hopeful blue eyes.

Chris didn't know why he felt so betrayed. It wasn't as if she were abandoning him by the roadside.

"Listen," he said, drawing her away and returning to his purpose, "I have something to ask you. You got a minute?"

They went out of the barn into the pale sunshine. A hazy layer of cloud was drifting in, and darker clouds hovered on the horizon. "I know this is short notice, but are you free next weekend?"

She jammed her hands on her hips and kicked at the gravel. "As free as I am every weekend. With Daniel gone, it's kind of impossible to get away from the diner."

He decided to ask anyway. "Remember I told you John Abrams is getting married in Las Vegas? That's this Saturday. I know it's late notice, but I was wondering if you wanted to come. I was going to bring Simon, but he hasn't been keen about going. So, I have a plus one that needs filling, and I hoped you'd be it."

He hadn't expected her eyebrows to knit together like that. Had he said something wrong?

"I'd have to check with my parents…you know." She toed the ground. "Also, money's a little tight. Daniel helped me pay for my car, and I want to pay him back as quick as possible, just in case he needs the funds. I'll have to see if I can pull some cash together. Can I get back to you?"

"Sure." He'd pay for her plane ticket if that was the issue. He probably should have said that to start, but he didn't want to sound desperate.

He wasn't. It was simply an offer—a nice getaway for them both after everything that had happened, and a reward for surviving a summer of tutoring his son. They both deserved the break and…well, he thought it would be nice to show her he could get away now and again. He wasn't a workaholic.

But then, maybe she was.

A WEDDING IN *VEGAS*. The words circled her brain as she ate dinner, her grandmother's cooking sticking in her throat.

It wasn't as if Chris had asked *her* to get hitched in a quickie Elvis-chapel wedding, so why was she sweating bullets over the idea of going away with him?

Because you know it's not right. Not when you have other things you should be focusing on.

That must be it. Handling things at the diner should be a priority. She owed it to Daniel to make sure things went smoothly. After all, she'd been instrumental in her brother's breakup with Selena, which had led to his departure. She had to deal with the consequences of her actions.

Yeah, right, because you've felt so responsible for what's happened here in the past.

A lump formed in her gut. She'd avoided her family, disassociated herself from them as much as she could since she'd

left home. She was only taking responsibility now because…
well, because.

That she was using her family as an excuse not to go to
this wedding with Chris made her feel like a heel. A weekend away with him should have been a dream, but the idea
unnerved her. Going out as a couple to a big public event like
a wedding put expectations on her, made it look to everyone
else as if they were together for the long haul. And she wasn't
good in big social gatherings. Inevitably, people would try
to make conversation, ask how she and Chris had met, how
long they'd been together, what their future plans were. And
then they'd force her to try to catch the bouquet, which was
the stupidest and most excruciating of wedding traditions in
her opinion. Not everyone wanted to get married. And she
knew if she hung out at the back of the crowd of single ladies, Chris would be hurt.

She dutifully finished her bowl of rice. There was no reason for her to go all the way to Vegas for this event. She really
couldn't afford the trip, or a gift for the happy couple. Chris's
friend barely even knew her, and wasn't it kind of rude to
invite her last minute? Besides, flying to Vegas and staying
in an oasis city would make her carbon footprint look like a
Sasquatch's. Surely Chris could appreciate that?

Not that she could tell Chris any of these reasons. He would
insist on paying her way, which she couldn't allow. He would
tell her his friend didn't care. And he'd probably go vegetarian
for a year to offset the environmental impact. She was inexplicably terrified he'd offer to do any of that for her.

She cleaned up and gave her grandmother a hug. *Poh-poh*
exclaimed, "What is this for? What's wrong?"

"Nothing's wrong. Thank you for cooking for me. Your
food is the best."

She waved her hand. "This is nothing. It's easy to make.
Not like what they make at the fancy restaurants."

"I missed your food when I was away," Tiffany told her sincerely.

Sunny turned her gaze up to her, smiling and shaking her head. *"Moh gum hac hay." No need to be so polite.* "There wasn't enough salt in the greens and I overcooked the beef."

Tiff smiled wryly. It was something she would never get used to, her family's way of not saying "thank you" or "you're welcome" to each other. "Still, I appreciate it."

"You want to say thank you, you come home and see me more," *Poh-poh* said primly. "I know you don't eat well enough on your own."

"But I'm learning so much from you now," she said, and it was true. Helping with meal preparations had reminded her of all the tasty things her grandmother had cooked for her as a child. When she moved back to the city, she was going to have a whole new culinary repertoire to work with. Impulsively, she gave Sunny another hug. *Poh-poh* shook her off and told her to stop crushing her old bones.

As Tiffany cleaned up in the kitchen, her mother walked in and handed her a slip of paper. "I found this by the phone. *Poh-poh* must have forgotten to mention you got a call."

On the piece of paper was a name, a phone number and the words *Hot Dog Books.* She puzzled over the message until her heart leaped into her throat. *Poh-poh* must have misheard the name Haute Docs Books, a small publishing house that had made its mark in the world by printing one of the most popular young adult series that year.

She thanked her mother and hurried to her room. Haute Docs Books was in Jersey City, and she'd applied for an editorial assistant's position at the start of the job hunt. It was one of the positions at the top of her list.

It was past seven-thirty. She decided to call so that Caitlyn Beauchamp, the senior editor, would get her message first thing in the morning.

She was surprised when a woman picked up, croaking, "Caitlyn speaking."

Her stomach pitched. "Hello, Ms. Beauchamp? This is Tiffany Cheung. You contacted me about the E.A. position. I'm sorry for calling so late. I just got your message now."

"Oh, not to worry. I was probably going to be here another two hours anyhow. It's been so busy, these twelve-hour days are starting to become a regular thing." She gave a short, nervous laugh. "I hope that doesn't scare you off."

"I'm not afraid of a little hard work," she replied stoutly.

Caitlyn's laughter rose an octave. "That's good to hear, 'cause there's nothing but hard work to be done. Listen, I read over your résumé and I was hoping you'd come in for an interview."

Tiffany shot to her feet. "Yes, absolutely."

"There's only one problem. I was wondering if you could come this weekend. I know it's short notice, but there's so much to do and I can hardly fit in time for these interviews during the week. I wouldn't be surprised if I had to sleep here in my office to get it all done." This time, her laughter sounded nearly hysterical. Tiffany laughed along with her anyhow. "So, if you're available…"

"Yes, absolutely, I can make it to New Jersey, no problem."

They set up an appointment, and when Tiff hung up, she danced on the spot and squealed.

Relax, she told herself sternly, *you don't have the job yet.*

But she would get it, dammit. New Jersey wasn't exactly where she'd pictured she'd end up, but it was a job in the field she'd trained for, and it would put her back on the road to success. Haute Docs was going to grow fast, and she was determined to grow with it.

Tiffany upended the garbage bags of unpacked clothing in search of her good work clothes. She needed to get them cleaned and pressed right away. When she unearthed a bunch of pretty evening dresses, she remembered with a pang Chris's invitation to Las Vegas. She couldn't say no to the opportunity at Haute Docs. She'd have to turn him down.

Was it wrong to feel relief and guilt at the same time?

She picked up the phone.

"Chris," she greeted, a lump rolling heavily around her stomach. "Listen…I'm sorry, I can't make it for the weekend…."

"Of course," he said quickly. "I should have asked earlier. I know your parents need you."

She held her tongue. There was no point in telling Chris about the interview. She might not get the position, after all. It would be senseless to prepare him for something that might not even happen. "Summer is a busy time for the diner," she said. The lump in her gut got heftier. "But you'll tell John congratulations?"

"Of course. I'll get to see you before I leave Saturday morning, though, right?"

"Sure." She decided to keep her mouth shut about the interview for now. She didn't want him brooding over it while he was in Vegas. He deserved to have worry-free fun.

Besides, he knew she'd never intended to stay, and they hadn't talked about a future beyond the end of summer.

Why should she spoil what time they had left together? He would understand. In fact, he should be happy for her.

CHRIS LUGGED HIS SUITCASE down the stairs, a little less enthusiastic about his upcoming weekend in Vegas since Tiffany had told him she had obligations at the diner. A getaway was exactly what he needed, but it wouldn't be nearly as fun without her.

Simon was having breakfast at the dining-room table, reading George Orwell's *1984*—a gift from Tiffany. Clover sat by his feet, watching his cereal bowl slowly empty. "You sure you don't want to come?" he asked his son. "Last chance to see the Strip until you turn twenty-one."

Simon looked up at him flatly. "No offense, Dad, but I'd rather stick pins in my eyes."

Chris chuckled. He didn't want to admit that he was kind of dreading being alone at this event. Ever since his divorce, his buddies had been trying to set him up with a series of comely female acquaintances. In the same way that a teenage son would have held the marriage hounds at bay, Tiffany would have been a good shield to hide behind. But she was more than that. Much more.

"Too bad Tiff couldn't go with you." Simon reached down and scratched the kitten's chin.

"She's working at her parents' while her brother's out of town. It couldn't be helped."

"Maybe I should go down to the diner and see if Mrs. Cheung wants to try me out for a few days."

"That's a good idea. Tiff will be there, so she can help train you." Chris had consented to Simon taking on a job as long as it didn't interfere with his studies and he could get to and from work safely. He'd work no more than ten hours a week. He'd talked with the Cheungs about it, as well. Tony was open to the idea, but stressed he couldn't pay more than minimum wage plus free meals. Rose had reassured him they would train him properly, too. They actually sounded quite excited about it.

Chris also made it clear to Simon that if the Cheungs' fighting made him uncomfortable, he had his permission to quit at any time. This part-time job was about learning and earning a little side money, not committing himself to a toxic environment.

Simon grinned. "I'll give Cindy a call and see when she can bring me down."

"All right." He gave him a hug and slapped him on the

back. "Take care of Grandpa while I'm away. Don't let him feed you too much junk food. He shouldn't be eating so much salt and fat."

"I'm not a child," William barked from the kitchen.

Chris went to the kitchen doorway. "Are you going to be okay for a few days?"

He glared. "In my day, we didn't leave the farm during the busiest time of year."

"I'm not missing John's wedding, Dad."

His father dismissed him with a wave. "Go on, then. Abandon your responsibilities and have a grand old time in Vegas. You're not leaving anything important behind."

But in fact, he was leaving something important behind. Tiffany had chosen to help her parents with their business over spending time with him. This was a good thing, he told himself staunchly. Maybe she was finally finding her place here and changing her mind about Everville. She might even find a reason to stay.

"You packed water, right?"

"Yes, Mom."

"And a blanket? Flares? A road map?"

"Mom, I'm only driving to New Jersey."

"But you'll stop at least once for a break, right? You can't stay on the road if you're sleepy, you know."

Tiffany summoned her patience. It was because Daniel was gone that Rose hovered. "I'll be fine."

"You probably thought that on your way driving here, and look how that turned out." She shook her head. "Why couldn't you take the bus instead?"

"Mom. I have to go now or I'm going to be late for the interview."

"Right. Of course." She looked her over, frowned. "You're not going to wear *that* to your interview, are you?"

"Ah-Teen—" Poh-poh scurried after her and handed her a plastic bag *"—cha siu bow."*

Tiffany opened up the bag. A cloud of steam rose from the fresh barbecue pork buns within. "I thought you gave Daniel the last ones?"

Sunny made a noise that was half tsk, half snort. "Of course I saved some for you. *Ah-Day* looked like he needed to feel special, though, so I lied."

She laughed and bussed her grandmother's cheek and got in the car. She dropped her mother off at the diner. Her father had gone in earlier to do some prep work.

"Are you sure you don't want to pop in and say hello to Dad?" Rose asked as Tiffany pulled up to the curb.

"Nah. Just tell him hi for me. I don't want him to feel like both his kids are abandoning him." She knew how petulant her father could be. "I'll be back by dinnertime." Part of her thought this would be a good opportunity to hang out in the city, eat at her favorite restaurant and enjoy the nightlife. But she couldn't afford to stay overnight, and she didn't want to drive home in the dark.

Her mother wished her good luck and shut the door. She settled herself, readjusted her mirrors and put on a nice long driving playlist on her iPod. "Magic Carpet Ride" came on, energizing her. She turned on her signal, checked her mirrors and started pulling away from the curb.

And nearly plowed straight into Simon as he crossed the street.

She jammed on the brakes and was thrown hard against her seat belt. He'd frozen midstep, and stared back at her wide-eyed. Her heart pumped hard. She started to lift her hand in a wave, but then realized she'd told the Jamiesons she'd be working.

He smiled tentatively and made some motions with his hands that clearly asked, "What's up?"

Tiffany didn't have a response. All the neurons in her brain were firing blanks.

Putting the car in gear once more, she pulled around him in a wide arc and sped toward New Jersey.

CHAPTER NINETEEN

TIFFANY DIDN'T COME HOME in time for dinner. In fact, she didn't come home until nearly eleven, after her mother and grandmother had been whipped into a frenzy.

"Why didn't you call?" her mother demanded as she dropped her purse on the sofa. "*Poh-poh* was scared you were in another car accident."

Tiffany settled her hands over her grandmother's shoulders. "I'm sorry, Grandma. I'm okay. Really." She couldn't hide her smile any longer and took her mother's hand. "I got the job."

Sunny and Rose cheered and clapped their hands. They looked genuinely happy for her, and real pride swelled in Tiffany. She'd half expected they'd accuse her of abandoning the family. But they didn't. Instead, they settled her at the kitchen table, pulling out all the dinner leftovers from the fridge and insisting she eat and tell them about the new position.

She would start next week. Caitlyn wanted her in as soon as possible, and was so enthusiastic about having her work there that she'd gone ahead and arranged a few showings for apartments in the area with friends' properties. Tiffany couldn't say no to such an accommodating boss, so she'd happily gone on a whirlwind apartment hunt. That was why she'd been so late getting home.

It wasn't until close to midnight that she had a moment to think about Chris. Now wasn't the best time to be telling him her news. He was probably still at the wedding reception, dancing with a bridesmaid and taking advantage of the open bar. Or cruising along the Strip in a limo. Or winning big money at a high-stakes poker game at the Bellagio, all while wearing a tuxedo and flashing fancy silver cuff links.

She smiled at the thought, because she could hardly imagine Chris doing any of those things. When she pictured him, it was always in jeans and a T-shirt, boots caked with dirt, sweat on his brow and bits of grass caught in the dark gold stubble on his dimpled chin. She tried to imagine him rumbling away on his old motorcycle, but it didn't seem to fit with his persona anymore. The boy she'd crushed on had grown into a man she was falling for....

A full-body shudder rippled through her like an earthquake. She wasn't falling for him. She'd had a crush, sure, and sex with him had been phenomenal. But she wouldn't say she was in the *L* word with him. The *L* word required an ability to see a future together. And she didn't. She was heading to New Jersey and her dream of becoming an editor at a big publishing house.

But first, she'd have to tell Chris.

A sour taste filled her mouth and her heart palpitated. She sat down hard. Maybe she was getting sick.

A glance at the clock, and she decided she could wait to tell him her news. He'd be back tomorrow afternoon. He'd be jet-lagged, but it was better she tell him sooner rather than later. She'd have to break the news to Simon, too. Another doubt smacked her between the eyes: How was he going to cope through the rest of school?

You don't need to worry about him. He'll be fine. He's responsible for himself.

Of course he was, the same way Chris was responsible for his own well-being and she was responsible for hers. She hadn't promised Simon anything, either.

Not that that made her feel better.

She drove to the farm the following afternoon. Chris's flight was scheduled to arrive at the airport at 2:30 p.m. Tiffany wanted to be there when he came home.

William was sitting stiffly on the porch in an old ladder-back chair. It didn't look comfortable. His palms were planted on his upper thighs, and he watched her with a cold expression.

"Hello, Mr. Jamieson," she greeted. He nodded in response, unsmiling. She waited for him to invite her in or tell her where Chris or Simon was, but he simply sat there. "Is Chris home yet?"

"No."

"Oh." She looked at her watch. "How about Simon? Is he around?"

The old man inclined his chin and nodded toward the barn. "You'll find him in there."

"Thanks." She hesitated, wondering if she should ask if everything was okay. He was probably just feeling grouchy. The weather had been somewhat oppressive lately, gray and wet with a leaden sky.

Simon was cleaning the horse stalls. He had his earbuds in and his MP3 player blared some loud hip-hop beats. She approached and called his name, but he didn't respond. She touched his shoulder and he turned. Hurt and betrayal clouded his features and his eyes became two hard stones.

"How's it going?" she asked brightly. He lifted a lip in a sneer and turned back to his work without acknowledging her. An uneasy feeling settled in her chest. "Simon? What's wrong? Did you get your summer school marks?"

He still didn't respond. Her stomach pitched. Oh, no. He'd failed. No, *she'd* failed him. She hadn't adequately prepared him for the essay portion of the exam, had she? She'd seen he had some difficulty expressing himself on paper. Why hadn't she worked on that more?

"The exam?" she asked tentatively, dread dragging her spirits to the ground.

A pitchfork full of manure scattered across her sandaled feet and she squeaked. "Hey!" She shook off her toes.

"I got an A-minus on the exam," he blurted. "I passed the course with a B-plus."

"Simon, that's fantastic. Congratulations." The clenching of her stomach eased. *Thank God.*

But still he would not look at her. Another steaming pile nearly landed on her toes.

"Simon, what is it? What's your problem?"

"*My* problem? What's *your* problem?" He finished with the stall and went to wheel the full barrow out.

Part of her wanted to believe he was mad at her for almost running him over, but she had the sickening feeling it was something much worse than that. Before she could explain why she hadn't been at the restaurant yesterday, he'd disappeared around the corner, obviously in no mood to talk.

She walked back toward the house. William was still on the porch, and as she approached, he gave her a long, steady look. "What's going on with Simon?" she asked.

"Not talking to you, is he?" He said it matter-of-factly, and his tone grated.

"Is it something I did?"

"What do you think?" He picked up his crutches and eased out of the chair, hobbling inside slowly.

She followed him into the kitchen, guilt and anxiety making her fidget. "I'm guessing he's mad about something I did—"

He whipped around, eyes blazing. "What are your intentions with my son, Miss Cheung?"

Her throat closed. "My intentions?"

"You told Chris you couldn't attend that wedding in Vegas with him because you were helping your parents at the diner.

Then my grandson spots you hotfooting it out of town and finds out you were driving to New Jersey for the weekend. Do you have any explanation for that?"

Dammit. She should have explained herself from the start. "I was going to a job interview."

"I know. Your parents told him. So, let me ask you, why are you involving yourself with my family if all you intend to do is leave?"

"What are you talking about? I never said anything to make them think—"

"You told Simon you'd help him find an internship. You promised you'd be here for him." His eyes burned with cold fire. "How could you do that to him? Don't you know what his mother's like?"

With a sinking feeling, she realized he was right. She'd made promises she couldn't keep. She'd told Simon she'd help him figure out his future. She'd told him he had a lot of time. But *she* didn't. Not enough to be there for him the way he needed her to be.

The contempt in the old man's hard expression made her feel lower than dirt. "I've had to endure a lot of grief since Daphne left," William said, locking his hands together. "I carried this family through some of the toughest times we've had to face. I raised Chris on my own after his mama died, and then I raised Simon while Chris dealt with his divorce." His glare nearly sliced her in half. "We don't need another woman drifting in and out of our lives. My son and grandson have been stomped on plenty enough. I don't need to be picking up the pieces after you leave and break their hearts."

Her stomach clenched. "I swear, it's not like that—"

"Don't you dare lie to me." His face reddened. "You always planned on leaving. I knew the moment I set eyes on you that you thought you were better than us, better than your family and far too good for Everville. You're a selfish girl, and you don't know anything about commitment or love." He shook his head. "I thought it was in your culture to be cruel. But I see it now. It's *you*."

William's proclamation knocked the breath out of her. Tears built in her throat, the pain of the truth nearly choking her.

He wasn't done yet. "I've seen you with Chris and Simon. Playing at something you're not, pretending you care. But you don't give a damn. They're only a means to an end." His face was purple now, and spittle flew from his mouth. "You don't think about how you make them feel, how you change things around here. But I see it every day you come. The way Simon tries to hide how much he wants to please you. And Chris...all you've done is make him happy and give him hope. Well, what's going to happen when you leave? How do you think he'll feel when you tell him he's not good enough to keep you?" His anguish showed clearly on his face. "You're a heartless bitch. I pity any man who wants to be with you."

"What's going on here?"

Chris stood in the doorway, his suitcase on the ground. His hair was mussed and dark circles hung beneath his eyes. The floor beneath her wobbled. She took a tentative step forward, but stopped herself. She wanted to throw her arms around him and hold him back, explain it all, get him away from this crucible of anger. But she could see the flexing of his hands and knew from the darkening of his features that he'd heard everything.

He strode in front of his father, placing Tiff behind him. "I can't leave here for a day without you pulling some kind of garbage, can I?"

Oh, no. He must not have heard everything. "Chris, please, it's all right." Tears blurred her voice, and she struggled to clear them from her throat. "Let me explain—"

"No. It's not all right. It was never all right. You don't deserve to be treated like this." He cupped her cheek tenderly.

The fire burning in his red-rimmed blue eyes made her want to cry.

He whipped back around to face William and stabbed a finger into his chest.

"You don't say those things to Tiffany. Ever. You don't say those things to anyone. You don't get to judge her, or me, or Simon or anyone else, do you hear?"

William slapped his hand aside. "How dare you. Don't you point and accuse me. You have no idea—"

"Shut up. I'm sick of hearing you talk and making excuses and telling me about the way things were. Wake up, Dad. Things change. The world changes. And you've been so stubborn about how they should be that you can't see how they could be." He half turned toward Tiffany. "I love this woman. I don't care what you think about that."

Tiffany gasped. *Love her?* No, no, Chris couldn't love her. She covered her mouth, sick to her stomach.

"You're a damned fool," William rasped harshly. "She won't make you happy. She won't do anything but leave your sorry ass."

Chris lost it. He grabbed his father by the shoulders and shoved him against the wall. His crutches clattered to the ground. Tiffany screamed.

William's face flushed dark red, then purple, then drained of all color. He was sweating profusely, and he made a grunting noise.

"Chris, stop!" Tiffany hauled on his steel-cable arm. "Something's wrong."

He let go, and the old man slumped to the floor, clutching his chest, breathing heavily, his eyes going distant with pain.

Chris's hands trembled as he fell to his knees next to his father. "Call 9-1-1."

THEY KEPT WILLIAM COMFORTABLE until the paramedics arrived. He was still awake and breathing as they strapped him into the gurney, but he clutched his chest and moaned in pain. Chris rode in the ambulance with his father. Tiffany followed with Simon in her car.

The teen didn't say anything as he glared out the passenger-side window. She could smell the acrid fear coming off him, but she didn't try to placate him with meaningless words or platitudes. And she didn't think it was appropriate to try to explain herself while William could be dying.

She had too much on her mind to form a coherent thought anyhow. Chris's declaration had sideswiped her. How could he possibly love her? Why did he have to tell her before she'd had a chance to give them both the out they needed? Then she thought about what William had said and realized he was right—she was cold and selfish. She was more worried about telling Chris about her new job than she was about William's health.

When they arrived at the E.R., the nurse informed them William was being taken into surgery. Chris was with his father now as he was being prepped. The nurse let Simon in to see him, but because Tiffany wasn't family, she had to stay in the waiting room.

She perched on a chair, hands clutched in her lap. It was almost two hours before Chris and Simon reappeared, both of them looking weary.

She stood shakily. Chris went straight to her, and though he engulfed her in his arms, she realized he was seeking comfort more than offering it. The smell of stale sweat and antiseptic soap wafted from his skin. Delicately, she wrapped her arms around his waist. Simon glared at her over his father's shoulder.

"My father had a heart attack," Chris told her bleakly. "They said it's pretty bad. He's going to need a double bypass. Surgery's going to take a while." His voice sounded distant and hollow. "This is all my fault."

"No, it's not." She gripped his forearms. "He had high blood pressure and other health problems. You didn't cause this."

He shook his head, not believing her. If anyone was to blame for all this, it was Tiffany. She'd been the one William was yelling at before Chris had stepped in.

"Do you want me to drive you back to the farm?" she asked. "You could get a shower, a change of clothes."

"No. I want to stay in case—" He cut himself off. "Simon should go back, though. He could grab a book or something."

The teen turned his full glare on Tiffany. "I'm not going anywhere with *her*." He stormed off.

"Simon—" Before he could even ask, his son had disappeared out the E.R. doors. "What is going on around here?" Chris forked both hands through his hair. His knees gave out as he dropped into a chair, exhausted, as though he'd aged ten years in the past few hours.

It was time to fess up. She hated that she had to do it now, but it wouldn't be any better after William was out of surgery.

"I have something to tell you," she began unsteadily. She sat next to him and tried for a smile to soften the blow. "I got a job."

It took him a moment to process that. "That's great. Where?"

"In New Jersey. I'm starting next Monday."

She didn't think he could go paler. He glanced away from her, then around, searching for answers. "Quite a time to be springing this on me," he murmured lowly.

"I'm sorry." All she wanted to do was put her arms around him and never let go. But she didn't. "There's something else I have to tell you. I wasn't working at my parents' diner yesterday. I was in New Jersey doing the interview. That's the real reason I couldn't go to the wedding with you. The editor at Haute Docs Books called me the day before. I didn't have a choice." She swallowed thickly. "That was why your dad was yelling at me. Simon found out before I had a chance to explain."

He stared at her, then hung his head. The silence was worse than his anger.

She forced herself to go on. She didn't want him to take the blame for anything—not his son's outburst, not William's heart attack. It was probably selfish of her to think of this as her final gift to him. But it was all she had to offer. "Simon saw me when I was heading out. My parents told him where I was going. That's why he and your dad are mad at me. I lied to all of you, and I'm sorry."

He sat unmoving, unblinking. She waited for him to acknowledge her. "Chris?"

"Why didn't you tell me the truth to start with?" he asked quietly. His glassy gaze slowly traveled up to her face. He looked at her as though she were a stranger. "Why didn't you say you were going to a job interview?"

"I wasn't sure I was going to get the job. I didn't think it would matter to you."

"Of course it matters to me. *You* matter to me. And I want to be in on the loop when you make life-changing decisions." He blew out a long breath, rubbed his palms over his face.

"I'm sorry." She would never be able to say it enough. His disappointment was clear. This was almost as bad as the moment she'd told her parents she'd won a scholarship to NYU and was majoring in English. At least then she'd felt justified and righteous in her decision. Right now, she felt like crap. "I didn't want to spoil the time we have left."

"What time?" he demanded, voice rising. People glanced over. More quietly, he said, "If you're starting work on Monday, that's barely a week. And instead of telling me so I could figure out something… A way for us…" He shook his head, pressed a fist against his mouth as his eyes went distant.

"No. Never mind. You told me at the very start you would leave." All emotion drained from him. He turned his ice-blue eyes on her. "That's why you kept your distance. That's why you didn't think to share even this little piece of your life with me. I should've known better." His voice hitched and he clenched his jaw, meeting her gaze unflinchingly. "Look, my dad might be dying. I have too much to deal with right now to have to handle you on top of it, so could you just…leave?"

That last word punched her in the chest. "You don't have your car here. You—"

"I'll call Jane. Go. Live your life, or whatever it is you think you're doing. Just do me a favor and stay out of mine from now on."

She rose, light-headed and off balance. She wanted to say something to make Chris feel better. But he'd turned to stone in his chair, staring straight ahead, pain digging deep trenches in his brow and around his eyes and mouth. Hesitantly, she started for the door. When he didn't stop her, she turned away and didn't look back. She refused to acknowledge the jagged emotion clawing in her chest, ignored the hot sting in the back of her throat.

Outside, the air-conditioned chill slid off her skin as she readjusted to the summer heat and fading sun. She smelled a summer storm brewing. A migraine drummed lightly on her temples.

A different sensation filled her when she spotted Simon sitting on the walkway with his back against the brick wall, hugging his knees.

She padded up to him. "Simon?"

He hastily wiped at his wet cheeks. "What do you want?"

That question was getting harder to answer by the minute. "Will you give me a chance to explain?"

"Explain what? That you're going to leave? I don't care."

It hurt more than she thought it would to hear him say that. "I have a life to get back to. A career—"

"I already have a mom who screws around with me. I don't need you to play house with us, too."

She didn't think she could have handled another blow, but there it was, and she staggered. "I'm sorry." She could say it a thousand times, but she doubted her apology would sound any less pathetic or make her feel any better.

Simon shook his head and let out a long breath through his nose. For a hopeful moment, she thought he'd forgive her. "If you leave…don't come back. I can take it, but Dad's not that strong. Don't call him. Don't email him. If you're going to visit your family, fine. But I'll know, and I'll make sure you don't go near my father, you hear me?"

The lump in her throat stuck as she acknowledged unhappily, "Loud and clear."

She turned, made her way to her car, got in and started the engine. Every muscle and joint in her body was stiff. A weight settled in her chest as she pulled onto the long, deserted road back to her parents' house.

The sky opened. It started to rain.

CHAPTER TWENTY

Four weeks later
New Jersey

"'It was a dark and stormy night....'" Tiff read aloud in her most ominous voice.

"Holy crap, people actually write like that?" Maya laughed.

"This isn't even the worst of them," Tiffany said as she put the manuscript back onto the reject pile and rubbed her aching eyes. "I need to talk to the boss about putting some restrictions on these submissions. They won't stop pouring in."

"Admit it. You love it."

Tiffany didn't say anything at first. The work had been nonstop since she'd arrived at Haute Docs. At first she'd wanted to write personalized letters back to every author, but there simply wasn't time. No matter how quickly or efficiently she worked, she couldn't dig out from under the massive piles of unsolicited manuscripts. She didn't want to admit she was nearing burnout only three weeks into the job, though, so all she said was, "Yeah."

Maya picked up her momentary hesitation. "Hey, if nothing else, you have somewhere to wear your nice business clothes."

"I still can't believe you didn't tell me." She glanced at the big paper shopping bag sitting in the corner of the room.

"Hey, my clients have a right to privacy. I can't run around telling everyone who bought what."

"Yeah, but this is my dad we're talking about."

Her father had helped her move out. Before he'd left, he'd presented her with a gift. "Your mom told me how happy you were to get this job. I'm glad you're working and doing something you want to do. We're proud of you, *Ah-Teen*. So, I bought you some new clothes for your new job. I got a great deal for them, too." He'd grinned impishly. "Just don't tell your mother."

She'd been speechless as she drew out every piece of clothing she'd sold at the consignment shop. She wasn't sure if her dad had known they'd originally belonged to her. That twinkle in his eyes was hard to decipher. She didn't ask as she hugged him tight. "You have no idea what this means to me."

"Bah." He waved her off and said, "I'm your father," as if it explained everything. And in a weird way, it did.

Outside, someone leaned on a car horn. It was nearly ten at night, and she made a noise of frustration.

"Ah, the sounds of the city." Maya snickered. Tiffany cradled the handset between her neck and shoulder as she pulled the window down, leaving it cracked an inch. The mild breeze was the only thing keeping her from cooking alive indoors. Freakin' global climate change, she muttered to herself. Mid-September and it was still in the high eighties. "I gotta say, I don't miss the noise one bit. Never had a better sleep than I have in Everville," Maya added a touch smugly.

"Jersey has its charms," Tiffany insisted, then wrinkled her nose at the stench of garbage from the Dumpster below. She closed the window the rest of the way. Despite the sounds and smells and lack of air-conditioning, she couldn't complain. The beautiful old apartment was only a few blocks from the Haute Docs offices, and it was three times the size of her old apartment in Manhattan.

"Well, if nothing else, I'll have someone I can stay with when I go on purchasing expeditions?" Her voice rose in a question, and Tiffany chuckled.

"The couch is yours anytime you like." She surprised herself by how easily she'd issued the invitation. The old Tiffany would have felt manipulated, but Maya had been a good friend these past few weeks. She hadn't been nosy and asked about what'd happened between her and Chris, though Tiffany was certain rumors must have been going around town since her departure. Instead, they talked about books, movies, music and girl stuff. They had a surprising amount in common, and had already planned to get together in the city for a weekend. Talking with Maya over the phone kept the loneliness at bay.

Tiffany glanced over at the stack of manuscripts haunting her coffee table and grimaced. "Listen, it's getting late, and I should finish this reading before I go to bed."

"Such a hard worker," Maya admonished. "All work and no play…"

"Makes Tiffany a better editor," she quipped dryly. "I'll call you tomorrow with more chilling tales from the slush pile."

"Can't wait."

They hung up, and the evening's levity fizzled. She faced the sterile, empty apartment and sighed into the silence. Everything inside her rebelled at the thought of doing any more work today.

She abandoned her duties and turned on the TV to a rerun of *Frasier*. The crotchety old dad, Martin Crane, reminded her of William Jamieson. She wondered how he was doing after the surgery. Rose had told her he'd been released from the hospital about two weeks after his heart attack. Simon had been working part-time at the diner and seemed to be doing well there, too. She wondered if he was having any troubles with his classes. It couldn't be easy working and doing school on top of taking care of his grandfather. She couldn't begin to imagine what Chris was going through.

Her heart squeezed. She wondered how he was holding up, whether he was still mad at her. She'd been so stupid to lie to all of them. The weight in her chest grew as she mentally recited all the accusations the Jamiesons had leveled at her.

Moh gwai young.

She was heading for a shower when someone knocked. Wondering who would be calling on her this late, she peered through the peephole and squeaked in surprise.

Tiffany quickly unlatched the door chain. "What are you doing here?" She threw her arms around her brother. Sudden tears sprang to her eyes. He smelled a little stale, and his stubble scraped her cheek, but he was solid and alive. "Where have you been? How did you know I lived here?"

"Mom told me. I'm sorry. I should have called before I came."

She ushered him in. She'd never been so glad to see Daniel. She cleared the couch for him, then fussed as she made him a cup of jasmine tea and put together a plate of dinner leftovers.

"This is pretty good," he said, shoveling the fried rice, beef and broccoli into his mouth. She wondered when his last meal had been—he looked thinner. "Takeout?"

"I cooked it," she said proudly. "There's an Asian grocery a couple of blocks from here. I even got ingredients for one of *Poh-poh's* soups, but I haven't mustered up the courage to try making it yet."

"What's to make? You throw the stuff in boiling water and it's soup."

"Well, I've been thinking about writing a blog about it. You know, doing the *Julie & Julia* thing."

He grinned. "Go for it. Maybe someone will want to turn it into a book."

She looked him over, noting the dark shadows under his eyes against his pale complexion. "I don't see a tan, so I'm guessing you didn't make it to Florida. Where have you been?"

"Here and there." He wiped his mouth and set the plate

down. "I drove along the coast mostly. Visited a couple of friends in Boston. Nearly made it to the Canadian border, but decided to turn around."

"What happened to Key West?"

"I couldn't go that far," he said quietly, staring at his hands.

"Selena?"

He nodded, unable to meet her eyes. "I tried to get away. I really did. But I kept driving back to New York. I'd trap myself in traffic just for an excuse to hang around. I was getting seriously stalker-y." He rubbed at the hollows beneath his eyes. "I passed through her neighborhood and drove by her office three times, thinking I should try talking to her. But I couldn't."

Pity wasn't something she thought he'd appreciate, but he sounded so forlorn all she wanted to do was hug him. "Are you heading home?" she asked instead.

"I'm not sure." His gaze was fixed on a spot on the floor between his feet. "How can I go back? You were right about me. No woman's ever going to want a man who lives with and works for his parents." He rubbed his temples. "I've wasted my life."

Tiffany felt a spurt of outrage. "Hey, you're a catch, okay? Any woman would be lucky to have you."

"You're just saying that because you're my sister." His words were muffled by his hands.

"No, as your sister, I'm obligated to make fun of you and push your self-confidence into the mud. Unfortunately, I did my job too well." She rubbed at her aching head, shame sweeping through her. "Look, you love Selena, don't you?"

Slowly, he nodded.

"Then nothing else matters. Not what she does or what you do or who you live with or any of those things I said. When have you ever listened to me, anyhow? Have I ever said a smart thing to you in all my life?"

His brow wrinkled in confusion. Tiff hated that she'd been so hard on him.

"Look, when I said all that stuff about you and Selena not being suited or whatever, I was being a petty bitch. I was jealous you had someone in your life." Feeling lighter as the sour admission left her lips, she pushed on. "Forget everything I said about what Mom and Dad will think. All that matters is how you feel for each other."

"I'm not sure she'll take me back after all this."

"At least give her a chance to tell you that herself. If it's really over like you think it is, what's the worst she can say?"

"How about 'you're a worthless human being and I never should have dated you and you smell funny and I hate the way you dress'?"

"Okay, what *else* could she possibly say?"

He smiled crookedly. "Does this spurt of relationship wisdom mean you've worked things out with Chris?"

The ache in her chest returned twofold. "It's more like he worked me out of things." Haltingly, she told him what had transpired, trying hard to keep the tears out of her voice.

Daniel sighed. "Man, what a pair we are. Sorry about Chris. I know how much you lov— Liked him."

She didn't miss his slip. "It's for the best."

"'For the best'?"

"Well, of course. I'm finally where I should be. Chris has his life, I have mine." She gestured vaguely around her with a tight smile. "I'm doing work I love, work I was trained to do. And look at this apartment—I'd have to pay through the nose for a place this size in Manhattan. I'd say I'm doing pretty well."

Daniel's sage look bordered on pity. "There's more to life than having a dream job and a nice apartment. What about a husband? A family? All that domestic stuff?"

She collected his empty plate and made herself busy re-

BACK TO THE GOOD FORTUNE DINER

filling his tea and washing up. "That's not for everyone. I certainly never wanted any of that. I'm not a people person. Marriage and the white picket fence aren't for me. Besides, I could never have anything with Chris." That bone-deep ache expanded painfully until she thought she couldn't breathe.

"Why not?"

"Because..." Because it wouldn't work. This was where she belonged. Lamely, she went on, "He's already divorced."

Her brother arched an eyebrow. "So? Lots of people get married a second time."

She struggled for a logical, straightforward explanation, but her feelings mixed themselves up with the facts and the cold hard truth. "There's baggage. I abused his trust. I made promises to Simon I couldn't keep, and to him, that's unforgivable."

Daniel rubbed his jaw. "Chris isn't like that—"

"He is," she snapped. "He doesn't want to be involved with someone who can't be satisfied with what life has handed him, the way he is. Don't you get it? I want more in my life than a farm. But all he sees is Daphne and the way she's treated Simon. We can't have anything together," she said, voice cracking. "We're too different. We want different things. I can't share my life with him—he'll only drag me down and it'd end horribly." She was getting too close to the raw nerve where her pain lived, but she plowed on, driven by the momentum of her fear and hurt. "Look at Mom and Dad. They've been together more than thirty-four years, and they fight all the time. They've never met eye to eye on anything. All these years, and they still can't work things out. Compare me and Chris to that. We wouldn't stand a chance."

Her brother's eyes rounded. "Are you seriously judging your ability to have a relationship based on *Mom and Dad's* marriage?"

She blinked slowly. Okay, when he said it like that, it sounded like the silliest thing ever. She dropped onto the couch and drew her knees up. "I know I wouldn't be good at it. Having kids probably makes things worse. I'd make a terrible mother and an even worse stepmother. You know I don't…get along with people easily. I'd be a selfish mother. Any kids I had would be screwed up."

"Good God…if I could get Dad to pay for therapy…" Daniel's head hit the back of the couch as he stared at the ceiling. "Just because Mom and Dad's marriage sucks doesn't mean you're going to end up the same way. There are tons of people from stable families who don't know how to have a relationship. We can all suck at it equally with or without our parents' help."

"Thanks. That's cheery, knowing so many of us are doomed to relationship failure."

He gave her a stern look. "You're not selfish. You're focused on surviving. We went through a lot of shit as kids, and you dealt with the situation however you could. Maybe it meant you closed yourself off emotionally from other people, but who's to say being alone isn't what's right for you?"

She pictured a lifetime of quiet solitude in her stuffy apartment. The idea had suited her just fine two months ago, but now, she wanted more, yearned for it. A handful of awkward first dates and impersonal work-related get-togethers did not constitute a social life. She hadn't been able to admit it to herself until now. Work alone was no longer enough to fulfill her. Unfortunately for Tiffany, work was all she had.

Her brother's next words pierced her heart. "However it happened, Chris fell in love with you. It wasn't a mistake and you didn't trick him into it. So now, there's only one question you have to ask yourself. Do you love Chris?"

She stared. She didn't know the answer.

CHAPTER TWENTY-ONE

CHRIS FOUND SIMON IN HIS ROOM, lying on the bed with Clover curled up on his belly. He had a book propped open on his chest, but his eyes were heavy-lidded and glazed.

"*Wuthering Heights,* huh?" Chris noted from the doorway.

Simon let the book fall against his chest and blinked rapidly. "It's. So. *Boring.*"

He laughed. "We'll rent a movie version. I thought you might want to work downstairs at the table. Grandpa's finished watching *Jeopardy!*"

"It's okay." He yawned. "I'm going to finish up these chapters. I'll probably pass out while reading anyways."

A mew from the corner of the room had Chris glancing over to the towel-filled basket where the little black kitten named Mack peered up. He hopped out of the basket and galloped to Chris's feet, rolling over to chew on his big toe. Chris scooped up the troublemaker and rubbed him behind the ears before putting him back down. "Still no takers, huh?"

"No." A guilty look stole across Simon's face. "I asked around at school, but no one wants him."

Chris didn't believe that for a minute. All the other kittens had been snatched up by Labor Day. He didn't blame Simon for wanting to keep him, though. Mack was so full of personality, even Chris had grown attached. "Well, he's good company for Clover, I guess." The little gray cat watched her brother frolic, thoroughly unimpressed as Mack wove around Chris's ankles purring loudly.

"If you have any questions about your homework, you'll let me know, right? We can go looking for the answers on the internet together."

"Sure, Dad." Simon resettled Clover and picked up the book once more.

Mack followed Chris down the stairs. His father sat at the kitchen table, a bunch of papers and folders scattered across the surface and a small collection of pill bottles on top of those. He squinted at the label of one, holding it up to the light.

"Need help?" Chris asked cautiously. When they'd come back from the hospital after the surgery, William had been infuriated by how much his son and grandson hovered around him. But a minor infection had weakened him, and the cocktail of medications he took had some powerful side effects. He could barely get out of his chair without assistance now, and had to rely on them for help with even the simplest tasks.

William shoved the pill bottle at him. "I don't see why they can't print this stuff in bigger letters with clearer instructions. I might as well be reading Chinese."

Chris ignored that little dig and helped him with the pills, taking out the prescribed doses of each and lining them up on the plate in front of his father. Mack hopped onto the table and batted the pill containers around until Will grabbed him by the scruff and put him forcibly in his lap. The kitten curled up and promptly fell asleep.

William grumbled at the rainbow of capsules. "From steaks and burgers to *this*." He took them two at a time, swallowing them with water.

"I'm sure the doctors will take you off these once you've shown improvement." He hoped so anyhow. His father had been so tired since the surgery. "Can I make you some coffee?"

"Can't have that. I have to lower my blood pressure, remember?" He rattled one of the bottles. "I think there's some green tea on the counter there. Sunny sent it to me. Said it would help."

Tiffany's grandmother had spoken to his dad? More shocking was the fact that his father was listening to her. "I didn't realize you knew Sunny." He found the sachets of green tea and brewed a cup.

"She plays mahjong down at the community center sometimes. Taught a bunch of other folks, too. I figured, she looks pretty healthy. And five thousand years of Chinese medicine can't be wrong. Look how many people live there. The medicine's not killing them, that's for sure."

Chris pursed his lips, a reprimand on the tip of his tongue.

His father chuckled. "I'm kidding, I'm kidding. I thought I could make you laugh, but I guess you miss her too much."

Chris made himself busy clearing the kitchen counter. "Miss who?"

"Don't be coy, Christopher." He sipped the tea, his face brightening as he took a second bigger gulp. "Have you talked to her?"

Chris didn't want to talk about Tiffany. Since that awful night in the hospital, he couldn't decide whether he was mad at her for not telling him about the job interview or mad at himself for the way he'd reacted. "I gave her last paycheck to her parents. They'll forward it to her." The paltry sum he'd sent made him feel queasy. Even with a modest bonus, which he'd included because he knew she hadn't been honest on her time sheet, he hadn't felt right paying her when she'd given him so much. He brewed a second cup of tea for himself to settle his roiling stomach.

"Now you're being plain stubborn. I realize things didn't end well, but you and Simon both have to forgive her at some point."

"I've forgiven her." He simply wasn't sure he could ever forget the way she'd treated him. He and Simon both deserved more than to be cast aside, but she'd made it quite clear they didn't fit into her life. That she didn't need their opinion on how to run her affairs.

And she didn't. They were both adults and responsible for themselves. They didn't owe each other anything, despite what they'd shared. She'd never made any promises. In fact, she'd been explicit about her intentions from the get-go. "I thought you were mad at her."

William lifted a thin shoulder. "I was. I got over it."

Chris snorted in disbelief. "Just like that?"

"Just like that," Will replied evenly. He folded his hands in front of him. "She's not Daphne, you know."

"I know that." He hadn't meant to snap. He repeated more calmly, "I know that."

"I don't think you do know."

"What do you want me to say, Dad? That there was nothing I could have offered to keep her here?" The fist around his heart squeezed and he laughed humorlessly. "I don't know why I ever thought she would stay."

"I don't see why you'd think she *wouldn't* stay."

Chris glared, then confusion struck him. Was he being sarcastic? He reexamined William's double negatives.

The old man put down his mug wearily. "Listen, son." He rubbed at his chest above the stitches. "Looking death in the eye makes you think about things. About how you've treated people, how they'll remember you when you're gone. I don't want to die with you hating me."

Chris stared into his father's pain-filled face. "I don't hate you, Dad."

"Well, I sure don't make it easy to like me." He held his gaze. "I'm proud of you, Chris. Proud of what you've done for this farm, for your son. You did right by them both…and by me, even when I've been at my worst. You don't owe your old man a damn thing. I've been a son of a bitch at times. I know it. But I always believed I was doing it for the right reasons."

Chris swallowed dryly. He was really starting to worry something was wrong with his father.

William went on huskily, "I know I've been hard on you since your mother passed. Losing her...well, it hurt all the time. If I hadn't had you to look after, I probably would've drunk myself into the grave. Fact was, I didn't know how to be a father to you without your mother around. She was supposed to give you all the softer things a child needs. And my job was to make you tough."

His dad almost never talked about his mom. She'd died suddenly of a brain aneurysm when he was six years old. Chris's memory of her came in little snatches, her presence almost entirely faded from the homestead all these years later. Nothing of hers had remained in the house after she was gone. Not even photos.

The grim twist of his father's lips softened. "It was my duty to raise you to be the man I couldn't be after she was gone. I was dying a little every day seeing you grow up. You look a lot like her, you know. I think I took that out on you, too. You were here and she wasn't, and it pissed me off every day you defied me."

Chris remained silent despite the old anger boiling up inside. He told himself firmly this wasn't about him. His father needed to get this all out of his system.

"When you told me you were haring off to college...I was crushed. I didn't want to be alone here." He shook his head. "I never meant to make you feel worthless. As if your dreams didn't matter. When you came back and Daphne moved in and had Simon...I didn't know whether to be overjoyed or miserable. I could see it in your eyes, too. Your entire future... gone. All because of her."

"Daphne didn't get pregnant on purpose, Dad." It had

crossed his mind over the years, though. He knew she could be manipulative, and she hated being left behind. Their last time together, she'd told him she wanted to feel him without any barrier. And he'd given in. Nine months later, he realized what a mistake that had been. Still… "I can never regret Simon." He said it with conviction as fierce love burned away all doubts in his mind. "And Daphne…she didn't know what she wanted in life. She thought all she wanted was me, but that turned out not to be good enough."

"She did the best she could," William declared, "but it wasn't enough in my books. All I've ever wished for was for you and Simon to be happy. I thought that would only happen if we could get back to the way things were when my Emma was still alive. At one point, I thought I should remarry, have a woman around the house to be a mother to you. But I couldn't do it. I was married to the farm, to the life me and your mother had built together. When you came back from school and started changing things…I didn't know what to do." He waved his hand. "I'm starting to ramble. Seems I am starting to get old."

"It's okay, Dad. I haven't heard you talk about Mom before. I don't remember much but…I miss her, too."

William's lips twitched. "Listen. I know how much you gave up for your son. I don't know that I gave up nearly as much for you. But you have to stop pining for the things you could've had and look forward to the things you can earn. You need to dream again, son. I remember when you used to ride that damn motorbike of yours and tell me you wanted to drive across the country. Would you believe I once thought the exact same thing about my bicycle?" He laughed.

Chris grinned, having a hard time imagining his dad as a young man, much less one riding a bicycle.

"You've accomplished all kinds of things I could never begin to think about. All these projects of yours…this crusade to save the planet…you're good at it. But I want you to start thinking about *your* future." He tapped his fingers on the table. "Simon will be going to college soon. I know you've been worried about money, so I'm thinking we should sell the farm."

Chris straightened in his seat. "What?"

"We've got a lot of land here, good equipment, a good staff and clients who trust us. Someone out there must want to buy a certified organic farm business. I even put some numbers together for you." He slid a folder toward him, and Chris opened it. Inside, his father had compiled a full report about the market value for the property and the business. They wouldn't be rich, but they would have enough to start over, be comfortable for a while and send Simon to college anywhere in the world. That was worth a fortune, as far as he was concerned.

"I don't know what to say." His thoughts whirled. He thought about what he could do with his life, what he might accomplish. The world had been offered to him on a silver platter. All the duties and chores and long, hard hours with the animals and the mud and the sun…he could give that all up. No more waking up before dawn. No more shit to shovel.

But the thought of leaving the Jamieson farm in a stranger's hands set off alarms in his brain. His hands clenched over the tabletop as if someone might steal it out from under him.

"You don't need to make a decision about it right now," William said. "But it's on the table. I want my grandson to find his way in the world and be the best at whatever it is he wants to do. I don't want him to be held back by a piece of land and an old man's stubbornness." He eyed his son critically. "The same goes for you, Chris. You've done well here, make no mistake about that. And you've made this your living now. I would be happy if you wanted to keep the farm. But I can tell you we don't always want what we think we want."

They finished their tea and his father retired for the evening. Chris picked up the folder, its weight more substantial than the pieces of paper within. William had given him everything he could possibly want. Except for the one thing he couldn't have. Not if he stayed.

And even then, he wasn't certain *she'd* want him.

He stared at the folder. He had a lot to think about.

"I STILL CAN'T BELIEVE you managed to pack a three-piece suit in your duffel bag for a soul-searching road trip," Tiffany said, watching Daniel iron his rumpled white dress shirt.

"Maybe I'm an international spy and I like to have a lot of disguises on hand." He hung up the now-crisp shirt and started on the red silk tie he'd wear to the job interview. Isaac had hooked him up with the HR department at Halo. There was an opening in the accounts department that Daniel was probably overqualified for, but he needed a foot in the door. Though he'd stopped driving, he still needed to find his place in the world. Nothing said settled like a nine-to-five daily grind.

Tiff watched him from the futon he'd been sleeping on all week, piles of manuscripts nearly burying her. If he were lucky, he wouldn't have to spend another night on that spine-twisting torture device starting Monday. "Are you sure you want to do this? I'm happy to have you here for as long as you need to stay, but if you get a job in the city, it means you won't go home."

"I need to do this," he told her, though it sounded as if he were trying to convince himself, too. Isaac had stuck his neck out for him. He was not going to throw this opportunity out the window.

It took forty-five minutes to get to Halo headquarters, which was located in the financial district. Daniel thought about what neighborhood he might afford an apartment in, but didn't want to jinx things by planning too far ahead.

He was ushered up to the twelfth floor of a sterile-looking glass-and-steel building where he shook hands with a primly dressed woman in gray and a man in shirtsleeves. They told him they were impressed by his background, and were a little surprised he'd spent all this time working at the family restaurant, but they said it "shows loyalty and dedication, a firm work ethic and the willingness to take on any responsibility."

Translation: *whipped.*

They asked all the requisite questions he had prepared answers for: What are your worst qualities? Where do you see yourself in five to ten years? Why do you want to work for us?

It was this last question that stumped him. The correct answer should have been "because I want to grow with a successful company and add my unique experience to help the company grow." Typical interview rhetoric.

Instead, he blurted, "Because I don't know what else to do."

"Excuse me?" the primly dressed woman said, glancing up.

Daniel opened his mouth, looked to the equally befuddled man. What was he saying? He should laugh it off and pretend he had a quirky sense of humor. Time slowed as he looked out of the glass-walled conference room at the blue and gray cubicle walls. Drones in suits sat hunched at their computers. The fluorescent lighting sent a harsh glare over the pale face of an office clerk who walked past. He made bleary eye contact with Daniel, and continued on, zombielike.

Suddenly, Daniel wanted to take his answer about the next five to ten years back. Because he knew exactly where he'd be in that time. He'd be here, walking around like that guy, in a slight daze, heading back to his cubicle to stare at some spreadsheets. He would have a chance to move up the company ladder, but would that matter? It would be the same thing at a different desk. He'd be a suit who played with numbers.

He shook his head. "I'm sorry. I just realized I have another appointment." He got up and shook their hands, then left the building and the miasma of despair he hadn't noticed before. He was going to have to apologize to Isaac about this.

The farther he got from the office, though, the more he knew it was the right decision. Enjoying the sun and the unseasonably warm September weather, he walked all the way to Chinatown and decided to have lunch at a popular barbecue and noodle house.

He'd been to this restaurant as a student because the food was cheap, the service fast. The waitress recognized him instantly. She asked after his family and whether he'd married yet, then speedily brought him his meal: noodles in soup with roast duck and a plate of *gai lan.* He relished the simple flavors of the egg noodles and broth with scallions, the tender, juicy meat of the slowly roasted duck. The parboiled leafy green *gai lan* was slightly bitter, but still crisp. He removed his tie and jacket, the steam from the front counters warm and redolent with spices and cooking oil. He ate slowly, every bite kindling a memory not only from his college years, but from his childhood, as well.

He'd had this meal before with *Kung-kung,* on his grandfather's birthday. Daniel's parents had wanted to take him to a fancy new dim sum place, but *Kung-kung* had insisted on the barbecue house. *The simple things often bring you the greatest happiness,* he'd said.

Daniel looked down at the empty bowl, swallowing his last bite. It was the most delicious meal he'd had in a long time.

As the waitress collected his dishes, she asked if he wanted anything else.

"Actually, yes. Are you hiring?"

CHAPTER TWENTY-TWO

TIFFANY LISTENED TO HER BROTHER'S enthusiastic chatter as she cleared off her desk. She'd gone to the office for a meeting and was buried hip-deep in work.

"So, let me get this straight. You gave up the chance to work at your friend's company to work as a *cook?*"

"And a waiter. The pay's not great, but the owner of the restaurant, Mr. Peng, said he'd be willing to give me a shot, see what I can do. He wanted someone fluent in English and Cantonese, so it works out perfectly."

He sounded nearly giddy about it. She wasn't sure she understood how he'd gone from putting on that suit this morning to donning another apron. He hadn't even gone back to the apartment to change—he'd started work right away. "That's… great." She could only be happy for him. It was his life, after all. "I hope this is what you want, bro."

"It is. I have to go. We've got to prep for the dinner hour. Don't wait up for me. I'll probably be working late."

She looked at her own pile of work and sighed. "Same here."

"I'll get the delivery guy to bring you some noodles, on me." With that, he hung up.

Tiffany turned back to the rejection letter she was writing, trying to find something positive to say about the abomination that had landed on her desk. By the time she was done typing the letter out, the receptionist knocked on her office door.

"Someone at the front desk to see you," Karen said. Tiffany

glanced up at the clock and was surprised by how quickly time had passed. "I'm about to leave. You sticking around?"

She slumped in her chair. "Probably."

Karen pouted in sympathy. "I'll wait until you're done with your visitor and lock the door behind me."

Tiff rummaged through her purse for a few dollars for a tip. It must be the delivery man with her brother's promised noodles. She'd never realized how thoughtful Daniel was—he'd always taken care of her, even when she'd been nasty to him. All this time, their relationship could have been so much better if only she hadn't been so hung up on how her mom and dad idolized him.

She owed him an apology big-time.

She headed toward the reception area and halted in her tracks. A familiar set of broad shoulders, wavy dark blond hair and sky-blue eyes was leaning against the counter, talking with Karen, grinning widely.

Tiffany's heart started pounding hard in her chest, and the edges of her vision went fuzzy. He stopped talking when he saw her, his eyes going bright and soft all at once. Karen looked her way and grinned. "Hey, Tiff. You and your... friend have a good weekend. And don't forget—Caitlyn's in her office." She winked.

"Um...thanks." What did she think they were going to do? Have sex on the conference table? Her brain smoldered at the thought, and she shut the image out.

Chris continued to smile at her. Her fingertips had gone numb, and her lips burned, as if they remembered his kisses. Determined not to show her weakness for him, she pushed back her shoulders and ground her heels into the hardwood floor. "Hello."

"Hi."

Even his voice seemed to beckon to her. His roving gaze

was as tangible as a touch. "What are you doing here?" she asked shakily.

"I drove up with Simon for a weekend in the city. Thought we might visit some campuses, look around. He's taking a nap at the hotel right now." Chris stuffed his hands into the pockets of his jacket, glancing down briefly. "I hope it's okay that I came to visit."

"No. I mean, yes, of course it's okay. How's your father?" she asked hastily. She didn't want to admit how glad she was to see him, how torn she'd been these past few weeks. She didn't want to talk about *them*.

"Dad's okay. He had a minor infection after the surgery, but he's doing better. Right now, he's taking care of things on the farm—well, from a backseat position, that is. Jane's doing all the heavy lifting, but keeping Dad involved helps him cope. Here." He pushed a potted plant wrapped in florist's paper across the receptionist's desk toward her. "This is from him. He wanted me to send you his congratulations on the new job."

Inside was a cactus. The card read:

Prickly and prone to hurt people. Not unlike yours truly. Sorry for being such an ass. Hope this thrives in your care. All the best, WJ.

She smiled wryly. The old man sure had a dry sense of humor. "Tell him thanks for me." She hoped this was the proverbial olive branch. She wished she could apologize to him in person.

Chris tapped his fists against his sides nervously and glanced around. "This is a nice office. Are you liking it here?"

"Oh, yes. Absolutely." She nodded. "Um…do you want a tour?"

There wasn't that much to see. Except for the boxes of

books everywhere, it looked like any other office within a converted loft space. But she pointed out the various desks, the cluttered library and her own overstuffed office, which remained devoid of any personal touches. She set the cactus by the window. It helped a little.

They passed Caitlyn's office, and when her boss looked up, she leaped out of her chair and introduced herself to Chris, pumping his hand vigorously. Her boss was a tiny powerhouse of a woman, exuberant and ultrafriendly. Her energy was infectious, though her workaholic tendencies made the rest of the staff feel guilty about leaving at five every day.

"Tiff's been such a trouper," she enthused. "I'm so glad I hired her. I couldn't have asked for a better assistant." She beamed at Tiff, making her blush a little. "So, you're visiting with your son?"

"Checking out the campuses. Seeing the sights. My main goal this weekend is to give him a taste of college life, make it less alien."

"That's terrific. What a great dad you are. Tiffany, you are going to host your friend, yes? Show off the old alma mater?" She turned back to Chris. "We both went to NYU, so I'd be a little biased in saying that you couldn't choose a better place to send your boy. Isn't that right, Tiff?"

Her brain was still hung up on the first part of her speedy speech. "Actually…I was going to take some work home this weekend…." She couldn't spend time with Chris and Simon. She didn't want to be reminded of what they'd shared, what she'd left behind.

Caitlyn put her strong hands on Tiff's shoulders and marched her toward her office. "You work too hard. You've been taking work home every day since you started."

"So do you," she pointed out.

"That's different. You need to take the weekend off. Catch

up with your friend, go see a movie, show off the city. I'll see you fresh on Monday morning."

"Um, okay. Thanks."

A few minutes later, Tiffany and Chris walked out of the building together.

"She's…energetic, isn't she?" Chris said.

"Caitlyn? Oh, yeah. That's what I like about her, though. She's a great boss."

He smiled. "We're staying at a hotel not too far from here. Would you like to join us for dinner? I was hoping you could recommend a place. I'm sure Simon wouldn't mind."

Tiff hesitated. Chris's choice of words seemed to indicate that all was not forgiven or forgotten. She hated to think Simon was still mad at her.

"I'd like that," she said, coming to a decision. "There's a nice Italian restaurant I used to go to all the time. It's in Manhattan on Canal Street. We can take a cab. After dinner, I could take you guys on a night tour."

"Sounds great."

Chris had driven a rented sedan, which was more comfortable and fuel efficient than his truck. They picked up Simon from the hotel. He greeted Tiffany with a wary "Hey," and didn't say anything else during the cab ride to Manhattan.

At dinner, Simon picked at his lasagna. Chris tried to engage him, but the teen stayed focused on his food. When Chris left the table to use the restroom, Tiff decided to clear the air. "You're not happy to see me, are you?"

"It wasn't my idea to come here." He slumped lower into his seat and looked away.

"Look, I'm sorry about the way things worked out. I know I was wrong to lie, and I'm going to regret that for the rest of my life, especially if you don't forgive me." She placed a hand over his forearm and he flinched, pulling away. She'd touched his burned arm, only the bandages had since been removed. She glimpsed a small patch of shiny pink scar tissue before he tucked his hands into his hoodie sleeves and hid them under the table. A lump formed in her throat. She'd brought this boy so much pain.

"My life is here, Simon. Even so, I hope we can still be friends," she said quietly. "I want you to feel like you can talk to me, especially if you want help with school." When he didn't respond, she pressed on. "I'm proud of you, Simon. You did an amazing job this summer. And I think if you keep working hard, you could do whatever you wanted. I'm sorry if the relationship I had with your father upset you, but that's between us. But you and me, we're friends, okay?"

He met her gaze, his bangs sliding over his eyes. "Whatever."

Chris returned, and he looked between them. "Everything all right here?"

She beamed up at him. "Everything's fine. Let's get the bill. We can get dessert at this awesome ice cream place not too far away."

They went for a stroll. Simon walked ahead of them, peering into shops and staring openly at the spectacle of native New Yorkers out on the town. Chris walked next to her, hands in his pockets. She resignedly followed suit and kept a few inches between them so they wouldn't bump elbows.

"Pretty, isn't it?" she asked when she noticed him squinting up at the skyline.

His lips pressed into a thin line. "I can't see the stars."

She thought about the night she and Chris had gone to Osprey Peak and how the stars had looked. That empty feeling inside her gaped wide.

They made their way north along Broadway, and she pointed out where the bulk of the New York University campus lay. Simon couldn't hide his avid interest as his eyes darted from building to building, and then to some of the coeds hurrying by to enjoy a night on the town.

They got ice cream and hopped on a bus to Times Square. Simon's eyes were like saucers as he gazed up and around to take it all in. He pulled out his cell phone and started snapping pictures. Tiff hopped into a souvenir shop and bought him an I ♥ NY button.

"Lame," he said, but pinned it onto the lapel of his shirt anyhow. His mouth pursed into a half smile. "How long would I have to live here until this became fashionably ironic?"

"A couple of months, I guess. I don't know. I've always felt like a bit of a tourist myself."

She caught Chris's odd look then. "Are you all right?" she asked when he rubbed his temples.

"It was a long drive. And I've got a headache." He squinted against the flashing rainbow of lights. "Call me an old man, but it's been a while since I've been out this late."

It was nearly midnight by the time they returned to the hotel in New Jersey. Chris insisted they drop Tiffany off at her apartment first, even though they would have to circle around.

"I'll walk you up," he said when they reached her stoop. He told Simon to wait in the cab. The teen stared balefully at Tiffany, as if to remind her of her promise not to play with his father's feelings. She waved and said good-night.

"I'm sorry about Simon," Chris said as they walked up four flights of stairs. "I'll have a word with him."

"No. Don't do that. I already talked with him and...well, neither of us can make him forgive me." She mused how she'd once said the same thing about earning Simon's respect. She'd lost it too easily.

When the silence stretched on, she asked tentatively, "Are *you* still mad at me?"

Chris stopped her on the stairwell. "No. I'm not. How can

I be? You love what you're doing. You're back where you belong, and you're happy. I can't be mad about that."

But I'm not happy without you, her heart cried.

"I'm sorry I didn't tell you about the interview," she said finally.

"I overreacted. The night of the wedding was rough, and my flight was delayed and I was tired after everything and Dad… Well, in any case, I don't have any excuses for the way I behaved."

"You did," she insisted. "I lied. I made you think—"

"You don't have to say anything, Tiff. I forgive you."

The words should have absolved her, but they only made her feel worse. She wanted him to yell at her, to hate her, to break things off and never speak to her again. She didn't deserve his kindness. She turned away from him and walked up the last flight of stairs, Chris on her heels. "Tomorrow," she said quickly, stamping out the emotions boiling under her skin, "we'll meet for breakfast. I'll take you guys to some of the college campuses I know a little more about. I can get some calendars for Simon to look at, too. It'd be easier if he had an idea of the area of study he'd like to focus on, of course. And then we can go to the Museum of Natural History. He'd like that. And we can hit Central Park, and—"

Chris turned her and covered her mouth with his, stopping the flow of words. His fingers tightened around her waist, but he didn't pull her closer. Tiffany arched into him. And though a feeling like warm honey filled her, his kiss brought her despair into sharp focus.

I may never get to kiss him like this again.

He pulled away and brushed a strand of hair away from her face. "I've missed that," he said quietly.

She didn't want to return the sentiment. If she admitted how much she wanted to be with him, she'd fall to pieces and allow him to sweep her up and take her back to Everville, where she'd remain a broken woman. So she said nothing.

"I'll call you tomorrow when we're up," he said after an awkward beat. "I better get back to Simon."

"Okay." He stood there a moment longer, as if waiting for her to say something more. But she had no idea what was supposed to come next. In the next breath, he turned back down the steps, his heavy footfalls echoing down, down, down, and out the door.

THE NEXT DAY, Tiffany dragged them all over Manhattan in a whirlwind attempt to show them everything about the city she loved. Something was off, though. She kept Simon between them, using him as shield and speaking mainly to his son, as if Chris were simply his chaperone. He suspected she was trying to win back his son's respect with the campus tour and museum visit. Surprisingly, it was working. He couldn't hide his growing excitement as they toured NYU's campus. By dinnertime, Simon was eagerly discussing living arrangements and ways to afford a place of his own.

Chris, meanwhile, struggled to stay upbeat. He'd had a terrible night's sleep no thanks to the constant whir of the hotel's noisy air conditioner, the traffic below his window and the glare of the streetlights peeking between the blackout curtains. The strange and constantly shifting smells of the city made his sinuses hurt. Now he had an inkling of what Daphne went through with her migraines. The exhaust fumes choked him and the tap water tasted funny. And there were so many people, all of them jostling him, glaring at him as if he had no right to be there.

Those little miseries were trivial, though, compared to the way Tiffany was trying to mask her pain.

He shouldn't have come to see her. After his talk with his dad, he'd thought bonding time with Simon would be good for them both. Involving Tiffany when they were both still hurting had been a mistake.

We don't always want what we think we want. He'd been almost certain of what he wanted: Tiffany, in his life. He'd come to see if it was a sure thing. But she hadn't even told him she'd missed him, never mind whether she felt the same way he did.

He should've left things as they were. He would have gotten over her eventually. He'd deluded himself into thinking he could win her back. Now he was hurting them both.

They ate dinner at a fancy steak house. Simon pored over NYU's course calendar. His son had been taken with Jenny, the pretty liberal arts major who'd conducted the tour. At the end of it, she'd handed him her number and told him to call anytime if he had questions. Chris couldn't help noticing his son was now keenly reading the section on liberal arts.

They dropped Simon off at the hotel after dinner. Chris drove Tiffany back to her apartment and asked to be invited in. "Just to talk," he assured her, despite that damned flicker of hope.

"Simon seems pretty enthusiastic about college now," she said once they were inside. She dropped her keys into a bowl on the small dining table.

"I think that had more to do with Jenny than the programs," Chris replied wryly.

"Well, he has time to figure it out." She brewed coffee for them both. He sat on the squishy futon and took the mug from her. "I'm glad you did this for him. I think he's really benefited from the trip."

"It wasn't just for him." He put the mug down. "There's something I've been meaning to tell you. Dad's been talking about selling the farm." Her mouth fell open, and he plowed on. "Before I came to see you yesterday, I was looking into some opportunities with a firm here that does policy advocacy for alternative energy programs."

Something brighter than hope sparkled in her eyes, but then dimmed quickly when he sighed.

"I'm not qualified, despite my experience. I don't have the right schooling for it. I don't have any schooling at all. Kind of ironic, really, considering everything I've done back home." He rubbed the bridge of his nose. "But even if I was qualified, I don't think I could do it. Being here, away from the farm… New York isn't the place for me." Admitting it out loud closed a bunch of doors in his mind. His gaze meshed with hers, even as she lowered her eyes, understanding clear in the slouch of her shoulders.

"To each his own." Her attempt at sounding trite fell flat. Her lips lifted in a tremulous smile. Dammit, he should have kept his mouth shut. He wanted to go to her, pull her into his arms, but if he touched her, he might do something stupid like promise to stay, sell the farm, buy some horrid little box of a condo in some stale little suburban borough and move in with her.

He couldn't do that. Not to his son or his father. But most important, he couldn't do it to himself. He was happy as a farmer. He'd always thought he'd been missing out on something bigger, grander, more important. But he'd achieved more in his hometown than he could have anywhere else. It wasn't on the same scale as working for an environmental lobby group, but he was making a difference.

For the first time in his life, he was truly proud of who he was and what he did. Tiffany couldn't give up her dream any more than he could give up his.

"We're leaving tomorrow afternoon," he said, throat tight. "Do you want to join us for brunch before we go?"

"I…I'd better not. I have a lot of work to do."

"I thought your boss told you to take the weekend off."

The corner of her mouth twisted up. "I snuck a few manuscripts home."

"Rebel." He chuckled, then slowly pushed to his feet. Dragging up the energy to be courteous and friendly was painful. "Okay. Well. Thanks for playing tour guide. And for... everything."

He waited, hoping beyond hope she'd reach out, show him *something*. She stared at him across the short space between the living room and the kitchen. It might as well have been miles. "You're welcome."

Every limb felt like wood as he forced himself to open the door. She started walking toward him to see him off, but he simply smiled, waved and shut the door behind him.

The next day, he headed home to Everville.

CHAPTER TWENTY-THREE

WHEN DANIEL CAME HOME around midnight, he found his sister facedown on the futon, sobbing.

"Tiff?" He threw his jacket aside and knelt by her. "What's wrong?"

"I can't be with him," she wailed, and hiccuped as she tried to take a breath. "I can't be with him. This is where I'm supposed to be, and he can't be here. He doesn't want to be here. I can't be with him." She was hyperventilating. The emotional dams had at last crumbled, and grief swamped her.

Daniel brought her tissues, brewed tea, then comforted her as best he could while she remained curled up in fetal position.

"Oh, God, Daniel, why am I so miserable?" she blubbered.

He patted her back. "Love is funny that way, I guess."

"I don't love him," she said staunchly, blowing her nose. "I can't love him. We don't belong together. We're too different."

"Sure, sure." He was too tired to point out how much she sounded like she was trying to convince herself.

"I love my job," she asserted, fist clenched. "It's a great job. It's what I've always wanted. What I trained for. This is where I am supposed to be."

"No, it's not." He clasped her shoulder and gave it a squeeze. "I saw it the minute you opened the door. Tiff, your job is making you miserable."

"It is not. I love my job. I worked all my life for this. If you're going to sit there and question my feelings all night—"

He burst out laughing, hearing his own words echoed back to him. His sister stared at him as if he'd lost his mind. "Like I haven't heard *that* before."

"What?"

"Remember when you first found out about Selena and you were all 'What do you have to offer her blah, blah, blah?' You told me we were too different, that she could never leave her practice and move to Everville, that I'd never figure out how to live apart from Mom and Dad—"

"I never said those things." She smacked him in the arm.

"You didn't say them out loud, but I got the message. And now it's the same for you, isn't it? You think you love your job, but really, you're in love with Chris."

"I am not!"

"You'd do anything for him," he went on relentlessly, "but you're too stubborn to because you're too focused on what you think you *should* want. You think you want all this, but in the week I've been here, all I've seen is how hard you work and how unhappy you've become. You don't have time to have the life you're dreaming of. I'm not sure you even know what that dream life is supposed to be. Make your own happiness, sis. Success is how you define it, not how someone else does."

As the words tumbled out of his mouth, it was as if a window had opened in his mind. It was all so clear now, and he took a deep breath.

He settled both hands over his sister's shoulders, looking her straight in the teary eyes. "We're both idiots," he said.

"Gee, thanks."

"You're welcome. Also, you're an ugly crier, so snap out of it and clean yourself up." He got to his feet and grabbed his jacket.

"Where are you going?" she asked. "Are you going to leave your poor, heartbroken sister all alone in her hour of need?"

"Tiff. Chris drove all the way here with his son to see you

during *harvest* season. You need to think about that and what you really want in life." He snatched up his keys. "You already know what that is. You just have to admit it to yourself." He hurried out the door, praying he could win back what happiness he could for himself.

IT WAS CLOSE TO ONE by the time Daniel arrived at Selena's condo. He buzzed her code, and when she picked up, he said, "It's Daniel. I'm sorry for calling so late. I'm not drunk. But I am an idiot and I need to tell you to your face how much of an idiot I am."

Silence answered him, and then a loud buzz. He nearly wrenched the door off the hinges going in.

His heart was hammering so hard, he could feel his sweat-and food-stained T-shirt jumping against his skin. He should have showered and changed before walking into this conversation, but he couldn't waste another minute of his life without telling Selena how he felt.

She opened the door at his knock. She had on pajama shorts and a T-shirt with a dancing kitten on it. Her hair was piled in a bun on her head, and she wore glasses rather than her usual contacts. Even so, she was the most radiant woman he'd ever seen.

"I love you, Selena," he said.

Her eyebrows climbed into her hairline. "Are you high?"

"Only on your love. Can I come in?"

"Depends." She cocked a hip and leaned against the door. "Are you going to pass out on my couch again and leave without saying thank you? Are you going to tell me your parents won't like me because I'm a *gwai-mui?*"

He chuckled at her use of the Cantonese slang term for *white girl.* "I promise never to do either of those things ever again. If you don't want to let me in, that's okay, but I have something to say and I might get a little loud about it."

She glared, considered him a moment. "In case you haven't picked up on it yet, I'm mad at you."

"I know."

"I can't begin to tell you how ticked off I was when you showed up here drunk after you told me I wasn't good enough for your parents."

"I know."

"I don't owe you a goddamned thing. And I'd probably be better off without you."

He swallowed thickly, glanced at his shoes. "Yeah. I know that, too."

Her fingers flexed over the edge of the door, but then she swung it wide open and waved him through.

He followed her into the living room, as if he were walking up to the edge of a precipice. He knew exactly how far he had to fall if Selena didn't return his feelings. The way she was eyeing him now, he might already have lost her. He must look slightly crazed. But now was the time for leaps of faith.

"I was making excuses," he declared. "I got it into my head that my parents wouldn't approve of you because you're white. Because you don't meet this strict list of qualifications that I made up in my mind based on nothing. My parents don't care what you are. In fact, I don't care what my parents think about you. The reality is that *I'm* not good enough for you. I'm the one who doesn't meet my own standards. I'm the one judging our relationship against some nonexistent benchmark." He breathed deeply. "I'm sorry I ever tried to put any of my own insecurities on you. I'm ashamed of myself."

"Go on," she said flatly when he paused for breath.

"When I met you, I was…overwhelmed by the fact a beautiful, smart, caring woman like you would want to have anything to do with me. I haven't stopped thinking about you since you first messaged me online. You're everything I could possibly ever want. And I was terrified that you'd see how much of a loser I am."

"Loser?" She appeared genuinely puzzled. "Why would you say that?"

"C'mon, Selena. Look at me. Thirty-four and living with my parents, working for them in a small-town Chinese restaurant with no real income of my own. Someone must have said something about how I might only be with you for your money."

The discomfort that flitted across her features confirmed his suspicions.

"It was my sister who made me face the facts. You were right, talking with her was helpful. Even if she kind of knocked me for a loop at first." He grimaced. "But she also made me realize nothing else matters except what I feel for you. I was bogged down by the idea that I should be the breadwinner and supporting you. It scared me that I could want something so bad and realize I hadn't earned it.

"I can't tell you that one day I'll make as much as you do in some job here in New York. Right now, I'm making fifteen dollars an hour working in a Chinese barbecue restaurant as a cook and waiter on the dinner shift. Frankly, I don't know that I want to do anything else. I love cooking. I love the restaurant business. But I would give all that up to become your trophy husband and raise our children if you would do me the honor of becoming my wife."

Tears shone in her eyes behind her glasses. She pressed a trembling hand against her heart. "Shouldn't you be on your knees or something?" she asked in a choked whisper.

"I would already be on them if I had a ring." He dropped to his knees anyhow. "Selena, will you marry me?"

She shook her head. "All this melodrama and you come here in the middle of the night, expecting me to give you a life-changing answer now?" She laughed shakily, and Daniel smiled.

"I'll stay on my knees until you do give me an answer."

"Get up, you goof." She flung her arms around him as he shot to his feet and wrapped her in his embrace.

"Is that a yes?"

"Yes, you idiot," she choked out. "God, I've missed you so much."

Hot tears of happiness welled in his eyes. He squeezed her tight. "I'll do whatever it takes to make up for what I've done. Anything you want, Selena, just name it."

"Shut up and kiss me."

He did. And he didn't stop.

TIFFANY HAD A LONG THINK ALL SUNDAY.

Puffy-eyed and exhausted from a night of emotional diarrhea, all she could think about was the week ahead. If she could focus on taking one step at a time, taking things day by day, it would all be more manageable.

But the thought only drove her into a deeper depression.

Daniel hadn't come home last night. She'd worried about him briefly, but then received a text around three in the morning, informing her he'd gotten back together with Selena and wouldn't be coming home. How nice for them, she'd thought bleakly, though in the light of the morning, over a strong cup of coffee, she had to admit she was happy for her brother... and a little envious.

She tried to settle down to read, but found herself staring blankly at the page, the words blurring together. She was watching the clock, she realized, counting down the minutes to Chris's departure.

Ridiculous. What was she going to do? Run to his hotel and fling herself in front of the car to stop him from leaving? He had to go home. Simon had school. William needed to be cared for and the farm needed its farmer.

What did Tiffany need? A brain transplant, apparently, because the way her thoughts were headed, she couldn't believe she wasn't going crazy.

There was absolutely nothing for her in Everville—not careerwise, anyhow. If she went back, she'd be throwing her hard-earned English degree out the window. That act of rebellion that had broken her away from her parents' expectations would be for nothing. If she went back, what would she be facing except humiliation? Failure? She would become Tiffany, the brainy Chinese girl who couldn't keep a job, poor thing.

She closed her eyes. Here, she was something. She was editorial assistant at Haute Docs Books. She was a gatekeeper, a publishing demigod.

But she was tired. And overworked. And alone.

And she was miserable.

She had to face it. She woke up every day dreading her life. She went through the motions, but her work was joyless, Sisyphean, even. But she was sticking around because she was certain it was what she'd been born to do.

There was only one thing she could think about doing, now.

She opened her laptop and started typing out her letter of resignation.

Three weeks later

TIFFANY DRANK IN the crisp smell of dried leaves and rich earth newly turned after harvest. She'd forgotten how much she'd loved this time of year in the country. The fall fair would be coming up soon; she thought about painting something to enter into the arts contest. Perhaps a view from Osprey Peak.

Her heart rate doubled as she pulled into the gravel driveway at the Jamieson farm. A familiar figure strode toward her from the field.

"Hi, Jane," she greeted. The farm manager didn't say anything as she gathered her into a hug. Tiffany hugged her right back.

"Thank God you're home. It hasn't been the same around here since you left." She held her away. "They're all in there." She nodded toward the house. "Don't know if you need backup, but…"

"I'll be sure to call for you if they chase me off with pitchforks and torches." She chuckled. "Here. Insurance." She handed the woman a large double espresso mocha latte with extra foam from the Grindery.

"You'd better marry that fool of a man," Jane called after her as Tiff walked up the veranda.

The door was unlocked. It always was. It was something she'd have to get used to, she supposed, though she wasn't sure she'd ever shake her city habit. Locked doors around here seemed to suggest you didn't trust your neighbors, though. And she was through shutting people out of her life.

The door opened on silent hinges. She stepped in, breathing in that slightly stale smell of old food, animals, grease and men. Another thing she would have to become accustomed to.

She hoped.

She heard voices raised in heated discussion coming from the dining room. As quietly as she could, she peeked around the doorway.

Chris and William were sitting on opposite sides of the table, with Simon sitting at the head between them, a laptop and several books spread open in front of him. His gaze bounced between father and grandfather, and he was scratching his scalp with the tip of a pen.

"It's not about love. It's about duty," William argued hotly. "Those girls, Regan and Goneril, they had the right idea.

Just smile and nod and say what they were supposed to say. If what's-her-face had gone along with it, Lear would have given her his kingdom."

"And there wouldn't be a play," Chris said tiredly. "Look, Cordelia loved her father the most. She owed him the truth. King Lear overreacted and cut off his nose to spite his face."

"You make it sound like he's crazy."

Simon raised a finger. "Uh, spoiler alert, Grandpa…."

Tiffany cleared her throat, and all three of them looked up. Their expressions ranged from surprise to shock to befuddlement. Chris lurched to his feet.

"Please," she said, staying him with an outstretched hand. "I have something to say first."

He sank into his chair. Her pulse hammered in her throat and she took a deep breath to steady her nerves.

"Simon was right about me. I was playing house. I jerked you all around. I never meant to. I'm sorry."

"Apology accepted." William grabbed his crutches and hopped out of his seat more spryly than she ever would have imagined. "C'mon, Simon. I need your help in the greenhouse."

"Greenhouse? What do you—"

"There are seedlings we need to…um…plant. Or…hell, let's just go already."

Simon looked between his father and Tiffany and followed his grandfather out. He paused at the kitchen doorway and gave her a narrowed look before disappearing. She deserved his suspicion. She vowed then to do everything she could to make him believe she'd never hurt his father or him again.

Before she could get a word out, something nudged her ankle, and she looked down.

"Mack!" she gasped, and scooped up the kitten. Her heart

swelled as she cradled the purring black cat and nuzzled him. "Look how much you've grown. You kept him?"

"Simon did, actually. I don't think he was willing to give him up." Chris stayed seated, hands clasped on the table.

Tiffany sniffed. Dammit, she was not going to cry. She hadn't even gotten to say what she had come to say yet. She was supposed to save her tears—happy or sad—for after Chris had answered her question. She set the cat down, and Mack trotted away.

"I've never felt like I belonged here," she began, gripping the back of a chair. "I never fit in with my family, with school or in town. But when I came back and I started working with Simon and being with you…it all clicked. I'd spent all these years thinking I could never love this place or my place in it. I thought I knew where I belonged. And then you changed my mind, and it terrified me.

"I've spent so much time trying to become someone else that I've ignored the person I actually am. I turned away from my family, my culture, turned away from the people who tried to be friends with me. I allowed others to define me in narrow terms, and I started defining myself in even narrower ones. And I've paid for it. I've become someone I don't like. Someone I don't understand."

He watched her with a slight frown. She was rambling.

"I quit my job, Chris. I've moved back into my parents' place for the time being."

He flinched. "But…why? You were happy…."

"I wasn't. I was miserable and tired and I couldn't stay on top of all that work. I thought it was because things were too new still. I didn't want to admit to myself that I couldn't do it. But I couldn't work under those conditions. So I quit."

"And moved back here? Just like that?"

"Just like that." It had taken a little longer than she'd

thought it would, but Daniel had promised to take care of things for her. He would be staying in her apartment until he could get a tenant to sublet the place, and then he'd move in with Selena.

She laced her fingers to keep from raising them in a plea. "This is the only place I've ever felt…at home. Like I belonged." She licked her dry lips. "I want roots, a family. I want to rediscover who I am. I was always afraid that I'd get stuck here…that if I stayed and tried to have relationships, I'd become like my parents.

"But I'm not going to get stuck," she said staunchly, "because I'll make my own opportunities the way you have. It's going to take time and a lot of work. I'm thinking of offering tutoring services, maybe see if any assistant teaching positions open up. I'm not sure I want to do more school right now, but I will if that's what it takes." She knew she was going to sound desperate and needy, but she would never let love in unless she cracked the armored shell around her heart and opened herself up.

She took a step closer. "I'll do whatever it takes if I can be a part of your life. I don't expect you to let me in for nothing. I can work on the farm, clean out stalls, dig in the dirt, whatever you need—"

"No."

The one word sliced through her. She faltered, ready to fold into herself and disappear. "No?"

"You don't need to do that." He stood, and in two long strides was in front of her. He grabbed her around the waist and tugged her toward him, slanting his mouth over hers.

Radiant joy burst inside her like fireworks. She clung to him, drinking him in as tears streamed down her cheeks.

"Don't cry," Chris whispered, pressing his forehead against hers. "Please, don't cry. I've been trying to fight it, but the minute I left you behind in New York, all I could think about was how to be with you." He cupped her chin. "I didn't try hard enough. I gave up too easily on that job. But I found out I can get a certificate through online courses. I'm going to do it."

"Chris, you don't need to do that, not for me."

"It's not for you, it's for me." A smile as deep and warm as an embrace spread across his face. "All I really want is a future with you. I love you, Tiffany."

"I love you, too," she said as fresh tears flowed. The tangled knot inside her heart loosened and her emotions unraveled. The armor was finally gone, and she felt invincible. "I love you. Oh, Chris, I love you so much." She laughed. "Sorry, I can't help it. I've wanted to tell you that since forever."

"You have?"

"Since the day you begged me to tutor you."

"I think I loved you the moment you walked back into my life." He cupped her cheek. "But I knew it for sure when I thought I'd lost you."

"When I left for New Jersey?"

"When you locked your keys in your car by the side of the road."

She laughed, and her heart soared. More solemnly, she said, "I'm serious about staying, you know. But…I can't live with my parents. I need to find a place of my own—"

"Say no more. We've got plenty of room here. I'll kick Simon out of his room if I have to."

"You'd put me in a separate room?" she asked in mock horror.

"You're right. I'll build a separate cabin for you and me. Wouldn't want Dad and Simon to hear all the things I'm going to do to you." He buried his face against the crook of her shoulder, kissing his way down as his hands moved to unbutton her top.

"That sounds like a fantastic idea," she said as Chris pressed her against the dining-room table and shoved *King Lear* aside.

* * * * *

COMING NEXT MONTH FROM
HARLEQUIN® SUPERROMANCE®

Available February 5, 2013

#1830 WILD FOR THE SHERIFF
The Sisters of Bell River Ranch • by Kathleen O'Brien

Rowena Wright has finally come home to the Bell River Ranch. Most townspeople thought this wild child would never be back, but Sheriff Dallas Garwood always knew it. She *belongs* to this land. He's doing his best to steer clear of her. The last time they tangled, he almost didn't walk away. And now there's too much at stake for him to risk a second round with her.

#1831 IN FROM THE COLD
by Mary Sullivan

Callie MacKintosh is good at her job. That's why she's been sent to this Colorado town—to persuade her boss's brother Gabe Jordan to relinquish his share of the family land. But she soon learns there's more to this situation than she knows. And her skills are no match for a family feud that runs deep...or for her growing attraction to Gabe!

#1832 BENDING THE RULES
by Margaret Watson

Nathan Devereux has big dreams—and they don't include family. After years of raising his siblings, he's ready for some time to himself. But what is he supposed to do when faced with an orphaned thirteen-year-old daughter he didn't know about? He can't turn his back on her—or ignore her very appealing guardian, Emma Sloane. But when Emma announces that she wants to adopt the girl herself, all Nathan's personal rules about family suddenly seem to change.

HSRCNM0113ENHA

#1833 THE CLOSER YOU GET
by Kristi Gold

As a country music superstar, Brett Taylor seems to have it all. But appearances are deceiving. He's learned the hard way that relationships and family don't mix with a life on the road. Then Cammie Carson joins his tour group, and the pull between them is intense. Suddenly he sees an entirely new perspective...with her by his side.

#1834 RESERVATIONS FOR TWO
by Jennifer Lohmann

Opening her own restaurant has been Tilly Milek's lifelong dream—and she's finally done it. And all it takes is one bad review to derail everything. Of course The Eater, the anonymous blogger all of Chicago reads, was there on the worst possible night! But when Tilly meets Dan Meier and discovers that he's the reviewer, she's determined to make him change his mind—no matter what it takes.

#1835 FINDING JUSTICE
by Rachel Brimble

For Sergeant Cat Forrester, there is only right and wrong. But when former lover Jay Garrett calls to say their friend has been murdered, those boundaries blur. Especially when he admits he's a suspect in the case. She needs to think like a detective and find the truth. But can she balance these instincts with her feelings for Jay?

YOU CAN FIND MORE INFORMATION ON UPCOMING HARLEQUIN® TITLES, FREE EXCERPTS AND MORE AT WWW.HARLEQUIN.COM.

HSRCNM0113ENHB

Wild for the Sheriff

by Kathleen O'Brien

On sale February 5

Dallas Garwood has always been the good guy, the one who does the right thing...except whenever he crosses paths with Rowena Wright. Now that she's back, things could get interesting for this small-town sheriff! Read on for an exciting excerpt from *Wild for the Sheriff* by Kathleen O'Brien.

Dallas Garwood had always known that sooner or later he'd open a door, turn a corner or look up from his desk and see Rowena Wright standing there.

It wasn't logical. It was simply an unshakable certainty that she wasn't gone for good, that one day she would return.

Not to see him, of course. He didn't kid himself that their brief interlude had been important to her. But she'd be back for Bell River—the ranch that was part of her.

Still, he hadn't thought today would be the day he'd face her across the threshold of her former home.

Or that she would look so gaunt. Her beauty was still there, but buried beneath some kind of haggard exhaustion. Her wild green eyes were circled with shadows, and her white shirt and jeans hung on her.

Something twisted in his chest, stealing his words. He'd never expected to feel pity for Rowena Wright.

She still knew how to look sardonic. She took him in, and he saw himself as she did, from the white-lightning scar dividing his right eyebrow to the shiny gold star pinned at his breast.

Three-tenths of a second. That was all it took to make him feel boring and overdressed, as if his uniform were as much a costume as his son Alec's cowboy hat.

"*Sheriff* Dallas Garwood." The crooked smile on her red lips was cryptic. "I should have known. Truly, I should have known."

"I didn't realize you'd come home," he said, wishing he didn't sound so stiff.

"Come *back*," she corrected him. "After all these years, it might be a bit of a stretch to call Bell River *home.*"

"I see." He didn't really, but so what? He'd been her lover once, but never her friend.

The funny thing was, right now he'd give almost anything to change that and resurrect that long-ago connection.

Will Dallas and Rowena reconnect? Or will she skip town again with everything left unsaid? Find out in *Wild for the Sheriff* by Kathleen O'Brien, available February 2013 from Harlequin® Superromance®.

HSREXP0113